# A Man
# of Some
# Repute

# ALSO BY ELIZABETH EDMONDSON

*The Frozen Lake*

*Voyage of Innocence*

*The Villa in Italy*

*The Villa on the Riviera*

*Night & Day*

*Devil's Sonata*

*Fencing with Death*

*Finding Philippe*

ELIZABETH EDMONDSON

# A Man of Some Repute

THOMAS & MERCER

Published by Thomas & Mercer, Seattle

www.apub.com

Amazon, the Amazon logo, and Thomas & Mercer are trademarks of Amazon.com, Inc., or its affiliates.

ISBN-13: 9781477829349
ISBN-10: 1477829342

Cover design by Lisa Horton

Library of Congress Control Number: 2014959254

Printed in the United States of America

*Remembering Paul*

# Headlines

## England, January 1947

**PEER VANISHES**

Police are trying to trace the whereabouts of Lord Selchester, who walked out into a blizzard from his home, Selchester Castle, on Saturday and has not been seen since.

Foul play is not suspected.

**This is the BBC Home Service. Here is the news, read by Alvar Lidell.**

The hunt for Lord Selchester continues.

Detectives are searching for Lord Selchester, following his disappearance five days ago.

The fifty-six-year-old Earl of Selchester has not been seen since last Saturday.

Because of adverse weather conditions, no one at Selchester Castle, the Earl's seat, was able to communicate with the police until the blizzard conditions abated. Heavy snowfall continuing in the area is hampering search efforts.

Inspector MacLeod, who is in charge of the search for the missing peer, said it is likely that he ventured out into the storm and was unable to make his way back to the Castle.

Lord Selchester was last seen at about 9:00 p.m. when he left his guests to go to his study. Guests staying at the Castle included his son, Lord Arlingham; his daughter, Lady Sonia Richmond; his niece, Miss Freya Wryton; Foreign Office official Mr Charles Guthrie; the society photographer Mr Lionel Tallis; the actress Miss Vivian Witt; and local businessman Mr Stanley Dillon.

*March 1947*

## STILL NO SIGN OF MISSING EARL

Lord Selchester, who disappeared five weeks ago, has not yet been found. As the thaw begins, the Army has been brought in to help with the search.

## FURTHER TRAGEDY HITS EARL'S FAMILY

Lord Arlingham, only son and heir to the Earldom of Selchester, was killed in action in Palestine, it has been reported.

# Chapter One

## England, 1953

### Scene 1

By the time they reached Selchester, Hugo's leg hurt like hell. It was a gritted-teeth job, and he struggled not to wince every time he had to change gear. Georgia was sitting beside him; she gave her brother a glance or two but didn't offer any sympathy. She'd said more than once that since his leg was the way it was, he would just have to get used to it, which practical and pragmatic response to his injury rather pleased him. But at the moment he wasn't thinking of Georgia, or how he'd injured his leg, or regretting what it had done to him. He was just wondering if he could last out until they got to Selchester Castle and he could climb out of the car. They had stopped on the way, more often than he would have done in the old days, but nonetheless it was a four-hour drive from London and the longest stretch of time behind the wheel he'd attempted since he'd been shot.

They were driving now through the town, along a wide eighteenth-century street with pollarded trees on either side. Georgia had found an old guidebook which told her that Selchester was a town dating back to Roman times. She read out the entry to Hugo, who said irritably, 'Of course it dates back to Roman times; look at the name.'

'No need to be sarky. Lots of Roman towns just vanished without trace, but this one hasn't. It seems to have had a lot of history. There's a cathedral—St Werberga's; what an odd name—which goes back for ever. It used to be an abbey, although the monks were all kicked out in 1542 by horrible Henry VIII. Plague . . . hmm, not too bad—not like in London. It says that in the Civil War the Earls of Selchester were Royalists and held the Castle for six weeks against Cromwell's troops. That's not quite true, because it was actually the Countess of Selchester who defended the Castle. She sounds a spirited lady; she and the servants kept off the Parliamentary forces for three weeks. Her hubby, the Earl, was elsewhere. Typical man.'

'That guidebook does not call the Earl her hubby,' Hugo said, stopping to let a woman with a pram cross the road.

The street narrowed into a maze of mediaeval streets, where some of the half-timbered houses had upper floors that overhung the pavement. 'This street is called Snake Alley,' Georgia said, consulting the map in her book. 'I like the names here, some of them are really weird.'

Then they were driving through a gateway set in the remnants of the old city walls and out on to an ancient bridge arching over a placid river. Hugo said, 'The turning should be coming up. It's supposed to be just the other side of this bridge.'

Georgia gave a triumphant cry that nearly caused her brother to step on the brakes. 'Look!' A weathered wooden signpost, on which was written 'Selchester Castle', pointed to a pair of wrought-iron gates.

They were open, and as he turned off the road and drove through, Hugo said, 'They're rather fine. I wonder how they survived being melted down in the war.'

'Clout,' Georgia said.

'Probably just the War Office.' Hugo manoeuvred the car round the first bend of the drive. 'They requisitioned the Castle, and I expect they needed gates and a guard.'

They drove round another bend, climbing now, and Georgia let out a vulgar whistle as Hugo slowed down, his attention riveted on the Castle, whose massive stone walls seemed to grow out of the hillside. Narrow slits for archers told of its fortress days; more modern mullioned windows spoke of peaceable times.

Power, thought Hugo. Selchester Castle dominated its landscape, just as its inhabitants must have dominated the town for centuries.

'Wow,' said Georgia. 'When you told me we were going to be living in a castle, I thought it would be one of those crenellated houses, but this is the real thing. It's even got towers. It's like something out of a fairy tale.'

Or a horror film, Hugo said to himself.

They drove up the rest of the mile-long drive and then through an archway that led into the inner precinct.

'A portcullis,' said Georgia, leaning out of the window and squinting up. 'It's all frightfully grand. Do you think we're being lodged in the stables, or in the servants' quarters?'

Hugo was so eager to stop the car and get out that he would willingly have accepted accommodation in a loose box. He said, 'I'm supposed to go round to the left to the stables. No, we aren't being lodged there as far as I know; it's where they garage cars.'

'That way then,' Georgia said, pointing to another archway set beneath a handsome clock that had stopped at ten past eleven.

The car rumbled over a cobbled courtyard, every jolt making Hugo grimace, and he thankfully rolled the car into an open space in a kind of barn.

He sat back in his seat, his hands off the wheel, his eyes shut, and gave out a long sigh.

Georgia said, 'Buck up, old thing. We've made it. You can go and stick your leg in a mustard bath or Epsom salts or whatever does it good. I expect you'll be hopping about for a day or two, but at least we're here and your precious car, too. I told you we should have come by train.'

Hugo now heartily wished they had, but Georgia was right. He was here, and so was the car.

It wouldn't have been his choice of accommodation, rooms in Selchester Castle. But Sir Bernard had written to him, saying that here was this pile, unoccupied except by one member of the family and a couple of live-in staff to look after the place. 'Lord Selchester disappeared a few years ago, and so the Castle is in the hands of the trustees. You'll be more comfortable there than putting up in some boarding house in the town.'

Hugo wasn't sure *comfortable* was the adjective he would have chosen. This vast and ancient edifice looked as though none of its builders or occupants had ever cared much for comfort. It spoke of violence and force, not of cushions and good food.

As he limped round to the boot of the car, a man who looked like a large gnome appeared from the stables, touched his finger to his forehead in a very peasant-like way and said, 'You leave that to me. I'll see to your cases and the young lady's.'

Hugo held out a hand. 'I'm Hugo Hawksworth, and this is my sister, Georgia.'

The man gave him another nod and said, 'Ben's my name. We're expecting you. If you go through that door over there, and along the passageway, you'll come to the kitchen. Miss Freya's there.'

Georgia had been gazing at a horse, whose inquisitive head had emerged from a stable half-door. As Ben jerked a thumb towards the door, she switched her attention to him and whispered, 'He looks like something out of a film set. That apron and everything.'

Hugo said, 'Don't you think this whole place is rather like a film set?'

Brother and sister stood looking up at the stone walls that towered above them. Then Georgia, keen to break the spell, said, 'Come on, let's see if you can make it to the kitchen without toppling over.'

With the help of his stick, Hugo didn't do too badly over the cobbles, but he was glad to get inside, where there were only flagstones to trouble him.

Georgia said in an awed whisper, 'Gosh, it's huge. I wonder what's in all these rooms. This can't even be the main part of the Castle, if the kitchen's here.'

Hugo said, 'This would have been the heart of the old Castle. Still rooms, the laundry, ironing room, butler's pantry, housekeeper's room and heaven knows what else. They used to have a lot of staff in the old days to keep a place this size running. Here we are, I think this must be the kitchen door.'

Voices came from behind it, and so Hugo turned the handle and limped in, followed by Georgia.

He stopped on the threshold, looking round the large kitchen. There was a long wooden table in the centre, an old range, a modern cooker, a wide door that seemed to lead into a scullery and a fireplace that took up almost the whole of the far wall.

There were two women in the kitchen, and a cat. Georgia, giving her brother a shove from behind that almost upset his balance, said, 'I like the cat.'

Hugo's attention was focused on the two women.

One was no longer young. Lean, with intense dark eyes, she looked as though she should have been stirring a cauldron. He pulled himself together; this place was getting to him. She was smiling at him in a friendly manner; no brimstone after all.

The other woman, about his own age, looked him up and down, not a trace of a smile on her face. Then she said, her voice cool and distant and not at all welcoming, 'You must be Hugo Hawksworth, and this is your sister. I'm Freya Wryton.'

# Scene 2

Freya didn't feel welcoming. She was still annoyed, bordering on furious; she wouldn't forgive Sir Bernard for this.

She had come back from her ride that morning in a cheerful mood, trotting through the archway and into the stable yard. She slid down from the saddle, ran the stirrups up the leathers and handed the reins to Ben, who'd come out to greet her. It was no part of Ben's job to look after Freya's horse, but he did so whenever he could. Once Lord Selchester's chauffeur, and before that head groom, he was now a general factotum, fixing what could be fixed and informing the trustees when some bigger job needed doing around the Castle. But his heart was still with horses, and since the only horse in the stables was Freya's ugly, temperamental piebald, Last Hurrah got a lot of attention from Ben.

'Cussed beast he is,' he said, stroking the horse's Roman nose. 'I'll see to him, Miss Freya. I've mucked out the loose box, and I'll just rub him down. Give over now,' he added as Last Hurrah gave him a hefty shove.

Freya went in through the back door and along the passageway, so familiar she never noticed the chill or all the closed doors, and into the kitchen. She'd collect a cup of coffee to take with her up to her room.

There was Mr Bunbury, the postman; there was Mrs Partridge, titular housekeeper, just setting the kettle to boil on the range; there was the letter lying on the table, addressed to her.

Freya recognised the writing.

So did the postman. 'It'll be from Sir Bernard. I wonder they bother with the stamp—might just as well hand it to me and be done with it.'

'That'd be cheating the Royal Mail,' Mrs Partridge said. 'You don't want to go down that route, not the way all those government officials go poking their long noses into all kinds of things that don't concern them.'

Freya picked up a knife, slid it under the flap and took out the single sheet of paper. She read it, frowning, and then said to Mrs Partridge, 'It seems we're to have lodgers. Sir Bernard requests, only if it is convenient for us, that we put up some new employee of his. They've been unable to find anywhere for him to stay in Selchester.'

The postman grunted and gave his weak coffee an extra stir. 'And isn't that the truth. A gentleman working up at the Hall wouldn't be content with the room over the butcher's or anything like that, and that's all that's free at the moment. Although I dare say that couple in Nightingale Cottage won't be there so very long.'

Freya didn't ask why, though she was sure that both the postman and Mrs Partridge knew exactly what had been going on at Nightingale Cottage.

Mrs Partridge said, 'Would that be a single gentleman, or does he have a wife?'

'Sir Bernard says it's a Mr Hawksworth and his young sister, who'll be going to the High School,' Freya said. 'Oh, it's too bad, Sir Bernard using the Castle as a hostel for his beastly staff.'

Mrs Partridge said, 'Can you say no?'

Freya shrugged. 'I could try, but he wouldn't take any notice. You know what he's like. As he'd remind me, I don't own the Castle; I just live here. I expect he's had Lady Sonia's permission to inflict this pair on us, and she won't care who stays here.' Or at least she wouldn't until she got her hands on the Castle, at which point they'd all be looking for somewhere to stay. 'He's a trustee. If he chooses to throw his weight around, I can't stop him.'

There was a gleam in Mrs Partridge's eye that told Freya she didn't at all mind two strangers coming to roost at the Castle. Mrs Partridge found cooking for the three of them no fun at all, no challenge to her skill both with recipes and overcoming the restrictions of rationing. Mr Hawksworth and his sister had better have good appetites.

'Two extra ration books will be a big help,' Mrs Partridge said with satisfaction. 'When she was here yesterday and read the tea leaves, Martha said she saw two strangers coming.'

Mr Bunbury gave a snort. 'If everyone Martha saw in the tea leaves came, the population of Selchester would double.'

'When are we to expect them?' Mrs Partridge said. 'I'll have to get the rooms aired. If it's a young man and his sister, then we could give them the green room and the one next door, and the old Morning Room for a sitting room.'

'Yes, and he can use the dressing room as a study if he's going to bring work home.' The more these two kept to their own quarters, the better, as far as Freya was concerned. She looked at the letter again. 'You won't have much time to air anything, so let's hope they don't mind damp sheets. They're arriving this evening, Sir Bernard says.' His cool certainty that she wouldn't—or couldn't—raise any objections was infuriating.

'Which would account for the fact that there's a trunk and some boxes being brought up from the station,' Mr Bunbury said. 'I wondered what that was about. Unaccompanied luggage, the stationmaster told me. For someone driving down from London.' He rose with a sigh and wiped his moustache with a large handkerchief. 'I'd better get on with my rounds. Anything for the post, Miss Freya?'

'No, thank you.'

She got up from the table, poured herself more coffee and headed for the door.

'Going off to write,' Freya heard Mrs Partridge say with a certain pride as she went out. 'Work, work, tapping away at that typewriter of hers hour after hour. It'll be a big book by the time she's finished. Well, there've been a lot of Selchesters for her to put in the book.'

Mr Bunbury was doubtful. 'It doesn't seem a useful occupation for a lively young lady like Miss Freya, writing a history of the Selchesters. Whoever is going to want to read that?'

Freya closed the door behind her, paused for a moment to smile, and set off for the Tower.

It had been a family decision for her to become a kind of caretaker for the Castle after her uncle vanished. Everything was in limbo; nothing could be done with the Castle or the estate until and unless her uncle's body was found. And that wasn't likely. The police forces of three counties had, with the assistance of the Army, searched and dredged and scoured every hedge and barn and ditch in an effort to find the missing Earl.

But until firm evidence of Lord Selchester's death came to light, or seven years from his disappearance had elapsed and the legal formality of declaring him dead could happen, the Castle belonged to no one. Which hadn't pleased Freya's cousin Sonia, who stood to inherit the Castle and all her father's land and money.

Meanwhile, even Lady Sonia, used to getting her own way, couldn't do anything to get her hands on her inheritance. Castle and estate had passed into the hands of the trustees, and Freya had installed herself in the Castle, where she had lived more or less contentedly ever since, enjoying having the place to herself with company from Mrs Partridge and the ubiquitous Ben if she felt the need of anyone to talk to.

Now she'd had this pair dumped on her. Oh, well, maybe they wouldn't stay long. Winter was coming, and winter in Selchester Castle wasn't for the faint-hearted.

When Freya moved into the Castle, she had decided to take up residence in the New Tower. This dated from 1485, while the Old Tower, which stood some way apart from the main part of the Castle, was a couple of centuries older and more of an historic ruin than a suitable dwelling for anyone. Now, in the octagonal room which she had adopted as her sitting room-cum-study, Freya sat down at her desk. She pulled her Smith Corona typewriter towards her and settled down to work.

At least she could put in a few uninterrupted hours of writing before these wretched Hawksworths arrived.

# Chapter Two

## Scene 1

F reya didn't hold out her hand to Hugo, but got up from the bench where she was sitting and fetched a chair from the corner of the room. 'You won't want to be sliding along benches if you've got a gammy leg. This is Mrs Partridge, who looks after us all.'

Mrs Partridge was at the range, busying herself with a kettle and a large brown teapot. 'You two will be wanting a cup of tea after your journey. Then you'll have time to settle in a bit before supper. I dare say you'll be hungry.'

At thirteen, Georgia was always hungry. Despite having eaten a large, if not very tasty, lunch, she was more than ready to have a slice of Mrs Partridge's plum cake. Mrs Partridge said, as though reading her mind, 'You eat up, there's no shortage of food here at the Castle. That's one thing you'll find different in the country. Not like in London.'

There was something about the way she said 'in London' that made it sound like an exotic foreign land, probably full of sins and wickedness. Which was what made it such an interesting place to live. Not much sin and wickedness in Selchester. Hugo was depressed by what he'd seen of the town, however much the guidebook had enthused about it. It was undoubtedly beautiful, but he had no inclination for country life and did not want to live in any country town, however charming and historic.

He had no choice. Selchester was, in the end, the lesser of two evils. There was no possibility of his going back into active service, not with his leg. He'd been lucky in a way; the bullet fired at him on that dark, wet night in Berlin had ripped through his calf—missing the bone, the surgeons told him, by a fraction of an inch. Even so, it had done enough damage to put him in hospital for weeks, and they'd warned him he'd never again walk without a limp.

It was a desk job for him, if he wanted to stay in the Service. Valerie, who had no idea of what his real work was, urged him to quit and find a new job. 'After all, if your present lot say you aren't fit to travel and you'll have to stay in England all the time, then find a job where they'll want you to go abroad.'

Jobs for a man with his rather odd qualifications weren't so easy to come by in England in 1953, as he'd pointed out. Valerie was sanguine. She had lots of contacts; so had he. 'What about stockbroking, or banking?'

And marriage; the unspoken words hovered in the air. Settled in England, he wouldn't have the excuse of his irregular life to postpone the trip to the altar.

'I'd hate it. I don't understand money.'

'You don't have to.'

He couldn't explain his strong sense of loyalty, his belief that the work the Service did was vital and he wanted still to be part of it. Which was why he was here in Selchester—and already regretting his decision.

Mrs Partridge set a steaming cup of tea in front of him and a slice of cake he didn't really want.

Freya was saying to Georgia, 'Yes, the piebald horse is mine. Do you ride?'

Georgia shook her head. 'In the holidays, I've been in London, and riding is not a thing they did at my boarding school.'

Freya said, 'You're going to the High School here, aren't you? People speak well of it.'

Georgia's face grew sullen. 'I expect it'll be like most other schools; wish I didn't have to go to school.'

'Where were you before?'

'Yorkshire Ladies College.'

'Good heavens,' Freya said. 'That's my old school.'

They instantly began comparing horror stories, with Freya exclaiming over a hated English mistress who was still there.

'Making everyone's life a misery,' Georgia said.

Hugo supposed he must be grateful that they had this bond, as Georgia chatted away and Freya reminisced about her own, pre-war schooldays. It sounded ghastly; no wonder Georgia had hated it so much. Well, at least it showed that Freya Wryton could smile—an attractive smile, too. Thank goodness she wasn't freezing Georgia out.

Mrs Partridge was watching him with an amused gleam in her eye. 'If you'd like to come with me, Mr Hawksworth, I'll show you your rooms.'

## Scene 2

They had a bedroom each and a shared sitting room, with a small room for Hugo to use as a study.

Georgia liked her room. 'Gosh, I never had an armchair in my bedroom before. And all these cupboards.' She was enchanted to discover a basin hidden away in one of the cupboards and approved of the wallpaper, a riot of flowers and birds. 'And my bed's jolly comfortable,' she called out, bouncing up and down experimentally.

She went across the corridor and into Hugo's room. 'How about yours? Oh, you've got a four-poster bed. Look at those posts—you'd think they were made to hold up a roof, not a canopy.'

'We can swap, if you feel you'd like the four-poster.'

She shook her head. 'No, thanks. Even without curtains it'd make me feel shut in. I like all the panelling, though. The whole room's a bit Northanger Abbey, don't you think? Perhaps there's a ghost.'

She tried his bed. 'Not too bad, but it won't make any difference to you, since you ache whatever the mattress is like. I say, is that a gong? Just like in a film! It must be time for supper. Hope Mrs Partridge is right about the food, I'm starving.'

After a substantial portion of shepherd's pie, followed by apple crumble and custard, Georgia went off, complaining, to bed. 'It's stupid, starting school on a Friday. It's the kind of thing they always do, spoiling your week so they can give out timetables and all that. At least I won't have to worry about buses; Freya says there's a bike I can use.'

They'd eaten in the kitchen. Freya hadn't felt any need to apologise for it, and it was Mrs Partridge who said, 'You'll excuse us eating down here, but it's a Sabbath day's journey to the dining room and I haven't got two pairs of hands and feet.' But after dinner, when Freya had removed herself with almost indecent haste, Mrs Partridge took Hugo along to the library. 'You just sit down here, and I'll bring you a whisky. Or would you prefer brandy?'

Hugo was taken aback. 'I really don't expect . . .'

'Don't you worry about that.'

And she'd brought him a stiff whisky, which seemed like manna from heaven for his tired head and throbbing leg.

'No shortage of wine and spirits here, that's one thing, and Miss Freya said you were to have whatever you wanted. It's all from his lordship's cellars.' She went over to the windows and began to draw the curtains.

'It's a beautiful room,' he said, appreciating the mellowness of its polished floor and the shelves, stretching almost to the ceiling and filled with leather-bound volumes.

'His lordship liked his guests to use the library. He didn't spend much time in here; he had his study and sitting room where he kept his own books.'

Hugo took a sip of his whisky and raised his eyebrows. A single malt; fiery bliss in his throat. 'What happened to Lord Selchester? He disappeared, didn't he?'

Mrs Partridge gave a tsk of amazement. 'Don't you know? It was all in the papers. In *The Times* and on the wireless and every-thing. The town was full of reporters. It was that wicked winter of forty-seven. You'll remember that at any rate.'

Hugo didn't, except from hearsay. He'd been working in North Africa for several weeks while England shivered in sub-zero temperatures.

Mrs Partridge was delighted to tell him the story of Lord Selchester's strange disappearance. How he'd sent his guests to the library, gone to his study and was never seen again. Vanished. Walked out into the snow and got lost. 'A daft thing to do, to go out on a night like that. Bitterly cold, and a blizzard blowing up. They didn't discover he was missing until late that night, and by that time there was two foot of snow on the ground. Drifts higher than a man.'

It sounded improbable. Why on earth would a man in posses-sion of his wits go out into that?

Mrs Partridge, one hand raised to tug on the cord of the damask curtains, looked like a sibyl prophesying doom. 'When the police finally got through to the Castle, there wasn't much they could do, not with the snow lying and freezing temperatures. Then the thaw came, we had floods and what with one thing and another, no one was surprised they never found a trace of him. He'd vanished into thin air.'

'Who vanished into thin air?' said an interested voice at the door. Georgia stood there, wrapped in a dressing gown that seemed to belong to a previous era, an era of glamour and boudoirs.

'Where did you get that?' Hugo said. He didn't need to. He remembered, with a stab of sadness, his mother wearing it. He'd come early to say goodbye before going overseas, and she'd been in the Morning Room, reading her letters as she ate breakfast. It was the last time he ever saw her.

'What?'

'That robe you've got on.'

Georgia looked down at it in surprise. 'What's wrong with it? It was Mummy's. Aunt Claire said I could have all her things. My old school dressing gown got shabbier and shabbier, and then the arm came off. It couldn't be patched any more, so I gave it to the rag-and-bone man. Never mind about dressing gowns—who vanished? Are you talking about ghosts? Is the Castle haunted, Mrs Partridge?'

'I never saw a ghost here,' Mrs Partridge said.

'Why aren't you in bed?' Hugo said.

'I left my toothbrush behind, and I wondered if you had a spare.'

'There's no problem about that,' Mrs Partridge said. 'You'll find a new one in the bathroom cupboard.'

'Oh, thank you. So who vanished if it wasn't a spirit from the other world?'

'Lord Selchester vanished,' Hugo said. 'Several years ago. Now, go back to bed.'

'Oh, him. And there's no need to snap. I only asked.'

Hugo could feel sympathy emanating from Mrs Partridge as the door closed behind Georgia with a bang. 'Gave you a turn, did it, seeing her in your mother's robe? But if she doesn't mind, neither should you.'

'It's unsuitable for a girl her age.'

'Perhaps she likes wearing something that belonged to her mother, and she can't very well wear her frocks. Your ma was killed in the Blitz, wasn't she? It's hard on a girl to lose her mother. No father, either, since your dad died in the war, too. It's all very well for you, but a girl that age needs a family.'

How the devil did she know so much about him? He said, 'She has a family. There's me, and we have an uncle and an aunt, who looked after her when Mother died.'

'And where's your aunt now?'

'She's gone to America to get married.' Why was he answering her questions? He was trained to hold up under interrogation, but Mrs Partridge had no trouble getting information out of him. Nor out of anyone else, probably. Perhaps she was indeed a witch.

'So it's up to you now. It's hard on you, too, I'm not saying it isn't. But you're older and there's a big gap between you and your sister. Quite a responsibility for a young man like you having to look after a girl of thirteen. I've raised two of my own; right little madams they are at that age. And you aren't married, so you'll have to cope with her on your own. Mind you, it would be a bit of a burden for any young lady to take on responsibility like that, so perhaps it's just as well you're a bachelor.'

She finished drawing the curtains and went over to turn on some more lamps.

Hugo, annoyed at this foray into his personal life, changed the subject; missing Earls were safer ground than his family. 'So they never found Lord Selchester's body? What did the police think happened to him?'

'They reckoned he'd ended up at the bottom of a bog. We've a lot of boggy patches around here—you want to be careful if you go walking, especially down near the river, though I don't suppose you will, not with that leg. But in the end they reckoned he died out there in the snow, and his body was taken off by animals. Dreadful end for a man. Not dignified to have nothing left to bury, and his lordship was a dignified man, you have to say that for him.'

# Chapter Three

## Scene 1

The skeleton was discovered in the Old Chapel at half past eight the next morning.

Ben had reported a leak in the Old Chapel, and plumber Bill Dringley duly arrived to inspect the pipework. He knew the Castle of old and went straight to the kitchen. Mrs Partridge would give him a cup of tea before he got to work.

'On your own?' she said. 'Ben says there'll be flagstones to get up.'

'John Brodrick's coming along to give me a hand. Here he is, as we speak.'

John Brodrick refused the offer of tea, saying he'd have a cup after he'd finished in the Chapel, and the two men set off together, talking about the weather, the football pools and the darts match due to take place that evening at the Red Lion.

They went along the passageway and up the stairs leading to the baize door that had in former times marked the boundary between the family quarters and the domestic offices. It swung to and fro behind them as they crossed a small rectangular room, empty except for a bust on a pillar against one wall, and arrived in the main entrance hall, a marble-floored and silent space with a magnificent

Tudor staircase fading into the darkness above. Another passage-way, and they came to Grace Hall, which adjoined the older part of the Castle. A stone passage led off it; Bill paused at the entrance to switch on the lights. They gave off only a feeble glow, but as Bill said, it was better than bumping along in the dark. At the end of the passage, two steps led up to an ancient wooden door set in a stone archway.

Bill used both hands to turn the iron handle, and the door creaked open to let out a waft of damp air. He wrinkled his nose. 'They've got a leak all right. This place is usually dry as a bone.'

The Old Chapel was a bare stone chamber with seven pillars set in a circle, and an empty marble altar. Thin sunlight from high windows sent dusty beams across the flagstone floor.

'Chilly,' said John Brodrick, looking around him. 'It's a while since I've been in here. Didn't know there was any water here'—he drew a boot across a flagstone gleaming with wetness—'but I see there is.'

'They laid the pipes under here when they put in all those basins and the central heating. During the war, when all those Army types were billeted here.' Bill was inspecting a much-folded plan. 'Sloppy work, they'd no notion of how to lay a pipe or do a decent join. Just go the direct route, and never mind what trouble they were storing up for the future. They didn't have a clue what they were doing. Let's have at this.'

John heaved a leather bag of tools from his shoulder and took out a crowbar. They began to prise up the damp flagstone. 'Careful—up she comes.'

The flagstones in the Chapel had been laid long ago, on bare earth. Earth that now lay dark and damp from the leak in the pipe that ran somewhere down there. Bill inspected the plan again and thrust a pole down into the soil. It hit something solid. 'Gotcha,' he said, and picked up his shovel.

John bent over to have a closer look at what Bill's shovel had thrown up. 'That doesn't look like pipework. That's a bone.'

## Scene 2

Hugo had had a substantial breakfast, seen Georgia off to school on her bike and watched Freya ride off on Last Hurrah. 'Going over to Veryan House,' Mrs Partridge said. 'To see her aunt, Lady Priscilla. Lord Selchester's sister; my, she's a one.'

'Would it be all right for me to have a look round the Castle?' he asked.

'You won't do it any harm. Mind you, it's a melancholy place with everything under dust covers. You go where you like, Mr Hawksworth. Except the New Tower, which is the staircase off to the left from your landing. That's where Miss Freya has her rooms.' She gave him directions to the oldest part of the Castle, 'That's the best place to start. You'll find a couple of men over there, come about a leak.'

Hugo was walking along the dimly lit passage that led to the Old Chapel when he heard a man's voice cry out in sudden fear, 'My gawd, there's a body under there.'

A few limping steps took him into the Chapel. Two men turned shocked faces towards him.

'What's up?' he said.

'Lord help us, sir, there's something horrible buried under the flagstones.'

For a moment Hugo supposed that they'd inadvertently opened an old grave, but a quick glance round the Chapel told him that was unlikely. Wherever the ancestral Selchesters lay, it wasn't in here. He went over to look down at their grisly discovery.

One of the men, who'd been gripping his shovel with both hands so tightly that his fingers were numb, now released his hold, and as the head of the shovel hit the ground, a clump of earth came loose and with it a small object that landed at Hugo's feet.

He stooped and picked it up. 'A ring.' He placed it carefully on the altar. 'Don't do anything more. Do you know where the telephone is?'

The two men looked at one another. 'There's a phone in Grace Hall. Along at the end of the passage.'

'I'll phone the police. You two go to the kitchen and get Mrs Partridge to give you some strong, sweet tea. I'll come back here and wait for them. Quickly, now.'

His calm, authoritative voice had its effect. The two men let out relieved puffs of breath and made for the door, averting their eyes from the bare earth with its gruesome relic.

## Scene 3

Twenty minutes later, heavy footsteps sounded on the flagstones along from the Chapel. Hugo was relieved, not because he minded being here with the bones—he'd seen a lot worse in his time—but because his leg was beginning to ache.

Two uniformed policemen came into the Chapel, followed by a man in working clothes who was holding a spade and had a mixture of alarm and curiosity on his weather-beaten face.

The senior police officer looked at Hugo. 'You'll be Mr Hawksworth. We spoke on the phone. You're one of Sir Bernard's men, come to work up at the Hall. I'm Superintendent MacLeod.'

Hugo had given the police his name, but hadn't said anything about working at the Hall.

'Word gets about,' MacLeod said. 'Now, what have we here?'

He bounced down on his heels and looked down at the bone and hand with its spectral fingers projecting from the dark earth.

'Nothing been touched or moved? Where are the men who found this?'

'Being revived in the kitchen.'

MacLeod stood up and nodded at his Constable. 'Go and fetch them, Bill.'

'The only thing that was touched is this,' Hugo said. 'It was thrown up by the shovel and rolled across the ground.'

He held out the signet ring, and the Superintendent took it, lips pursed. He scratched carefully at the engraving on the ring with a fingernail. 'Gold. And a crest. The Selchester crest.' He sighed. 'His lordship always wore a signet ring. On the little finger of his left hand.'

The third man said, 'That's a left hand down there.'

MacLeod said, as though he owed Hugo an explanation, 'I brought Mr Gusby here with us to give a hand. He's the sexton at St Michael's.'

'More used to burying bodies than digging them up, Mr Gusby,' Hugo said.

'You'd be surprised what turns up, Mr Hawksworth. But I'll tell you one thing, Superintendent, before you asks me, you aren't going to find anything but bones here. Not in this soil. You won't find clues and all that, you can take my word for it. You've got a skeleton here, nothing more nor less. And we'll see when we get him up whether it's Lord Selchester, which is what you'll be wondering. Because his lordship was a tall man, so if this fellow here's a shortie, then it's someone else entirely.'

'Well, we'll have a look as soon as the police surgeon gets here and we get the rest of the body up. That's assuming there is a rest of the body, which we don't know for sure yet.'

For a ghoulish moment, Hugo wondered if the Selchesters were in the habit of burying various body parts; it seemed unlikely. No, he'd bet on there being a complete skeleton down there, and not a very old one either. This wasn't going to be a case for the archaeologists.

He would have liked to stay to watch them unearth whatever else was there, but once Bill Dringley and John Brodrick had come back to the Chapel and told the story of the discovery in a few halting sentences, MacLeod dismissed them. 'I'll need a proper written statement from you two as soon as I'm finished here, so don't think you can go haring off anywhere. And you, too, if you don't mind, Mr Hawksworth.'

'I need to get my pipe fixed,' Bill Dringley said.

'Well, you can't. It'll have to wait.'

'What about my next job?' John Brodrick was aggrieved. 'I only stopped off to give Bill here a hand. I've got a busy morning.'

'That'll have to wait, too. Now, where's Miss Freya?'

The two men looked at one another and shrugged.

Hugo said, 'She's ridden over to see her aunt.'

Bill put in, 'Mrs Partridge says she won't be back before this afternoon.'

'Mrs Partridge's in the kitchen, is she?'

'No,' said Bill. 'She said she was just going down into the town to get a few things, went whizzing off on that bike of hers like the hounds of hell was after her.'

The Superintendent raised his eyebrows. 'That'll be the news spread all round the town within five minutes of her getting there.'

The Constable, who had keen ears, said, 'I think I hear the doctor's car, sir.'

'Good.'

# Scene 4

Superintendent MacLeod came into the kitchen, accepted the offer of a cup of coffee and sat down on the bench with a sigh.

'All done?' Hugo said.

'Everything we can do for the moment.' MacLeod stirred several spoons of sugar into his coffee. Then he said, 'You haven't started yet at the Hall, have you? Pity, or you could have passed on the news to Sir Bernard. As it is, I'll have to give him a ring and tell him. He'll be on to London straight away.'

Hugo wondered why, but thought it best not to ask. Instead, he said, 'So you think it's Lord Selchester?'

'No one else has gone missing in these parts. And that was most likely his ring, we'll know for sure when Miss Freya gets back. Then it'll be a matter of dental records, I dare say. But yes, it's most likely his lordship.' Another sigh. 'Which answers one old question, but raises a lot more.'

'Were you involved in the search for him when he disappeared?'

'I was, but I wasn't in charge. They sent people down from London. And not just the Yard, but Special Branch as well.'

Hugo raised an eyebrow.

'Lord Selchester having been in government and involved in secret stuff during the war and all that, it was understandable, but it didn't make the work any easier. The Special Branch man was good, I will say that for him. He did a thorough job, but in the end it came down to solid police work, and nothing came of it. For a start we didn't have a body, and nobody who was at the Castle that night seemed to have a strong need to bump him off, even if we'd had any evidence that he had been done away with, which we hadn't. The conclusion was that either he'd gone out for some reason, and when that blizzard came sweeping down he got caught in it and perished, or he'd let in an outsider.'

'Not much to go on.'

MacLeod went on morosely, 'I expect we'll have the Yard down again, given who he was, although maybe Special Branch won't be bothered with him this time. And we'll have all the reporters poking their noses in and asking silly questions. I'll have to open the case again, find the original statements, and question all the people involved. It's a murder enquiry now; that's a different thing from a disappearance.'

Hugo said, 'Do you have a long list of suspects? Were there many people at the Castle when he disappeared?'

'Not as many as there would have been if the weather hadn't been so bad and people knowing that storm was coming. As it was, there were just four locals and family.'

'Family?'

'His son, Lord Arlingham; his daughter, Lady Sonia; and Miss Freya.'

'Where's his son now?'

'Dead. He was a soldier and got killed in Palestine only a few weeks after his lordship disappeared.'

'Hard on Lady Sonia, to have a father go missing and then to lose her brother. Was he the only son?'

Superintendent MacLeod's face was expressionless. 'Just the two of them. One son, one daughter.'

Hugo wondered if the man was always this laconic, or whether he was disturbed by what had been found. 'And there'd have been staff?'

'Only a butler and a housekeeper and a maid inside, and daily help up from the town. And Richard, from the Daffodil. He's a trained chef, used to cook for his lordship when he had guests. Nothing like the state they would have had before the war, of course, with footmen and chef and under chefs and all. The Castle was requisitioned during the war, and a lot of it was closed up afterwards when the Earl got it back. Great pile of a place it is, impossible to heat. And supposed to be haunted,' he added with a glint of humour. 'Servants don't care for that.'

'You'll have a job getting hold of the people after this time to question them again.'

MacLeod shook his head. 'No, they're all still here in Selchester. Even Mr Guthrie, who's abroad a lot, being in the Foreign Office, but he's on leave, so I hear.'

'How deep was the body buried?'

'About four foot down. That was some digging, that took a bit of effort. Although I seem to remember there'd been some work done shortly before in the Old Chapel, and so lifting the flagstones wouldn't have been such a problem.'

Hugo was surprised at how informative MacLeod was being. The Superintendent enlightened him. 'I'm sure you won't go talking about this, not when you're one of Sir Bernard's men. You people at the Hall know how to keep your mouths shut; I will say that for you.'

'No marks on the skeleton, no signs of injury of any kind?'

'Clean as a whistle, so the doctor says. The police surgeon will do a more thorough examination, but it's going to be difficult to tell, after this much time has passed, just how he died. He didn't fall down the stairs and break his neck, that's for sure. And he didn't put himself under the flagstones either. No, he was put there, which means someone at least knew he was dead. More than one person, probably; hard for one person to dig a grave.'

'I don't know,' Hugo said. 'I expect your sexton does a job of it in the churchyard.'

'True enough, but it takes time.' He looked at his watch. 'I think I'll make a telephone call to Veryan House, tell Miss Freya she'd best get back here.'

'To identify the ring?'

The Superintendent stood up and stretched, then hitched his uniform tunic back in place. 'Not only that. Miss Freya was here at the Castle that night, and she and Lord Arlingham had quite a row with Lord Selchester. She's got some questions to answer.'

'Surely everyone has.'

'All the others vouch for each other, and besides, three of the guests hardly knew his lordship. No, the truth is, murder is often a family business. And since Lady Sonia was flat out upstairs with a migraine, and Lord Arlingham is dead, the family member I need to talk to is Miss Freya. Pity; she's a nice young lady, but murder is murder.'

# Chapter Four

## Scene 1

The news flew round Selchester. 'There's a skeleton been found up at the Castle. Buried under the flagstones in the Old Chapel,' said Mrs Wandsworth. 'It's bound to be his lordship. I'll take a few more carrots, Mr Graham, please.'

'Lots of bodies up there, aren't there?' said Mr Graham as he spilled potatoes from the scales into her shopping bag. The sign above his shop said in faded lettering, 'Fruit and Vegetables, Suppliers to the Gentry'. He was proud of his connection to the Castle. 'Didn't they used to put them all away there?'

'Unhygienic, I call it,' said Mrs Wandsworth as she stowed the paper bags into her shopping bag. 'I wouldn't live in a place with all those dead ancestors underfoot.'

'No room for ancestors in your cottage, so no need for you to worry, Mrs Wandsworth.'

'And this body wasn't tucked away in any vault,' Mrs Wandsworth said. 'It never had a coffin or any kind of proper burial, just in the earth, so Mrs Partridge was saying. Gave Bill Dringley such a fright, he nearly passed out. Well, who can blame him, coming on a skeleton like that when he was just expecting to fix a leaking pipe.'

'If it's his lordship, the police will want to know how he got there. It'll be murder, that's what,' Mr Graham said, shaking his head. 'Not at all the kind of thing one associates with a family like the Selchesters.'

Dinah Linthrop, whose family had lived in Selchester for generations, recalled some of the exploits of former members of the family, but she held her tongue as Mrs Wandsworth moved on to find more people to tell about the macabre discovery at the Castle.

People were in and out of each other's houses with the news. Sworn enemies stopped to tell one another about it in the street, and newcomers who didn't know about the Castle and the lost Earl were swiftly filled in.

'Nearly seven years ago his lordship disappeared. Walked out into the snow, they said. No one knew why or where he'd gone. Never to be seen from that day to this. And all the time he was there; he never left the Castle at all.'

'Wonder if he walks?' said Martha Radley, who was standing in the bakers' queue. 'There are a heap of ghosts up there. I dare say he's joined them; an uneasy spirit always walks.'

# Scene 2

Vivian Witt heard the news from Marcel, who was doing her hair in the beauty parlour. She had been feeling relaxed and soothed, having her nails done at the same time as a perm, but her blood ran cold when the receptionist brought her a cup of tea and said, 'Isn't it awful? Have you heard they found a body up at the Castle?'

Although clients of Marcel were attended to in separate cubicles, these were only divided off from each other by flimsy curtains, and soon the whole place was abuzz with delighted talk about the body and who had found it, and who it could be.

All the pleasure in the pampering had gone out of Vivian, and she sat with gritted teeth, waiting for the whole procedure to be over so that she could go home and think. She must get hold of Stanley Dillon. She couldn't ask to use the telephone here; all these women would listen to her conversation with flapping ears. Of course, most of them knew that she had been one of the people up at the Castle that night. Anyone who hadn't known ten minutes ago would know now.

One bold soul, the offensive Mrs Raymond, who didn't know the meaning of the word *tact*, popped her head round the cubicle, exclaiming, 'Of course, Vivian, my dear, you were there. You and those others must have been the last people to see Lord Selchester alive. You'll all be suspects, I dare say.'

'Thank you, Moira,' Vivian said coldly. 'Since we were all together the whole evening, and can vouch for one another, I hardly think we're going to be high on any list of suspects.'

Vivian escaped as soon as she could, furious at the extra burst of conversation that broke out when she left and knowing full well that they had all been longing to talk about her presence at the Castle on that fatal night.

She went straight back to her cottage and picked up the telephone to ring Stanley Dillon. He hadn't heard the news. He let out a long, low whistle down the phone. 'I never thought that they would find him. Always assuming it is Selchester, of course, but I don't see that it could be anyone else. I wonder if Lady Sonia knows? This will be good news for her.'

'Good news?'

'Well, she'll have long assumed that he is dead, so it's not going to come as a shock to a grieving daughter. But it will affect her plans for the Castle. She couldn't put all the legal proceedings in place until the New Year, but if they've found Lord Selchester's body, then she can apply for probate at once. The trustees can wind everything up, and she can make her arrangements for selling the Castle as soon as she wants.'

'I hadn't thought of that.'

'I can't imagine they'll have much luck with an investigation after nearly seven years. The scent will have gone cold by now. And after all, none of us will have anything more to say than we had last time. It was a mystery then, and I reckon it'll still be a mystery now. Of course, I'm all right where I am, but you'll have the reporters hounding you; that's the price of fame.'

'I was thinking of decamping to London.'

' I wouldn't. It might seem as though you were running away.'

'That's exactly what I would be doing.'

'The police will want to talk to you. I think you'd better stay put for the moment.'

'You mean the police might appear at any moment? When I'm in such a state of nerves, heaven knows what stupid things I might say.'

'Probably not straight away. After all, they'll have to do the formal identification of the body.'

Vivian didn't like to think about the body. 'It'll hardly be recognisable, surely.'

'No, and I don't think Lady Sonia would fancy being dragged in to identify it. After all this time, it'll probably be identified by the teeth.'

Vivian shut her eyes. On stage or on a film set, she was indifferent to blood and violence; she could play Lady Macbeth or a gun-toting femme fatale spy without turning a hair. Off stage, she was distinctly squeamish. 'I wish you wouldn't say things like that, Stanley. It makes my stomach feel most peculiar.'

'Have you had any lunch?'

'I was in the hairdresser's.'

'Make yourself a cup of tea, or pour yourself a glass of sherry, and have something to eat. And don't dwell on it. It could be difficult or even unpleasant for a while, but you know what reporters are like. It'll be headlines for a day or two, and then they'll pound off after another story.'

'We'll still be left with the police. Superintendent MacLeod at the least, and that man from Special Branch with the soft voice might come back. He terrified me.'

'I doubt if Special Branch will get involved now.'

'What about Charles? He needs to know, but isn't he still abroad?'

'He finished his tour of duty in Washington, and he's back on leave.'

'How do you know? Are you in touch with him?'

'I am not. Mrs Bunbury, who helps out with the cleaning at home, also does for Charles, and she told me he's back. She's getting the house ready for him. I'll try to get hold of him in London, tell him what's happened. Then he won't be surprised to find a policeman standing on his doorstep when he gets to Selchester.'

'Oh, it's all so ghastly.'

'My advice to you is to get on with some work. Nothing like work to take the mind off one of life's little problems.'

Vivian put the phone down with a sigh. One of life's little problems? How she wished it was just that.

# Scene 3

Stanley Dillon got up from his desk and went over to the window. He looked out towards distant Pagan Hill, noticing with half his mind that the grove of oaks on the crest of the hill were showing brown amid the dark green of their summer leaves, and thought about the late Lord Selchester.

Then he went back to his desk, picked up the telephone and told his secretary to get him the Foreign Office. 'I want to speak to Charles Guthrie.'

Charles Guthrie listened in silence.

'I suppose it was inevitable. I'm driving down to Selchester tonight, I've a month's leave. Does Lionel know?'

'He'll be at his studio in London, but he usually comes down for the weekend.'

'I'll give him a ring and see if I can catch him. He'll be in a panic when he hears—you know how sensitive he is. Best to give him some time to get over it before he's back in Selchester.'

Charles put the phone down, but he didn't make the call from his desk. Instead, he left the building and walked to the other side of Parliament Square to a public phone box.

A woman was in the phone box, having an apparently interminable conversation. He waited for a few minutes and then impatiently tapped on one of the glass panes.

The woman flapped a dismissive hand at him, but finished her phone call and came out of the box, glaring at him and deliberately not holding the door open. He went inside, fishing in his pocket for the requisite coins. With the receiver in one hand, he riffled through his address book to find Lionel's London number, and put the call through. The phone was answered by Lionel's secretary, and it took Charles a little while to persuade her that he needed to speak to Lionel urgently. 'I don't care if he's in a session with a client. This is important. I must speak to him.'

At last a peevish Lionel was on the line. 'Who is this? Charles? I thought you were in Washington.'

'I'm back in England. I just had a phone call from Stanley Dillon. Workmen have discovered a body up at the Castle, under the flagstones, and everybody is saying it's Lord Selchester. You need to know, because the reporters will be all over the place, and they're bound to come after you and all of us who were there at the Castle that evening.'

There was a long silence, and then Lionel said, 'Do they think it's murder?'

'I don't see how they can think it to be anything else. Bodies don't customarily bury themselves under flagstones. Are you coming down for the weekend?'

Lionel sounded as though he was about to burst into tears. 'I was going to come down this evening, but it's going to be beastly, quite awful, everyone full of gossip and malicious looks and then, as you say, the reporters. It's such bad publicity for me.'

Charles said bracingly, 'You know what they say: no such thing as bad publicity. Besides, the police will want to talk to you. They're bound to come back to all of us. You can't expect anything else.'

There was a wail down the line from Lionel. 'Oh dear, how horrible it all is. What a dreadful thing to happen.'

Charles said, 'Ring me when you're back in Selchester. I have to go. Bye, Lionel, and don't worry; it'll all blow over in due course.'

As the door of the phone box closed behind him and he set off towards St James's Park, Charles wished he believed that.

# Scene 4

Lady Priscilla Veryan was in the garden, attacking weeds with vicious stabs of a hoe. She wore a wide-brimmed and battered sun hat and didn't look up as Freya approached. 'Heard hooves, thought it might be you. Give me a moment. This one's a nasty, tough specimen.'

In earlier days, Lady Priscilla had kept her extensive gardens in immaculate order, with the help of several gardeners and under gardeners. War had taken all of them except her ancient and bad-tempered head gardener, so Lady Priscilla, in the time she could spare from her extensive WVS duties, had furiously 'Dug for Victory'. Lawns that had been mowed and rolled for centuries were planted with cabbages; flower gardens became neat rows of potatoes and onions; tomatoes flourished in the greenhouses.

With peace and prosperity, Lady Priscilla could have employed a team of gardeners again, but by this time she was passionate about gardening. Her grumpy head gardener now had a boy to help him, while she set about replanting a knot garden on its seventeenth-century site.

She triumphantly scooped up the recalcitrant weed and tossed it into the wheelbarrow. She stripped off her gloves and set off along the path at a ferocious pace, calling over her shoulder to Freya, 'Bring that hoe, you can put it in the shed as we go past.'

Used to her aunt's unsentimental greetings, Freya did as she was told and then followed Lady Priscilla into the house. Compared to the Castle, it was small, but by any other standards it was large: an Elizabethan prodigy house built in the local pinkish-red brick with zigzag patterns on its numerous tall chimneys.

Lady Priscilla might take care of her gardens herself, but she kept indoor staff and rang for a maid to bring coffee. Freya enquired after her uncle, Sir Archibald, a busy MP who spent most of the week in London, and her cousins.

Her aunt dismissed them with a wave of her hand. 'All fine as far as I know. If I don't hear from them, I assume they're well. Helena's expecting again, but that's hardly news.'

Freya couldn't remember if this would be her cousin Helena's fifth or sixth child.

'Time you got married, Freya.'

A familiar suggestion. 'I do very well as I am, thank you.'

'Nonsense. What kind of a life is that? Alone in the Castle, digging out all that information about the family? No one will ever want to read it. Much better to leave all that sort of thing to the professionals, get an historian in to snuffle about among the parchments and leases. Dry as dust, those archives.'

'The family letters are interesting,' said Freya.

They weren't. Most of them were extremely dull, domestic, often petty, full of trivia. Some items of pure gold as far as Freya was concerned, but she wasn't about to tell her aunt about them.

'Besides, I'm not alone in the Castle any more.'

'I heard that Bernard had billeted a young man on you.'

'With his sister.'

'Is he another statistician?' Lady Priscilla's voice was ironic. She no more believed the official story of the Hall's statistical purpose than did most of the rest of Selchester. It had been known as the Hush-Hush Camp during the war, and few people had any doubt that was what it still was. 'What's his name?'

'Mr Hawksworth. Hugo Hawksworth.'

Lady Priscilla gave her a startled look. 'With a sister, you say? About thirteen? Called Georgina?'

'Georgia. Do you know them?'

'No, but I knew their uncle. Leo Hawksworth.' A faraway look came into Lady Priscilla's eyes. 'I haven't seen Leo since before the war. We rather lost touch, although we exchange cards at Christmas.'

'Are you sure it's the same family?'

'It's an unusual name, and Leo has a nephew called Hugo.'

'Then it probably is. Why did you lose touch?'

'During the war one did lose touch with people. Leo is a priest. He was a professional soldier but left the Army after the war. The Great War, that is. He converted, and was ordained.'

'No wife or family to stand in the way?'

'He was married, but his wife died. In India, when he was serving out there, attached to the Viceroy. Cholera, I think, or typhoid. They had no children. I'd have expected him to marry again; he was a good husband, so people said, and he liked women. No, he wasn't a rake. When I say he liked women, I mean exactly that: he liked the company of women. Understood them, got on well with them.'

Freya gave her aunt a sharp look. There was an unusual warmth in her voice when she spoke of this Leo Hawksworth. She was generally brisk, if not brusque, and regarded most of humankind with tolerant contempt. But not, it seemed, this man.

Coffee came. Lady Priscilla cradled the delicate china cup in her hands and looked back into the past. It was rare for her to reminisce, and Freya was content to sit in a shaft of sunlight and listen.

'The last time I saw Leo was at the Castle, strangely enough. 1935, the year Helena did the Season. We held a ball for her there. You'll remember it, although you and Sonia were too young to attend. It should have been here, but we'd had trouble with death-watch beetle and the house was full of workmen. So Selchester offered the Castle.'

'And Leo Hawksworth came?'

Lady Priscilla nodded. 'Archie knew him, they'd been in the same regiment. Leo was a house guest at the Castle. Got on well with Selchester, and Hermione liked him. That was just before she went off to Canada.'

They were both silent for a while, thinking of Lady Selchester, whose visit to Canada had stretched from weeks to months and who had stayed there when war broke out.

'Selchester did us proud that evening,' Lady Priscilla said, coming back to the ball.

Freya remembered it well. She and Sonia had been wild with excitement at all the preparations for the great ball and angry that they were excluded, although Sonia was taking notes for her own ball. Which never took place; Sonia was deprived of her year of glory as a debutante. By the time she was eighteen, Selchester Castle was in the hands of the War Office; balls and court presentations were no more than a dream from the past.

'Flambeaux lining the drive. Wonderful ices, and a tip-top band,' Freya said.

'And Helena in a foul mood. That was how I really got to know Leo. He took her in hand in the calmest way. I don't know what we would have done without him. I think Helena might have spent the evening howling in her room.'

Freya remembered Helena's tantrums. Extraordinary how that highly-strung—one might almost say neurotic—girl had turned into a placid matron.

'If this nephew has half his uncle's brains and charm, he'll be worth knowing.'

Although she liked the sound of Hugo's uncle, Freya had no intention of getting to know her lodger. 'I hope they won't be with us for long. It's only a stopgap until there's a place free in the town.'

'Nightingale Cottage might do for them. What's he like, this Hugo?'

Freya considered. 'Like something out of the Renaissance. Courteous, obviously has his wits about him, but I can just see him sliding through marble halls or dark streets, a dagger in his hand. Except that he has a limp.'

'You're being fanciful. You always did have too much imagination. I shall ride over to the Castle one day and meet him. Hear how Leo's getting on.'

'Hugo's an English Odysseus, perhaps. A wily pie.'

'A what?'

'It's from Golding's translation. He called Odysseus that.'

'Nonsense. This man hasn't been sailing the seas for ten years, has he, succumbing to sirens and witches and goodness knows what?'

'No, but I bet he's good at intrigue. A man of secrets.'

'Inevitably, if he's working at the Hall.'

In the distance, a telephone rang. A few minutes later, a maid came in. 'There's someone wanting to speak to Miss Freya, my lady. From the Castle.'

# Scene 5

Superintendent MacLeod had been circumspect, unforthcoming and definite about only one thing: the police would prefer that Freya didn't leave Selchester for the time being.

'It's likely we'll need to question you.'

'You questioned me back in 1947. Why should I say anything different today?'

'The questions might be different now, Miss Freya. This is a murder enquiry.'

'Well, set your mind at rest; I've no intention of going anywhere at the moment. Has anyone told Lady Sonia?'

'Not yet. We don't inform the next of kin until we're sure of the identification.'

The moment Freya heard the police car going down the drive, she ran into Grace Hall, picked up the receiver and asked the exchange to put her through to a London number. Mabel was on duty at the exchange, marginally better at not spreading the news than Irene was. 'Mabel, this is strictly private. Please don't listen in. Or if you must, keep it to yourself.'

She could almost hear Mabel's thoughts as she weighed up the pros and cons of keeping her mouth shut.

Gratifying as it would be to pass on whatever Miss Freya and Lady Sonia had to say to each other, Mabel felt it was probably more satisfying to madden the likes of Irene by making it clear she knew something but wasn't telling. She liked Miss Freya, no side to her. On the other hand, she didn't like Lady Sonia. No one did. Miss Freya won. 'I never listen in, Miss Freya, it would be more than my job's worth.' The lie was so blatant as to be not worth a moment's discussion. 'You go ahead and talk to Lady Sonia. Don't worry that what you have to say will get out, I'll see that it doesn't. You'll be wanting to tell her about the skeleton; ever so sorry for you, Miss Freya, about that. What a thing to have buried under your feet all that time and never knowing it was there. Your uncle and all. It is a shame.'

In Lady Sonia's London flat, the bell pealed for a full minute before her maid lifted the receiver and told Miss Freya that her lady-ship was resting and couldn't be disturbed.

Which, roughly translated, meant that Sonia had been out on the tiles, had got back in the early hours and was sleeping it off. 'I'm sorry, Rose, but you'll have to disturb her. This is urgent. No, don't argue. She can talk to me lying in her bed since she has a telephone in her room.'

'That instrument isn't switched through.'

'Then switch it through and put her on the line. Now, please, Rose. She'd rather speak to me than have Lady Priscilla ring her up, which is what will happen if you cut me off.'

The threat worked, and Sonia came on the line. Sleepy and annoyed, she demanded to know why on earth whatever Freya had to say couldn't wait.

Freya told her.

A long, long silence, and then Sonia's muffled voice—she'd put a hand over the mouthpiece—telling Rose to bring her cigarette case. The click of a lighter, a deep inhalation and then Sonia said,

'His signet ring? I don't see anyone else would be wearing that. The police? Oh, Lord, the provincial Superintendent Whosit and his PC Plods stamping around in their regulation boots. What a bore. Murder enquiry? Darling, why? Bodies don't bury themselves under the flagstones? No, I suppose not, but I'm sure there's a perfectly reasonable explanation for why he was there. I'll drive down after the funeral. There are a few things I'll need to do at the Castle now he's finally turned up. Darling, please, let's not pretend to have feelings we don't; we both knew he was dead. A shock? I suppose so, but you didn't dig him up, did you? Who did, by the way? Bill Dringley and John Brodrick? I see. And where, exactly? In the Old Chapel. Well, consecrated ground in a way; he'd have preferred that, not that it'll help him come Judgement Day. I just wish they'd found him at the time. It would have saved me a lot of bother.'

With that she rang off. Mabel let out a scandalised hiss, and Freya slowly put the receiver down and stood there, lost in thought. Selchester, lying there in the Chapel all this time. Did Sonia care so little about that? Or the fact that he'd been murdered?

Mrs Partridge found her standing irresolute beside the phone. 'With all the upset, I clean forgot to get vinegar. I've none left, and I've a salad planned for this evening, so I need it for the dressing.'

Mrs Partridge never asked Freya to do anything directly, but Freya knew what was expected of her.

'I'll ride down and get it for you.'

'It'd have to be soon. The shops will be closing.'

'I'll go now.'

# Scene 6

Hugo heard the sound of hooves coming up behind him, and he drew to one side to let the rider go past. He recognised the horse before he saw the rider; the big piebald horse with the ugly head was unmistakable. Instead of trotting past, Freya reined in.

'Good evening. Stretching your legs?'

Hugo looked down at his lame leg. 'Literally. I'm supposed to walk as much as I can. I thought I'd try a different terrain.'

He'd left the Castle through the orchard at the back and then gone along a wide grassy track. He didn't know where it led, nor did he care. He'd walked for half an hour and then turned to walk back, knowing it would take longer as his leg was hurting. The unevenness of the ground, with its tufts and hummocks and ruts, meant he had to concentrate. Balance was something you took for granted until you lost it.

He put out a hand to caress the horse's velvety nose. Last Hurrah gave a snort and jerked his head up, then lowered it and looked at him with a wicked eye.

Freya kicked her feet out of the stirrups, swung her leg over the pommel and slid to the ground. She drew the reins over the horse's head. 'I'll join you, if you don't mind company.'

'Not at all,' Hugo said. He eyed Last Hurrah, who was dancing on his hooves. 'As long as your horse doesn't tread on my feet.'

Freya laughed. 'It's a habit he has; he thinks it's playful, but he's never learned that an iron shoe and quite a weight of solid horse-flesh isn't exactly comfortable on human toes. Walk on the other side, and then he won't bother you.'

Hugo moved round, keeping a wary eye on the horse.

'Do you ride?' Freya said.

Hugo lifted an eyebrow, and she said, 'Tactless question; sorry—although all kinds of people with injured legs or even missing a leg do seem to ride.'

'I can ride, but I've never had a horse of my own, and it wasn't a favourite sport.'

'Cricket? Rugger?' Freya asked without a trace of sympathy in her voice. 'Bit of a blow then, not being able to do those any more. But I expect you'll find something else.'

'And you could reasonably point out that lots of people had far worse injuries during the war and they've all had to keep going. Keeping fit is the real problem. I'm not used to a sedentary life.'

'So you weren't going anywhere in particular, just walking for exercise? You won't be able to come this way in winter. If we have any snow, this bridle path will be blocked, and when it rains and then freezes, it's treacherous even if you aren't lame.'

They walked along together in silence, Last Hurrah occasionally throwing up his head and rolling his eyes at Freya as though indicating that this was slow work.

Hugo said, 'I'm sorry about your uncle. Distressing for you.'

Freya ran a hand down Last Hurrah's neck and said, 'I'm on my way back from the town. I went to get something for Mrs Partridge. I hadn't realised what it would be like there; it was stupid of me not to think of it. It's a gossipy place, as I suppose all country towns are, but somehow I hadn't expected . . . Well, you know the kind of thing. People stare at you and then look away and you can see them thinking, "She was there that night. What does she know?" I suppose you've heard all about Lord Selchester's mysterious disappearance.'

'Merely what happened this morning and what Mrs Partridge told me, which isn't a lot. Just the bare bones.'

Freya pulled a face. 'Bare bones is about right.'

'I apologise, I spoke thoughtlessly.'

'Don't let it worry you. Words slip out.'

'There were only a few of you at the Castle that night, weren't there? Mrs Partridge said you could all vouch for one another.'

'In a way,' Freya said. 'I left early. I had a bit of a row with my uncle because he'd been beastly rude to his son, Tom. I was always close to Tom. We were first cousins and we more or less grew up together. So we both stormed out, and it wasn't until days later, when they finally got through the snowdrifts to the Castle, that I heard the news about Selchester's disappearance.'

Last Hurrah dropped his head to snatch at a juicy tuft of grass. Freya waited for a moment and then pulled him away.

Hugo said, 'It's going to be difficult for all of you who were at the Castle while the investigation is going on. A murder enquiry has a way of turning up things that one might prefer not to have brought into the light.'

'You mean things that have nothing to do with the murder? We were all questioned at the time, when they were trying to work out what had happened to Selchester. But none of us thought for a moment that anything violent had happened to him.'

'The questioning will be tougher now. Disappearances are all very well, especially when it's a man in your uncle's position who's vanished, but murder's quite a different matter.'

Freya said, 'The police would be questioning Tom if they could. It must be frustrating for them that they can't. Not that it matters—not for this enquiry. How could either of us be suspects when everyone saw us leave halfway through dinner, when Selchester was very much alive?'

Could she be that naive? He wondered what the row had been about, and if there were witnesses to where they went after they'd left the Castle.

Freya changed the subject. 'If you go walking, be careful of boggy areas. There are lots of dangerous places, here on the hillside and down by the river.'

'Mrs Partridge mentioned bogs.'

'Some of the patches and holes are deep. Bottomless, the locals say. Which is nonsense, but they're certainly deep enough to swallow up the occasional animal. And people, too, in the past. Especially when you get near the river. It's like quicksand in some places.'

'Aren't you worried when you go riding?'

'I know where the worst places are, and Last Hurrah keeps me on the straight and narrow, don't you, old thing?' She gave the horse's neck an affectionate slap. 'He has a sixth sense. Horse sense, you might call it.'

# Chapter Five

## Scene 1

Georgia had school on Saturday morning, and ate an early breakfast with Hugo. He watched with fascination as she finished her boiled egg, turned the shell upside down, and returned it to the egg-cup before crushing it into bits with her spoon.

'Whatever did you do that for?' Hugo said.

'To make sure a witch doesn't take up residence, of course. Don't you know anything?'

One thing he did know, and that was how little he knew about girls of Georgia's age. His aunt had warned him that Georgia was going through a difficult stage. From his recollection of her, there'd never been a time when she hadn't been at a difficult stage.

He was looking at her as these thoughts went through his mind. She looked back at him with her eyes full of suspicion. 'You're thinking evil things about me, I can tell. Disapproval is written all over your lean countenance. Don't worry, I'm used to being disapproved of.'

She got up vigorously from the bench, almost sending it flying. 'I'm going to be late for school.' She picked up the lacrosse stick she'd left propped against the table and bounded towards the door.

There she stopped abruptly to turn round and say, 'Don't forget it's Uncle Leo's birthday on Monday.'

He had forgotten. 'Thank you for reminding me. I'll see if there's a bookshop in town. If so, I can buy him a detective novel.'

'It's amazing he's allowed to read them. I thought priests weren't allowed to read anything but the Bible and prayer books. There's a new Agatha Christie out—get that for him, and then I can borrow it.' With that she was gone, banging the door shut behind her.

Mrs Partridge came in from the scullery. 'That sister of yours seems to be messy in her habits, clothes strewn all over her room, but maybe she'll be planning to tidy it when she gets home from school.'

Hugo felt obliged to apologise for Georgia. 'I expect she was looking for her games kit. She has games this afternoon.'

'It was all hung up on the door, so no need to throw things about. She'll have to keep it tidier than that, or I won't be able to clean. Then the moths will get in, and all sorts of grubbiness, and she'll regret it when she's nothing but dirty clothes with holes in them. Girls don't know they've been born these days. Now, on Saturdays I don't do lunch, Mr Hawksworth, so you'll have to fend for yourself. Miss Freya won't be in either, but there's a nice piece of ham in the larder, and cheese, so you can make yourself some sandwiches.'

# Scene 2

Hugo decided to drive into Selchester. He would find a bookshop and then go to the garage to have the sparking plugs checked. He parked in a side street, asked a passerby for information and directions and found himself in a street of higgledy-piggledy houses, some mediaeval, some from later centuries. There were several shops with bow windows, and above one of those was a swinging sign depicting an open book.

There wasn't much room in the bookshop, but every available space was pleasingly crammed with shelves of books from floor to ceiling. A desk stood beside the door, with a till on it and an empty stool beside it. Hugo ventured further in and saw a spiral staircase that led to an upper floor. A voice called out, 'Hello, is that a customer? I'll be down in a sec. Feel free to browse.'

He called out, 'Thank you,' and went over to some shelves labelled 'Detective Fiction'. Footsteps rattled on the spiral staircase, and he looked up to see Freya jump down the last steps.

'I thought it was you,' she said, and came over to him. 'Good morning. Are you looking for anything in particular? Can I give you any advice? And before you ask, it isn't my shop, but the person who owns it is a friend, and I give her a hand on Saturdays.'

'I was looking for the new Agatha Christie.'

'Some copies of her latest one came in yesterday. Are you a fan?'

'I don't read much detective fiction. It's a present for my uncle.'

A few quick steps took her into a curtained-off area at the back of the shop, and she returned, brandishing a copy of *A Pocket Full of Rye*.

'It's supposed to be a good one. I'm sure he'll enjoy it.' She took it over to the till, took his money, wrote out a receipt and wrapped the book in brown paper. 'It's quiet this morning. I was just going to go over to the Daffodils for coffee. Why don't you come with me? You'll have to meet them sooner or later, and they'll want to know all about you.'

Who the hell were the Daffodils? Then he saw she was pointing across the road to a shop front above which was written in flowing letters, 'Daffodil Tearooms'.

She pulled on a jacket and held the door open for him, closed the door without bothering to lock it, and joined him on the pavement. 'The locals know where to find me, and if there are any strangers, I'll see them from across the road. There's Jamie waving at us.'

They waited for a butcher's van to pass and then crossed the road. Freya said, 'The proprietors are Jamie and Richard, but everyone calls them the Daffodils.' She pushed open the door to the tearooms to the sound of a cascade of tinkling bells, and went in.

There were about a dozen round tables, covered with yellow gingham tablecloths. Only three were occupied. As they came in, a cherubic man came bouncing towards them, beaming all over his face and fluting, 'How nice, how nice to meet you, Mr Hawksworth. I did so hope that you would pop in when I saw you coming down the street just now. But I can tell you're the literary type; books come first. Freya, darling, how are you?' He ran a critical eye over her. 'Not looking your best this morning, sweetie, if I may say so. We mustn't let difficult times get to us. Extra skin cream always helps the complexion when nerves start to show, don't you think?'

'Thank you, Jamie, kind of you to mention it,' said Freya, sitting down at a table.

Jamie pulled out a chair for Hugo. 'Now, let me introduce myself. I'm Jamie, and I run the tearooms with Richard, who is in the back baking. Let me take your stick and I'll pop it here in the brolly holder. I'm so sorry to see you limping. Is that from the war?'

This wasn't at all how Hugo had intended to spend his morning, but he appreciated that Freya was making an effort to be friendly, and he had a feeling that the Daffodils were destined to become part of his life in Selchester.

Friends in London had warned him about life in country towns. 'You're never alone for a moment; everybody knows everything about you. If you want privacy, you need to live in a busy street in London where nobody cares what you do. Either that or take root in the depths of the country where you have no neighbours. Poor Hugo, doomed to live in a place like Selchester, where if you go to the lav ten minutes later than usual one morning, your neighbours will comment on it. Still, you've got a car so you can nip up to London at the weekend to keep in touch.'

'I'll sit with you for just a minute,' Jamie said, 'since I want to know all about Mr Hawksworth. May I call you Hugo? We're very friendly here and all on first-name terms, and you have that long-legged sister whose school uniform doesn't fit at all well. What's her name?'

'Georgia.'

'And we know all about your terrible family tragedy, but we won't talk about that. Anyway, there's only one topic of conversation at the moment. Freya, dearest, have you heard anything more about the late lamented?'

Freya laughed and said she knew no more than the rest of them. More customers came in, and Jamie bustled over to attend to them, calling over his shoulder, 'It'll be your usual, Freya, and how do you like your coffee, Hugo?'

Hugo said to Freya, 'It must be tough for you, all this talk about your uncle.'

She gave him a direct look. 'I'm not overcome by sorrow, so there's no need to tread delicately. I accepted years ago that he was dead. After all, there was no reason why he would disappear and not come back. It's not like he was a Burgess or Maclean, setting off to vanish behind the Iron Curtain with a briefcase stuffed with secrets. Even if he had been, he'd have surfaced in Moscow long ago.'

Jamie came back and hitched his plump behind on to the table. 'Tell me, Freya dear, have you heard anything from Lady Sonia?'

Freya said to Hugo, 'Sonia is Lord Selchester's daughter and my cousin. She inherits the Castle and the money, although the title will lapse. With Tom dead, there isn't a male heir close enough to inherit.'

'It's a big responsibility, the Castle and the land and so on,' Hugo said.

Freya shrugged. 'Not one Sonia has any intention of taking on. She already had a plan for when the seven years were up and Selchester could be declared legally dead. This makes it easier for her.'

Jamie pursed his lips. 'And isn't that going to be a bad day for Selchester.'

'Why?' Hugo said.

Freya finished her coffee. 'Because she plans to sell the Castle to a go-ahead hotel group who want to do all kinds of things that locals aren't happy with. I must go, I spy a customer.'

She rose swiftly, leaving coins on the table before Hugo could offer to pay.

As the bells tinkled behind her, a door at the rear of the room swung open, and a tall man in chef's trousers and white jacket came out. Clearly, he was the other half of the partnership. He didn't bounce, but glided over to their table. 'Jamie told me that our new neighbour was in, and I had to come and say hello. I'm Richard; no, I won't shake hands because I'm all floury. Things are quiet just now, so I can take a few minutes off before our lunchtime rush. How are you settling in? Do you like life at the Castle? It isn't what one would call cosy, but of course in these days one has to be grateful for what one can get.'

Hugo agreed, and said, 'Have you had the tearooms for long?'

'Coming up to eight years now. It was the worst time to start, so soon after the war, with such shortages—quite dreadful. But we were determined. It was the only thing we wanted to do, settle in a peaceful and beautiful town like Selchester and forget all about the guns and bombs and death.' He looked across at the other customers, stolidly eating their way through cakes and buns. He lowered his voice and said, 'Selchester is the most tranquil place on God's earth, but you'll not believe it, coming here just now. You were there, weren't you, when they unearthed the skeleton? How dreadful for you.'

Jamie gave a dramatic shudder. 'I shall go about in fear and trembling, because the dreadful truth is that we have a murderer in our midst.'

# Scene 3

As soon as Hugo had turned the corner into Snake Alley, Jamie was out of the tearooms and across into the bookshop. Freya didn't need to look up to see who was coming in; she knew perfectly well it would be Jamie, eager to discuss the newcomer.

'Do you think he's good-looking?' was his first comment. 'Quite attractive with that limp and the stick. If you like those lean, keen-looking men. Of course, being a roly-poly myself, I always envy them.'

Freya said, 'He seems a pleasant enough person.' She didn't add that she'd much rather he weren't staying at the Castle.

'Come on, Freya—you must say more than that. What did he buy? Don't you think that a man's choice in literature gives you an insight into him?'

'Since he bought a book as a present for someone, no, I don't think it does.'

'A present? Who for?'

'Jamie, a narrow line divides inquisitiveness from nosiness. All right, if you must know, he said it was for his uncle. And he bought the latest Agatha Christie, and no, I'm not lending you a copy to read. If you want one, you'll have to buy it or put your name down for it at Boots Library, which is what you usually do. If Dinah had to rely on you and Richard as customers, she'd soon be out of business.'

Jamie was unrepentant. 'They say he's working up at the Hall. Maybe Army, he has that kind of look about him.'

Jamie's own career in the Army had not been distinguished by any gallantry awards since he had been a conscientious objector. But he had served with courage as a stretcher-bearer, and no one in Selchester bore him any ill will for his pacifism. He'd done his bit as far as they were concerned; he hadn't scuttled off to America like a lot of people did. And there was no question about Richard, who'd served in the Navy and been torpedoed twice.

'I know no more about him than you do. Probably considerably less, given that you're already gathering all the gossip. Why don't you go back and concentrate on keeping your customers happy? Then I can get on with unpacking a batch of books which arrived this morning.'

'Well, of course we take an interest in our neighbours. There's nothing else to talk about at the moment. I mean, we've all exhausted the subject of the body until we know for sure who it is. I don't suppose you've heard? Officially, I mean?'

'The first people to know will be the police, and then Sonia.'

Jamie's face took on a tragic expression. 'Oh, such a woeful day it will be, because it will mean that Sonia will be able to go ahead with her horrible plans much more quickly now she won't have to go through all that legal process. I spoke to a lawyer chum yesterday; we had a long talk on the phone. He'd been quite consoling about the seven years business, because apparently it does take a lot of formalities, and it might have helped to hold up things for a while longer. But if it is Lord Selchester lying there—nothing but a heap of bones, so I heard, the poor man—then she can apply for probate and sell the Castle as soon as she likes.'

'It's her Castle. She can do what she likes with it.'

'Selchester may have been a difficult man—or so people said; I hardly knew him—but he was a good landlord. So many of us have our leases coming up.'

All this had been thrashed out over and over again ever since the plan for the Castle to be turned into a luxury hotel first burst upon the town. Freya sighed, and, almost pushing Jamie out of the door, said firmly, 'Go back to the tearooms, and let me get on.'

'All right, there's no need to be so bossy.' And then, as a parting shot, 'Did you know the police from London have been here?'

'What? How do you know?'

'I saw the car go past, one of those discreet black cars. No bell ringing, but it might as well have had "Police" written all over it. Two men and a driver. That'll be Scotland Yard called in, and wasn't there a man from Special Branch last time? Bye for now.'

# Scene 4

Hugo bought a card and some paper at the stationer's then went to the Post Office, where he wrapped and addressed his parcel. As he handed it over to the woman at the counter, he suspected that here was another member of the Selchester information service. Her eyes gleamed with interest as she read the address out to him. 'Father Leo Hawksworth, St Giles College, Oxford.'

Hugo asked how much it was, handed over the money, and beat a quick retreat. He had a feeling the news that his uncle was a priest would be flying around the town before he reached the end of the street.

Mrs Partridge had recommended a garage. 'Wilf is who you want; he looks after all the cars. He's got a foreigner working with him, but you won't mind that.'

Hugo retrieved his car and drove the short distance to where a pot-holed road took him towards the river. The garage was opposite a livery stables, in a yard set back from the road. A sign above the entrance said 'Castle Motors'.

He got out of the car and looked around. There was a glass cubbyhole against the wall and a burly man with Army written all over him stepped out, wiping oily hands. 'Can I help you, sir?'

Hugo said, 'I wonder if you could check the sparking plugs. I drove down from London a couple of days ago, and I don't think she's firing quite right.'

The man said, 'I'm Wilf Farley. It's my garage, and it'll be a pleasure to have a look for you. We don't often see a Talbot Lago here—lovely cars they are.' He glanced at Hugo's stick and said, 'She'll have the turbo overdrive. I dare say that's why you drive her, if you have trouble with your leg.'

Hugo said, 'Yes. It's easier for me if I don't have to change gear so frequently.'

'War wound?'

'No, an accident.'

'But you were an Army man yourself, so I hear. I was in the REME.' A tall, thin, dark man with big feet and hands and an unmistakably foreign air came out from the workshop and across the yard. Wilf introduced him, 'This is Stefan. Stefan, this gentleman wants his sparking plugs looked at.'

Stefan nodded, loped over to Hugo's car and lifted the bonnet. He nodded his approval and bent his head over the engine.

Wilf said, 'Stefan looked after planes in the Air Force. Any time you need anything doing to the car, you just bring her in. We've no trouble getting parts, and you won't get better service anywhere, Mr Hawksworth.'

That startled Hugo. 'How do you know my name?'

'Oh, you're the gent as is living up at the Castle, come to work for Sir Bernard at the Hall. We look after his car. Nothing like yours; he drives a Rover.'

# Chapter Six

## Scene 1

U sed as she was to the Selchester grapevine, Freya was still surprised to find how quickly the news had spread.

Sonia had telephoned her yesterday evening. 'Darling, going out to celebrate, wanted to share the news with you.'

'Celebrate? What is there to celebrate?'

'Darling, Superintendent Thingie just rang me five minutes ago, to say he's had the report and the identification is confirmed. The body under the flagstones—sounds like a thriller, doesn't it?— is Selchester. The teeth prove it, and so I'm now the undisputed owner of the Castle and everything pertaining to it. Bye for now, off to drink buckets of champagne in my joy. See you soon.'

And here on Sunday morning, when Freya reached the top of the spiral stone staircase that led up to the ringing chamber in the Cathedral's bell tower, almost the whole band was already there, looking expectant. Ben had his hands on the tenor bell. 'Just waiting for you, Miss Freya.'

'Am I late?' she asked, taking hold of the rope to her bell.

Charles Guthrie stood opposite her, at 8. 'No, but Ben didn't want to start until you were here. The Dean asked him to ring a passing bell for Selchester.'

'Now he's been identified,' said Mr Graham, who rang 7. 'Now we know for sure it was him.'

Ben gave him a quelling look and, counting to himself, tolled the first of the nine bells that marked the death of a man. The sound died away, and then he rang fifty-six slow strokes, one for each year of Lord Selchester's life.

The tolling sent shivers down Freya's spine. It was no longer the custom to ring the passing bell, and it seemed to last for ever. The sound resonating in her head, she wanted to put her fingers in her ears and cry out, 'Stop!'

At last he finished; the silence after the bell was almost tangible.

At her side, Richard, a long-time bellringer, whispered, 'Chin up, duckie.'

The ringers were all in their places now, and they began to ring. The familiar, intricate patterns as the bells gave voice soothed Freya. For the moment, she forgot about Sonia and her uncle, her mind oblivious to everything except the sounds of the twelve bells in their cascading peals.

## Scene 2

Hugo had expected to have a tussle with Georgia about going to church, and he was geared up to reason with her: her aunt had always insisted on it; it was what her father would have wanted; her mother always went to church; she'd had to go to a Sunday service at her boarding school—no, that wasn't a good argument. Probably none of this would carry any weight. She was of an age and temperament to assert her independence, and that would mean not doing things that other people wanted her to do, and doing things that they didn't want her to do. Sins of commission and omission, in fact.

He was surprised when she made no objection. 'I thought we'd go to the service at the Cathedral,' he said. 'I haven't yet been in there.'

'That's what I was going to suggest,' Georgia said airily. 'Daisy's family go to the Cathedral, and she'll be there.'

'Daisy? Daisy who?'

'Daisy Dillon. From school. She said she'd look out for me. You'd better get a move on if we're walking, because Matins starts at eleven, and it's already twenty to.'

'We'll take the car. Are you going dressed like that?' Georgia was putting on a shapeless and over-large jacket that matched her ill-fitting brown tweed skirt. 'You look like some hairy creature that's died.'

'It's my Sunday best,' Georgia said, cramming on a pudding-basin hat to add the last touch of sartorial disaster. 'My only suit. It was part of the uniform at my old school. Aunt Claire bought it with growing room for me, but I've sort of grown in the wrong direction.'

'I suppose you could have it altered?'

'Nothing's going to make it look anything other than ghastly, so I might just as well wear it as it is and not be bothered.'

They parked the car and walked across the green to the Cathedral to join the stream of worshippers going in through the west door. A small cathedral, compared to York or Lincoln, but a ridiculous size for a town—should be city, of course—like Selchester. Hugo was about to take seats near the back, but Georgia's eagle eye had been darting over the congregation, and she'd seen her friend waving at her.

She grabbed Hugo's hand and tugged him to a row near the front, where she slid in, treading on toes as she went, and thumped herself down next to her friend. Hugo made a more polite passage along the seats, murmuring 'Sorry,' and 'Excuse me,' before sitting down next to his sister.

Georgia said to Daisy, 'This is my brother, Hugo. Hugo, this is Daisy. I told you about her.'

On Daisy's other side sat a pleasant-looking woman in a smart hat, and beyond her a big man who looked like a successful businessman. That must be Stanley Dillon. Mrs Dillon smiled at Hugo, and he nodded back at her, then rose to his feet as clergy and choir began their stately procession down the aisle.

Georgia whispered to Hugo, 'Daisy's brother's in the choir. He's that one with dark, curly hair. People think choirboys are angelic, but Daisy says they're all fiends, and she should know.'

Hugo found sitting through the service with Georgia's running commentary rather unnerving. She announced in a loud voice that they had the wrong tune for the opening hymn, complained about the hardness of the hassock, and commented on the peculiarities of the readings. Hugo was dreading what she might have to say during the sermon, but he needn't have worried. Georgia and Daisy had some kind of bet on as to how long the sermon would last, and their eyes were glued to their wristwatches.

At the end of it, Georgia said in a penetrating whisper, 'I win.' And Hugo heard Daisy say, 'Lucky you not to be here last week. The bishop was preaching, and he's an awful gasbag; he went on for twenty-seven minutes.'

Hugo couldn't say that the experience of going to Matins had refreshed his soul, although during the quieter moments, when Georgia wasn't whispering in his ear, he did take time to look around and appreciate the beauty of the Cathedral. He wondered vaguely about Saint Werberga as his eyes fell on a fine example of Victorian stained glass depicting a depressed-looking blonde woman in a mediaeval garment. Her bare feet were planted on a scroll with 'St Werberga' written in Gothic lettering, and she was clutching a goose. That didn't look to be in the best of spirits, either.

When he mentioned this after the service, Georgia put him right. 'You're woefully ignorant; she was the one who resurrected a goose. That's why all the Selchester arms have a goose on them.'

She then entertained him with the story, picaresque and peculiar even for a mediaeval saint, of the Abbess whose favourite goose had been eaten and then brought back to life again.

'I can't see how that qualified her for sainthood,' he said.

Georgia shrugged. 'Don't ask me. I'm just giving you the facts.' She added callously, 'Talking about eating a goose makes me feel quite hungry. Mrs P is cooking roast beef for lunch, so could we get a move on?'

They couldn't. The Dean, a round, merry-looking man with bushy eyebrows and twinkling eyes, was shaking hands at the door, and he was eager to greet the two newcomers. 'Are you just visiting our town and our lovely Cathedral? No? Oh, you must be Mr Hawksworth, who's going to be working with Sir Bernard. He's here with us this morning. And this is your sister?'

Georgia, her mind full of roast beef, scowled and then smiled, resulting in a strange grimace. The Dean looked taken aback and moved on to the person waiting behind Hugo.

'Just a mo,' said Georgia, who had spotted Daisy again, loping off across the green to talk to her friend.

Waiting in a patch of sunlight, Hugo caught sight of Freya, who had come out of the Cathedral with some of her fellow bellringers. She beckoned to him.

'I didn't see you inside,' he said.

'We slide in at the back, us bellringers,' Richard said.

'Did you walk or drive down?' Freya asked him. 'Drove? Then you can give me a lift back to the Castle.'

Hugo was introduced to Stanley Dillon, who had shrewd eyes and a firm handshake, and to Charles Guthrie, a pale, fair-haired man with a watchful expression.

He stood to one side, listening with half an ear to their conversation, the allusive talk of people linked by ties of friendship and familiarity. He felt out of it, removed from his company, and wished he were in London. Or better still, Budapest or even Bucharest. Anywhere but Selchester, a provincial backwater, this place where life moved placidly from one Sunday to the next.

'Teeth,' Richard was saying. 'They identified him by his dental work. Makes you think, doesn't it, when all that's left of a man's individuality are his fillings.'

Perhaps not quite so placid, after all.

'Do you know Sir Bernard?' Freya asked him. 'The one who's going to be your boss? Because he's kind of hovering, and I think he wants to speak to you. I don't want to talk to him, so I'll leave you to it. Where are you parked? Okay, I'll meet you there.'

Sir Bernard was a short man with a trim, silvery moustache, a ruddy complexion and unexpectedly dark, rather sad eyes. He greeted Hugo without formality. 'Ah, there you are, Hawksworth. Glad to see you attending the service. Makes a good impression if people from the Hall become part of the community. Settling in at the Castle? Good, good. You're starting with us tomorrow, are you not, now you've been passed fit?'

He glanced down at Hugo's leg. 'Not giving you too much trouble, I trust. Ah, there's my wife, making signs at me.' A plump woman, all perm and pearls, was beckoning to him, and he called out, 'Coming, dear.' He nodded at Hugo. 'See you tomorrow.'

'What did that man with the red face want?' Georgia said as she climbed into the back seat of Hugo's car.

'That was Sir Bernard. I'll be working for him at the Hall.'

'Secrets,' said Georgia, waving at Daisy as they drove past the Dillon family. 'Everyone says the Hall is run by the Secret Service. Are you a Secret Service agent, Hugo?'

'Nothing so exciting,' he said easily. 'All I'll be doing is sitting at a desk and pushing files about.'

'And pushing numbers, one assumes,' Freya said.

'What?' said Hugo, off guard for a moment.

'Aren't you all supposed to be statisticians up at the Hall? There's a big sign on the entrance saying "Government Statistics Department".'

'Cover,' Georgia said. 'Nothing is what it seems.'

# Chapter Seven

## Scene 1

F reya was expecting a visitor. Superintendent MacLeod had asked to see her again.

'On a Sunday?' she'd said when he telephoned her before lunch.

'This is a murder investigation, Miss Freya. I shall need to question all those present on the night Lord Selchester died.'

She wasn't going to be interrogated in her own sitting room. Nor in the library, which had always been a place of refuge. As was the kitchen—and in any case, that was too informal and friendly.

She decided on the South Drawing Room. It wasn't used now, and all the furniture was in dust covers. Well, she'd remove them. Mrs P might object, but it was her afternoon off, so she needn't worry about that.

Freya went into the huge room, hushed and eerie, threads of light coming through closed shutters and revealing pale shapes of shrouded furniture. She pulled back the shutters and opened a couple of windows before heaving the covers off. Where to put them? She took the bundled sheets across the landing and dumped them on the floor in the Countess's Morning Room.

Why did she want to talk to the Superintendent in here? Because she wanted the magnificence of the surroundings and the beauty of the room to trouble Superintendent MacLeod's austere Socialist conscience. He had the advantage of the law and its powers. She had nothing but her wits and her own clear conscience to stand in her defence, but she was on home territory and would make the most of that.

This room was full of memories for her. It was all so familiar: the exquisite Jacobean plastering, the Aubusson rugs, the enormous gilt-framed paintings, the vast tapestry of a mediaeval boar hunt which had hung on one wall ever since this part of the Castle was built.

There had been some wonderful holidays when her parents had been in England; a summer in France and another in Italy and a couple of joyful Christmases spent in London, but mostly, when her grim northern boarding school broke up, she would make the long train journey back to Selchester.

She used to arrive in the late afternoon, tired after hours of travel. In the summer, to tea on the terrace; in winter here in the South Drawing Room, sitting in front of a roaring log fire, toasting crumpets on a long fork.

In those days before the war, Selchester was one of the great houses of England, with a huge staff: dozens of servants from the boot boy up to a steward and butler, not to mention all the outdoor staff in gardens and stables.

She always preferred it when there wasn't a house party there on the day she arrived, so that it was just the family. Aunt Hermione would greet her with a hug and kind enquiries about her journey; Sonia, glad of her company, would nonetheless try to keep the enthusiasm from her voice and greet her with, 'Hello, squirt. What a sight you look in that uniform.'

Tom, back from school and then university, would slap her on the shoulder, tell her she'd grown and ask if she wanted a game of croquet before dinner. Her uncle would give her an avuncular kiss on each cheek, ask how she was, pass on any family news—and she would be wrapped once again in the comfort of the Castle.

Comfort by daytime, at least. In those days, she was afraid of the dark and the Castle ghosts, which she sensed and heard but never saw. She had been prone to nightmares as well. Strange that now, installed in the Tower, she never felt the presence of ghosts or suffered any disturbed or fearful nights.

When there were house guests, she and Sonia had to keep out of the way. They would be under the care of the governess up in the schoolroom, out of sight and allowed to come down, dressed in their best, at six in the evening. The glittering, glamorous people would look at them with indifferent eyes, commenting on how they had grown and how they all had the Selchester looks. Sonia, pretty even when a girl, was much more the centre of attention, but Freya didn't mind that. Sonia revelled in attention, as she always had and always would.

When the Selchesters weren't entertaining, life in the Castle was quiet and happy. Lord Selchester was away a good deal in London, attending to his parliamentary and government duties. Although they had a house in town, Lady Selchester rarely accompanied him. Freya, pleased to have her at the Castle, never questioned that arrangement. Now, looking back, she realised that they must have been estranged for a long while. Her aunt came to life when Selchester was away. She had boundless energy, loved to hunt and, Tom told her, managed the estate with enthusiasm and skill.

Holidays followed a pattern: large meals with good food from the Selchester estate, riding, hunting in winter, swimming in the river in summer. Weekly Mass in the chapel—not the Old Chapel, but the Victorian one, full of colour and gilt. Lord Selchester, meticulous in his observance, insisted that they all attend. Both chapels had been deconsecrated at the outbreak of war and wouldn't ever be used again. Freya wondered what the hotel group would do with them. Perhaps they would leave the Old Chapel as a kind of charming relic of history and turn the Victorian one into a sitting room, or even a bar.

Then the door opened, and the past fled as Superintendent MacLeod came in.

## Scene 2

Usually Freya spent her Sunday evenings writing, but not today. She wanted company. She needed to tell someone about that dreadful session with Superintendent MacLeod, but who was there to confide in?

She'd spoken to Sonia on the phone, but that was cold comfort.

'I hear they want to brush it under the carpet,' Sonia said.

A pause; Freya knew Sonia was smoking, and those puffing sounds were her wafting smoke rings into the air. She went on, 'Tom is a convenient scapegoat, since he's not around to protest his innocence or give evidence.'

'He murdered Selchester, and I helped him? Is that the story?'

'Don't be ridiculous, darling—of course you weren't involved. I know that, but the authorities don't actually give a damn whether you helped him or not any time. Don't fret; they aren't going to accuse you. Not formally.'

'Where did you hear this?'

'I have friends in high places. Don't make such a thing of it. It doesn't bother me that they'll never find out for sure who killed Selchester, so why should it bother you? Must fly now. Byeee.'

## Scene 3

Freya was used to Mrs Partridge's sixth sense, which this evening had brought her back to the Castle early in order to cook a hot meal instead of the usual cold cuts and cheese. So the kitchen Freya went into was warm and welcoming, and a delicious aroma hung on the air. Macaroni cheese. Comfort food from her childhood.

'With bacon bits,' said Georgia. She was seated at the long table, exercise book in front of her and Magnus the cat beside her. 'I caught a trout, and Mrs P is cooking it. Magnus is to have the head and tail as a treat.'

Hugo, who'd been helping Georgia with a tricky passage of Cicero, got to his feet as Freya came in.

Mrs Partridge gave her a long, hard look and then went silently out into the passage. She came back with a bottle of wine and two glasses. She handed Hugo the bottle and a corkscrew. He read the label and lifted an eyebrow. 'Rather special.'

'No point in drinking bad wine,' Mrs Partridge said. 'And no point in not making the most of the cellar while we're here. No, I didn't bring another glass. I don't touch alcohol.'

Georgia watched as Hugo poured the wine. 'You look like someone trampled all over you,' she said to Freya. 'Did Last Hurrah throw you or something?'

Freya had gone for a ride after the Superintendent had left. The weather had changed from benign sunshine to a cloudy, chilly drizzle, and she'd come back wet, the reins slipping in her hands and Last Hurrah shaking drops of rain from his tangled mane. 'No, it was rough going in places, but I didn't fall off.'

'It's the Superintendent who's made you look like that,' Mrs Partridge said, speaking over her shoulder as she checked the dish in the oven. 'Coming on a Sunday afternoon, I never heard of such a thing. Whatever did he want?'

Freya said flatly, 'Oh, merely to say that he thinks Tom murdered Selchester, with some help from me.'

'Tom?' said Georgia. 'And why do you call him Selchester and not Uncle Whatever?'

'We all do. Did. His children, his wife, his sister. We all called him Selchester. No one ever called him Ralph. Tom was Selchester's son. Poor Firecracker. He was in the Army and got himself killed in Palestine. In some pointless skirmish, which served no purpose and cost Tom his life. Goodness, I do still miss him. You'd have liked him, I think, Hugo. He was your sort of person. Energetic and honourable.' She gave a quick sigh and reached for the wine.

## Scene 4

Her remark had startled Hugo. How did she guess how much he valued a sense of honour in his fellow human beings? Something stirred in his memory. 'Firecracker?'

'That was Tom's nickname. He was like a firecracker, always fizzing and going off pop.'

'What was his regiment?'

Freya said, 'Fourth Hussars. But he volunteered for special duties and ended up in the SAS. That's one reason why Superintendent MacLeod thinks he did it. He was a trained killer.'

'I thought soldiers killed enemies, not Earls,' said Georgia. 'Let alone fathers.' She drew a doodle in the margin of her rough book.

'Then I knew him,' said Hugo. 'Or rather, met him for about five minutes.' Firecracker. A tall man with a lopsided grin. Thrusting bunched fists into the air and shouting imprecations at the heavens. 'Things were a bit tricky at the time. It was on Crete, and he'd just saved the life of a friend. The bravest thing I ever saw.'

Freya's face brightened for a moment. 'That sounds like Tom. But now he's going to be branded as a murderer, and there's nothing I can do about it.'

'How can it be a murder investigation if they already think they know who did it?' Georgia asked. She'd drawn a hangman's noose, but caught Hugo's eye and quickly rubbed it out. 'Aren't there loads of other suspects?'

'All with cast-iron alibis,' Freya said. 'Whereas I don't seem to have one.'

'You left early,' Mrs Partridge said. 'With your cousin Tom. His lordship was right as rain and in a nasty temper by all accounts. So that puts you in the clear.'

'Not according to the Superintendent. His idea is that we drove away to give the impression we'd left, but in fact came back, went in through the study window and . . .'

Hugo could already see flaws in this theory.

'It sounds as though they're clutching at straws. Georgia, can I have a piece of paper?'

Mrs Partridge went to the dresser, opened a drawer and took out what looked like a ledger. 'There are blank pages at the back.'

Hugo riffled through the pages with writing on them. 'What is this?'

'List of guests. The kitchen list,' said Freya. 'The housekeeper kept it. Who was coming, which room he or she would be in, any notes about food, name of servant waiting on them—all that kind of thing. Relic of a past age.'

'Hmm,' said Hugo, turning to the back. He smoothed down a page, took out his fountain pen, uncapped it and then looked at Freya.

'I'd like you to tell me what happened that night.'

Freya looked at her hands.

'I find it helps to write things down,' Hugo said.

'Superintendent MacLeod wrote it down.'

'You don't know what he wrote down.'

'Answers to the questions he asked.'

'Let's do it another way. You talk, and I'll write.'

Mrs Partridge said, 'Go on, Miss Freya, while it's fresh in your mind. Two heads are better than one.'

'Four heads, actually,' Georgia said, her eyes alive with interest. 'Five if you count Magnus.'

'Right,' Hugo said. 'You were there that evening, with Tom, and you left early.'

'Why?' said Georgia.

'Why was I there?' said Freya.

'Why did you leave early?'

'Wait, Georgia. Let Freya tell her story. Did you live at the Castle in those days?'

'No. I was living in the flat above the bookshop. Tom was driving down from London. He picked me up. He was late. I thought it might be the weather, but in fact he'd been delayed in town. He arrived just after six. We drove up to the Castle and joined the other guests for drinks before dinner.'

Hugo said, 'Drinks, then you went into dinner?'

'Not immediately. The others were all there. Hardly a crowd. Charles—you met him this morning. Mr Dillon. Vivian Witt, the actress. And Lionel Tallis. They were having cocktails and making awkward conversation. Not a lively gathering, I have to say. After a while, I slipped out to go and see how Sonia was.'

'She wasn't with you?'

'No, she was laid up with a headache. Well, headache doesn't begin to describe it. She gets migraines, stunningly bad ones. The doctor had given her some kind of a knockout pill.'

'So she was asleep.'

'Yes.'

The slightest of hesitations, a fraction of a second, but Hugo knew all about fractions of seconds in replies. He watched Freya rub the tip of her nose with a forefinger. She was lying. Or, if not lying, keeping something back.

'So she couldn't have got up?'

'No. Not then, not later.'

That had the ring of truth. Hugo wrote *Sonia, migraine* and ringed the words.

'Then I went back downstairs, and we went in to dinner. Vivian Witt was on Selchester's right, Mr Dillon on his other side. I was at the other end of the table.'

'And?' Hugo prompted. Freya had fallen silent, her eyes looking into the past.

'And Tom had rather a row with Selchester.' Now her words came out in a rush. 'All quite beastly. Tom had fallen in love with a girl, and despite Selchester's objections, he told his father he was still intending to marry her. So Selchester went off the deep end. Which wasn't like him. Cold, contemptuous fury was more his style when he was angry.'

'Why did he go off the deep end?' asked Georgia, intensely irritated.

Freya ticked off on her fingers, 'Antonia's half-American, isn't rich, is the daughter of a plumber and isn't a Catholic.'

'What's wrong with that?' Georgia said. 'All right, I can see why an Earl wouldn't care for the plumber bit, but for the rest of it. Is she nice?'

'Very,' Freya said. 'She was a nurse in the war, in all kinds of dangerous places. That's how she and Tom met; he was wounded in 1944. That wouldn't cut any ice with my uncle. He could be the most terrific snob.'

'Surely Tom didn't need his permission to marry,' Hugo said.

'No. And he couldn't prevent Tom from inheriting the title and the Castle. But he could leave most of his money to Sonia if he wanted to cut Tom out. Which he threatened to do.'

'And you stood up for him?' Georgia was doodling again, drawing a cat slinking out of a door. 'Did he get angry with you?'

'He hurled a few insults in my direction, and so when Tom flung out of the dining room, I went after him. I wanted him to come back, actually, but he wouldn't. I got into the car with him, saying he needed to reason with Selchester, not lose his temper. So he lost his temper with me instead, and we parted on fairly heated terms. That's it. End of story. I never saw Tom again. He flew out a week later to join his regiment and was killed soon afterwards.'

Wanting to break the tension, she stroked Magnus's furry head and said, 'The only good thing to come out of that evening was Magnus. I found him when I came back from the Castle that night.'

Georgia said, 'Go on. Tell us about finding Magnus. People say that a cat chooses you, not the other way round.'

Freya said, 'I think there's probably some truth in that. It was really a miracle for him. I'd made Tom drop me by the bridge—I was pretty annoyed with him by then. I'd left my galoshes behind, so I was wearing evening shoes and slipping and sliding on the snow. It was dark, of course, and then I heard mewing, and it was Magnus, looking like a drowned rat. So I scooped him up and took him home with me.'

'Why did you call him Magnus?' Georgia asked.

'Irony. Because he was such a tiny scrap of a thing. I had no idea he'd grow to be such a big cat.'

'You'd think that cat could talk,' Mrs Partridge said. 'Almost human, he is.'

'Pity he can't,' Georgia said. 'If he could, he would be your alibi.'

Mrs Partridge was taking the dish of macaroni cheese out of the oven. 'You cut some bread, Georgia. Yes, I couldn't think what Miss Freya was doing on her knees in the snow, and her in a long frock.'

'Did you see me?' Freya said. 'I didn't know.'

'I was sitting by the window, looking out at the snow,' Mrs Partridge said. 'I was lodging with my niece, just across from you—you'll remember that.'

'Yes.'

Hugo was listening intently. Did neither of them realise what this meant?

'She loves a stuffy room, does Eileen, and I was far too hot, with the stove going full blast. So I went to the window to get some fresh air. That's when I saw you pick the cat up and go into your house.'

Georgia knew what it meant. She said to Hugo, 'She could have gone out later.'

'No, she couldn't,' Mrs Partridge said. She put the dish on the table with a triumphant thump. 'Because by that time it was snowing hard, blowing a blizzard. No one could have gone out in that, and besides, I could see Miss Freya moving about upstairs. It stopped snowing after a while, and no one walked down that street after that, believe you me. I went down at midnight to put the milk bottles out, although I knew the milkman wouldn't be doing his rounds. Not in that weather. Snow like a blanket, and if anyone had walked in it, which they couldn't have done, it being that deep, there'd have been footprints. You were still up, Miss Freya, looking out of your window. I waved up at you, but you didn't see me.'

# Scene 5

Georgia had gone to bed. Mrs Partridge was washing up in the scullery, singing loudly. Freya and Hugo were still sitting at the table, drinking the last of the wine.

'Do you believe me?'

'Yes.'

'And you don't think Tom came back and killed Selchester?'

'He could have done. Theoretically. I don't have any details of that night after you and Tom left. I'd need to know exactly what was happening here to form any more of an opinion.'

Freya gave him a long look. 'What's it to you?'

'I don't like loose ends. I don't like what you told me Sonia said, about brushing it under the carpet. And I don't believe a man like Firecracker could ever murder anyone in cold blood. Least of all his father. If you and Tom are in the clear, then one of the others must have done it.'

'Or an intruder. An outsider.'

'Or an intruder, as you say.'

Another considering look from Freya. 'Have you done this kind of thing before?'

'What kind of thing?'

'Investigations.'

'In a way. I did some interrogation work during the war.'

'Spanish Inquisition stuff?'

'Pincers and the rack? No, we're more subtle these days. But one learns to have a sense of when people are lying.'

'And you don't think I'm lying?'

'No. Although I'm not sure you've told me the whole story.'

'We all have our secrets. I've told you everything about Tom and me, which is what matters. Listen, if you really want to find out more, you'll have to talk to Plinth.'

'Plinth?'

'Mr Plinth was my uncle's butler, and he's now landlord of the Dragon. Go and talk to him. Tell him I said you should. The servants were all shut away that evening—he'll explain—but he can tell you everything about what happened that night after Tom and I left.'

# Chapter Eight

## Scene 1

Hugo walked to Thorn Hall on the morning of his first day at work. There was a footpath through the woods, and the walk would be good exercise for his leg. Damn his leg. Brilliant work by surgeons had saved it from amputation, but there was no way, even with the best treatment and physiotherapy, that he would ever walk without a limp.

Sunlight filtered through the leaves of the trees around him. The soft noises of the wood should have soothed him: birdsong, leaves rustling in the breeze, sounds in the undergrowth as some creature went on its way. The air was warm. There was a scent of earth and the sudden fragrance of a late wild rose.

He hadn't set off in a joyful mood, and he didn't want to be soothed. The country might have its charms, but give him London any day.

When he'd come out of hospital, he'd wondered if the Service had offered him the posting as a way of getting him to resign. Then the Chief had invited him to lunch at his club. There, in the quiet surroundings—for he favoured the Athenaeum over the rather more raffish clubs used by the rest of the high-rankers of the Service—he had told Hugo what his new job involved.

There was nothing tactful about the Chief, and his opening words had been brutal.

'You're lame and no good for anything active, so you'll have to adjust to a different way of life. It comes to us all sooner or later. None of us can stay in the field for ever. Either we get a bullet put through us, fatally or not, or we lose our nerve.'

He hadn't lost his nerve, nor had the bullet been fatal. Just damaging enough to mean he'd never pass any fitness board.

'It's just happened to you sooner than might have been expected. Which is no bad thing; you won't have grown bitter, as people do in the end.'

Was the Chief bitter? Hugo doubted it. His intelligence work in the Middle East during the First World War had made him a legend, not to mention the fact that he'd been in and out of Berlin all through the inter-war years, when he'd been in his forties.

'You had a good war, and you've done excellent work since then, I grant you, but it's over. Times are changing. It's brainwork, not brawn, that we need now, and you've got plenty of brains and a trained mind. I dare say Selchester won't be as dull as you expect.'

No, probably even duller, Hugo thought.

'I gather you'll be staying at Selchester Castle, Lord Selchester's seat. He's not there at the moment, of course; he disappeared a few years back. He was at the War Office during the war, did an outstanding job on the secret side. He's the reason we have an outpost in Selchester.'

Hugo had wondered about that.

'Thorn Hall belonged to Lord Selchester, but he gave us a long lease on it at a peppercorn rent. The archives were sent there during the war for safekeeping. They were due to come back to London after the war ended, but we've decided to leave them there for the time being.'

Archives? That settled it. He reached for his stick and hauled himself to his feet. 'I'm grateful for your advice, but the truth is I don't want a desk job. I know, I know; I can't ever go back into the field. I'm a lame duck, but I'm damned if I'm going to moulder away among a heap of files.'

That had been the one thing that had kept him from handing in his resignation. Thorn Hall was used to train people in interrogation techniques, and he'd assumed that was what he'd be doing, and it was a job he could do well. Apparently not.

'Sit down.'

He sat.

'After the whole Burgess and Maclean affair, we've got to make sure that we haven't got too many other rotten apples in the system.'

'Because we've had a couple of traitors, there must be dozens more lurking in the woodwork?'

'Don't be facile. Of course there are. There's never just one cockroach, and usually more than two. And there's another reason I want you in Selchester. I want to know what's going on there.'

'Surely you know what's going on at Thorn Hall.'

'Don't play games with me, Hugo. You know perfectly well what I mean. Obviously I know the work that's being done at the Hall, and it's good. Sir Bernard is a capable man. But I have a faint tingling in my spine about Selchester.'

He paused and took a sip of port. 'There's something not quite right there, so keep your eyes and ears open. If anything crops up, keep it under your hat. Come to me first. That's an order, Hugo.'

Hugo opened his mouth to say, '*Too bad. My resignation will be on the desk of the head of Establishment Division tomorrow morning,*' but then shut it. The Chief was up to something.

'I took you on, Hugo. Trust me. Go to Selchester. You won't regret it.'

# Scene 2

The guard at the gate checked his name on a clipboard, looked at his ID and waved him through. 'Main entrance, sir. Round the corner and then keep straight on.'

Round the corner Hugo went, to be hit by the full glory of Thorn Hall. It was a Victorian pile, sprouting turrets and gargoyles with wild abandon, the extravagant creation of a tycoon who'd made a fortune in an earlier and more confident era. Over to one side was the inevitable collection of wartime Nissen huts; on the other, a small lake with a few ducks scudding among the reeds.

He went through a massive front door and into the entrance hall, a vast space with a crazily marbled floor, and was greeted by a competent grey woman in her fifties. Grey skirt and cardigan, grey hair, grey eyes. A thin nose, a thin mouth and thin legs clad in grey stockings. No fool, however; her light eyes were shrewd and knowing.

'I'm Mrs Tempest, Sir Bernard's secretary. Sir Bernard is in a meeting at the moment, so I'll take you over to Personnel. When you've completed all the formalities, someone will bring you up to see Sir Bernard. He's on the first floor.'

Mrs Tempest handed him over to a stout man in Personnel called Mr Dorsitt, who issued him with a pass, handed him a folder filled with sheets of information about everything from fire drill to security and told him, with some satisfaction, that his paperwork had all come through from London. 'Which is not always the case; very sloppy some of those clerks are at the London office. Everything's in order, and your salary will continue to be paid into your London bank account. You can make a drawing arrangement at a local branch, but we prefer our senior staff not to bank in Selchester. Your office is Room 19, top floor, next door to Mrs Clutton, who's the Assistant Archivist.'

Hugo filled in forms, signed his name in sundry places and waited while Mr Dorsitt flipped through the paperwork, stamped it here and there and finally placed it in a wooden tray on his desk. 'Thank you, Mr Hawksworth, that's everything we need to do for the moment. I'll get a messenger to take you to Sir Bernard's office.'

The messenger, a dispirited youth of about fifteen, led Hugo back to the entrance hall and up the main staircase, a marble affair with ornate banisters and a regulation strip of carpet running down the centre. He walked ahead of Hugo, along a wide landing, and paused in front of an open door to say, 'Here's the new bloke,' before heading back to the stairs, whistling tunelessly as he went.

Mrs Tempest came out, collected Hugo and knocked on the polished double doors at the end of the landing. She didn't wait for a reply, but was already inside when a voice called out, 'Come.'

'Mr Hawksworth, Sir Bernard,' she said, and left, closing the doors with a click behind her.

Sir Bernard rose from behind his large desk and came round to greet Hugo. He pulled out a chair for him, then went back to his own seat, a heavy, wooden swivelling affair. He put his fingertips together, pursed his lips and looked at Hugo over half-rimmed glasses. 'Are you comfortable sitting there? That was a nasty business with your leg. Hope it's healing as it should.'

'I'm fine, thank you, sir,' Hugo said.

'The medics say you still need regular check-ups, physiotherapy and so forth. No problem with that—you can ease yourself into the job. Take off whatever time is necessary; just let Personnel know. You've seen Dorsitt, dealt with all that? Good, good. Well, glad to welcome you aboard.'

He glanced at a folder laid on the desk in front of him. 'I expect you're wondering what you'll be doing here. I don't suppose they told you much in London.'

'It was all rather vague.'

'Quite so, quite so. We are rather a long way from London—Lord Selchester always maintained it was one of the advantages of the Hall. And to some extent, we operate at arm's length. A survival of the Hall's wartime activities is that we hold the Service archives, but you'll know about that. Those are what you'll be working on. Essentially, you'll be going through old files, looking for anomalies. Things in a chap's record that don't ring true or don't match up. I want you to take a long hard look at missions that failed. Find patterns, check the facts, worm out the truth, dig up the history.'

'When you say history—'

'Pre-war. Twenties, thirties to begin with. Those years when so many bright men at the universities started swallowing all the propaganda coming from the Socialists. And, worse, from the Communists. All that stuff that appealed to youthful idealism. Marxism, revolution, that kind of thing. Most of them grew up and left all that behind.'

'Only that didn't always happen.'

'No, unfortunately not.'

# Scene 3

Mrs Tempest came in with a tray of coffee and biscuits. Hugo had a sense of déjà vu. How often, before setting off on a mission, had he sat in an office with some deskbound superior, drinking weak coffee and eating biscuits.

This mission wouldn't take him to the wild spots of Eastern Europe. Now he was on his way to Room 19 on the top floor of this preposterous Victorian mansion. To a desk of his own, a regulation-size desk with regulation buff folders on it. And he'd no doubt end up with a regulation buff mind.

To hell with it all. The first and only thing he'd do at that desk would be to write a letter of resignation.

Then his attention was drawn back to what Sir Bernard was saying. He wasn't talking about files and history any more. He was talking about Lord Selchester's death.

'Altogether a very unfortunate affair, this murder. It would be very much better if his body had never been discovered. Then he would, in due course, have been declared dead, and that would have been the end of the matter.'

Hugo was taken aback. 'Surely, a murder in England—'

'Yes, yes, of course, murder is always a terrible thing, but this one is especially inconvenient for us.'

Inconvenient? Us? What was the man on about? Hugo thought.

'Who is *us?*'

'The Service. Me, you, everyone who works at the Hall. Lord Selchester's disappearance made no difference to our work here, but murder is a different matter. Where there's murder, there's the press, there's a spotlight on a place, especially when the victim was an Earl. However, don't worry. We're on top of things.'

Hugo wasn't worrying, except perhaps about Sir Bernard's sanity.

Sir Bernard went on, 'An officer from the Yard, a senior officer, came down yesterday morning, together with a man from Special Branch. I was present at the meeting, and it was all most satisfactory. We've quashed the story for the time being, and Superintendent MacLeod has been told he has to come up with a solution as quickly as possible.'

'Difficult after all this time, I would have thought.'

'Almost impossible, given the time lag and the circumstances. However, we need to name a murderer, even if he or she can't be brought to justice, so the inquest can bring in a verdict, and the whole business can be forgotten.'

'Just like that?'

His comment earned him a sharp look. 'Most murders are local affairs, so any investigation will focus on the family as well as anyone in the neighbourhood who might have had a grudge. It was agreed that Selchester's son, Lord Arlingham, is the suspect who best fits this profile, probably aided and abetted by Freya Wryton.'

Freya had been right. It was a stitch-up.

Hugo knew something about stitch-ups, didn't like them on principle and mistrusted anyone involved in them. They were an inevitable if disagreeable part of life in most organisations, so he'd objected to them when he could and learned to accept them when he couldn't.

Only he wasn't going to accept this one. Not just because it outraged his sense of right and wrong, but because the whole set-up aroused his suspicion. There was something seriously amiss here, something worse than the usual fudge and making the best of a bad business that he was used to in the Service.

'There were rumours of a close relationship between them. Women in love will do anything for the object of their affections, I think you will agree. Their moral sense is inclined to desert them.'

'You can't accuse Arlingham or bring him to trial. He's dead.'

'So much the better. Less publicity.'

'And Miss Wryton? An accomplice to murder?'

Sir Bernard made a whistling sound. 'All circumstantial, with the chief suspect no longer with us, as you say. No, I don't think a warrant will be issued for her arrest.'

'But it will hang over her. She'll always have to live with that presumption of guilt.'

'Oh, I shouldn't think so. People have short memories. She can move away from Selchester. She can't go on living in the Castle, after all, because Lady Sonia plans to sell it. Freya can go abroad, make a new life for herself.'

'And where do I come into all this?'

'I was coming to that. A watching brief, that's what you have to do with it. It was agreed at my meeting with the police that the Hall needs to be kept fully informed as to how the investigation is going. I don't have time, I'm a busy man, and I think it will fit in perfectly well with the work you're doing. It's hardly likely to be onerous, and I know I can rely on you to keep on top of everything.'

# Chapter Nine

## Scene 1

Mr Plinth greeted Hugo genially. 'You've been to see Dr Rogers,' he said.

How did he know that?

'Emily, our chambermaid, saw you going into the surgery. That'll be about your leg. Not bad news, I trust.'

'Just a check-up,' Hugo said.

'As long as they don't want to operate. Never go under the knife if you can help it.'

Hugo was beginning to feel his leg was public property. He'd already bumped into the postman, Mr Bunbury, and then Richard, while on his way to the Dragon. Both of them had enquired after his injured leg and recommended that he should do just as Dr Rogers told him.

'You'll soon be right as rain,' Mr Bunbury said.

Richard was courteous. 'You'll soon be walking without a stick, although I always think a cane adds a touch of distinction.'

Now here was Mr Plinth at it. Hugo was goaded into saying, 'I have to continue with physiotherapy, that's all.'

'The doctor will be sending you to Mrs Svensson, I expect. Swedish. But don't be imagining one of those blonde Swedish masseuses in a bikini.' A lascivious gleam came into Mr Plinth's eye and then died as he went on gloomily, 'Built like a tank, Mrs Svensson, and most come out of her treatment room hurting more than when they went in. Still, some folk swear by her, say all the pain is worth it in the end. What can I get you to drink? This one?' He touched the handle of one of his beer pumps. 'Our local brew, none of that nasty, fizzy stuff you get nowadays.'

'I've left it too late for lunch,' Hugo said, looking at his watch. 'It's just on closing time.'

'Don't you worry about that, sir,' Plinth said. 'Drinking-up time is flexible for locals. You just go into the snug—there's no one there. A plate of ham with pickle do you?'

He took Hugo his plate of food—thick slices of home-cooked ham and home-made pickle: 'I don't hold with serving my patrons shop stuff.' He accepted Hugo's offer of a drink, poured himself a small glass of port and lingered behind the small wooden counter.

'Faring well up at the Castle?' he asked. 'I dare say Mrs Partridge does you proud. Mind you, she's a tongue on her, and there's nothing goes on in Selchester but she doesn't know about it before the day's end. She'll have had your life story out of you by now.' He went on, 'Miss Freya will be worried by all this, I dare say. With the Superintendent nagging at her, so I hear.'

'She is. She told me something about that night, but of course she left early.'

'Nasty business. Miss Freya'll be keen for them to get to the bottom of it. She knows as well as anyone that mud sticks. I worked up at the Castle in those days, butler to Lord Selchester.' Mr Plinth paused and sniffed. 'The late Lord Selchester, I should say.'

'Miss Wryton told me you did. She said to come and talk to you about what happened later that evening.'

That earned him a shrewd look from Mr Plinth. 'Natural, you'd be curious, seeing that you were there when they dug up his lordship.'

'Was Lord Selchester a good man to work for?'

'Lord Selchester kept his distance with his servants, as you'd expect, but he was a fair man and gave me full responsibility. In return for which he expected to see his household run like clockwork.'

'An orderly man.'

'Indeed he was. He liked everything to be just so.' Plinth took down a pewter mug, inspected it, holding it up to the light, and set about polishing it. 'Which is why it pains me to think of him lying there all those years. If he had to die—and he wasn't an old man by any means, in his fifties and hale and hearty—then he should have been buried decent. In a coffin, along with all those other Selchesters. Everything as it should be, not under the flagstones. Hugger-mugger, as it says in the play. It isn't right.'

'You must have been one of the last people to see him alive.'

'I was that. Not,' he added, with a frown, 'that anyone can say I was *the* last man to see him alive, because that would be whoever killed him. Which wasn't me. It couldn't be, seeing as how I was shut away in the other part of the Castle and in company with Mrs Hardwick and Ben and the girl.'

'Girl?'

'Hattie, the maid, a useless girl. Always in a fright over something or other.'

'And Mrs Hardwick?'

'Mrs Hardwick was the housekeeper. She came to the Castle at much the same time as I did. They asked her to stay on when the trustees took over, but she didn't want to. She didn't like the ghosts.'

Mr Plinth spoke of ghosts in so matter-of-fact a tone, as though he were talking about rats or beetles, that it took a moment for Hugo to take in what he'd said. He was curious, but the ghosts could wait.

Mr Plinth wasn't lingering on the ghosts, either. 'Women tend to be fanciful, 'specially in an old place like that. And Mrs Hardwick was mighty upset by the police coming in, as they had to. She said she'd never worked in an establishment that had the police in.'

It sounded as though Mrs Hardwick ranked police on a level with rat-catchers. Or possibly ghost hunters.

'I wasn't asked to stay on, mind you. They needed a house-keeper, but what's the use of a butler in an empty castle?'

'Strange way to lose a position. Traumatic, you could say.'

'Traumatic was the word. And a bolt from the blue—not like when you can sense you're going to get the boot. Mind you, there was something in the air that day, and I don't mean bad weather. Martha Radley had been up at the Castle that morning, tipping over the tea leaves and talking nonsense about the future like she always does. But afterwards, I did wonder if she did see something in those dregs.'

'Did she foretell Lord Selchester's death? That would be remarkable.'

'Not exactly. But she went on about the Castle being given over to another, that evil was abroad and life wouldn't be the same for anyone in the Castle by the time the day had ended. Mrs Hardwick didn't like that at all, and Hattie had hysterics, said she was leaving at once. We calmed her down and told Martha to take her miserable forebodings off with her. Still, it left a sour taste in our mouths, and that's when things started to go wrong.'

Now they were getting to the heart of the matter. Hugo sent up a silent prayer that nothing would happen to interrupt Mr Plinth's reminiscences. 'Were things amiss before you discovered Lord Selchester had disappeared?'

# Scene 2

Caleb Plinth liked the look of Mr Hawksworth. He was the kind of man who'd have been a good officer in the war. One of the tricky ones, though; a rule bender if ever he saw one.

He was asking a lot of questions, but Plinth didn't mind that. Mr Hawksworth worked up at the Hall, and they were hand in glove with the police, so doubtless he had his reasons. The police were no more likely to find Lord Selchester's killer than his pot boy, but this man had a head on his shoulders.

Plinth ran the tap over a glass tankard, making a soft whistling sound between his teeth. His feet were firmly behind his counter; his mind was back in 1947, at the Castle, with the household in a bustle over preparations for the dozen guests expected.

He'd been in Grace Hall when he heard the raised voices coming from Lord Selchester's study. His lordship and his daughter had never got on, but from the sound of it, they were tearing into each other. Unusual for Lord Selchester, who preferred cold and cutting to shouting. Plinth hadn't lingered to hear what they were arguing about. He knew that to be found there if one of them stormed out could cost him his job.

'You could say so. Annoyances and hitches. And arguments, which always leave a bad atmosphere.'

'Arguments in the kitchen?'

'Oh, no. I wouldn't allow any arguing below stairs. The argument was upstairs, a father-and-daughter row.'

'A row on the morning her father was murdered could look bad for Lady Sonia.'

Plinth had taken down a glass and was now running his cloth around the rim in a thoughtful way.

'You might say so, but you'd be wrong. Only she and his lordship knew what they were arguing about, and he can't say and she certainly won't. The police did ask her, but she told them it was a family matter and to mind their own business. Besides, she couldn't have had any hand in killing her pa, leaving aside what a wicked thing it would be.'

'Why was that? Did she leave the Castle?'

'No, she took to her bed. With a migraine. She was prone to them, and it was a bad attack. So bad that Mrs Hardwick took it upon herself to call the doctor.'

'Was that Dr Rogers?'

'It was. He prescribed something for the pain and something to make her sleep. Ben had to go down to the chemist to get the tablets. But they worked all right. She went out like a light and didn't come round until the morning.'

'Thus upsetting the numbers. Was she acting as hostess?'

'She was. But as soon as Lord Selchester knew she'd be out of action, he said Miss Freya would have to take Lady Sonia's place.'

'And then, I gather, most of the guests cancelled.'

'They did, on account of the bad weather.' His lordship had become more and more annoyed as Plinth had conveyed the messages and telegrams from his guests. 'We were left with the family and four local guests. I really don't know why they came. They must have known there was a chance they'd be snowed in and, apart from Mr Guthrie, none of them were particular friends of his lordship.'

'And the ones coming from further afield were his friends?'

He pursed his lips. 'I don't know as I'd say that exactly.' And then in a burst of confidence, 'To be honest with you, Mr Hawksworth, I never could quite make sense of his lordship's house parties. I'd expected aristocrats, people from the best families. County types, maybe. Politicos, too, given his lordship was so active in such matters, often taking his seat in the Lords and serving on committees and so forth. But then there were what you might call Bohemians—like Miss Witt and Mr Tallis. Scientists, dons from Oxford, artists. All sorts, some of them with hardly a decent pair of trousers to their name. Eccentrics.'

'So you were down to four guests and Miss Freya and—'

'And his young lordship, Lord Arlingham. He lost his temper at dinner, which I don't blame him for, and then Lord Selchester turned on Miss Freya, saying some unpleasant things that I won't repeat, and she and Lord Arlingham left. Just like that. So there was the table, with great spaces between the guests, who weren't enjoying themselves at all.'

'Embarrassed by Lord Selchester quarrelling with his son and niece?'

'The guests didn't seem any too pleased to be there when they were having cocktails before dinner. Once at the table they looked miserable and apprehensive, as you might say. In the case of that photographer, Mr Tallis, downright frightened.'

'It doesn't sound like a merry gathering.'

'It wasn't. You could tell they were relieved at the end of the meal when Lord Selchester said he had some business to attend to and would join his guests later. He thought they might like to play bridge.'

His lordship had told him to take drinks into the library. There was a fire there, quite cosy, so he'd set up a card table and seen to it that they had the necessary cards and scoring pads and pencils. He could see the room now, in his mind's eye, warm and quiet in the soft lighting and the flickering flames of a good fire.

'I took in a tray with the decanters and Strega for the lady. A foreign drink. Italian. Not to my taste at all, but apparently it was her favourite, and his lordship had me get it in special. I asked if there was anything further that they wanted, and then I was about to take myself off to the servants' hall when all the lights went out.'

'A power cut?'

'Yes. Not unusual in those days, and what with the wind blowing up and the snow, I suppose it was only to be expected. The fire gave out some light, and there were always candles and oil lamps kept in the rooms in case the electricity failed. So I lit them and then went out to see if his lordship was all right. I could see some light under his study door, so I didn't disturb him. I supposed he'd lit the lamps in there himself.'

'And then you went off duty? Was that usual?'

'It was. His lordship had the habit of dismissing the servants after dinner. It was an absolute rule: no servants the other side of the baize door after dinner. Some of the ladies, if they'd brought a maid with them, weren't happy about it, but those were Castle rules. Besides, most ladies didn't have maids—not like before the war.'

'So you wouldn't be needed again until the morning?'

'That's what I thought. Little did I know what was going to happen, nor that Lord Selchester wouldn't be seen on this earth again.' Mr Plinth's tone was more sorrowful than dramatic. 'I went back down to the servants' hall, where they'd already lit the lamps. Richard wasn't there by then. He'd gone off earlier, leaving Mrs Hardwick to handle the rest. He was on his bicycle, you see, and it had started to snow, just a few flakes drifting down, but he didn't want to be stranded at the Castle.'

'What time was it when you went downstairs?'

'About ten. I gave Mrs Hardwick and the girl a hand clearing up from dinner, and then we all sat down to a late supper. We were just tucking in when Mr Charles—that's Mr Guthrie—appeared at the door. We were shocked; he had no business in the servants' quarters.'

'I'm worried about Selchester,' he said. 'He never came to join us in the library. I went and knocked on his door, and he didn't answer. The door's locked. Have you got a key?'

'Were you worried?'

'What I was worried about was his lordship's reaction if anyone went opening his study door when he'd locked it. Still, it did seem odd, him not replying to Mr Charles. I did have a set of spare keys, hanging in the butler's pantry, but I didn't want to hand them over. Then Mr Charles said, "It's blowing a blizzard out there. You don't suppose he could have gone out to the stables and come to some harm?"'

'I know there's a door out to the terrace from his old study,' Hugo said.

'There is, and his lordship was quite in the habit of coming and going that way. Mrs Hardwick said I'd best go and see, and so I got the keys and went back through to the main part of the Castle, along with Mr Charles. The other three guests were there outside the door, looking worried. Mr Charles took charge, and I was glad he did, as I didn't want the responsibility of disturbing his lordship. Mr Charles might get the wrong end of his lordship's temper, but I'd get the sack. And Mr Charles is the kind of man who takes command. You can see he must have been a good officer in the war.'

'You unlocked the door?' Hugo dabbed some mustard on to a mouthful of ham, but Plinth wasn't deceived; Mr Hawksworth was taking in every detail.

'We couldn't at first because there was a key in the lock on the other side. Mr Charles dealt with that. He had one of those pocket-knives with all sorts of attachments. He fiddled with the lock, and we heard the key fall on to the floor. Then I unlocked the door for him. He pushed it open a few inches, put his head round and called out, "Selchester?" There was no reply, so he opened the door and went in. We followed him. He went into the adjoining sitting room and called out, "He's not here either." And that was the truth, there was no sign of him. There was his desk with an oil lamp on it, and there was a fire and another lamp in the sitting room. Then Mr Tallis pointed out a big damp patch on the carpet, over by the door that led on to the terrace. That key was in the lock, too, but the door wasn't locked. Mr Charles opened it, and a great heap of snow came in. He and Mr Dillon had a real struggle to get the door shut.'

'Why on earth would Lord Selchester go out on a night like that?'

'It wouldn't have been so bad earlier. It didn't start blowing a real blizzard until a bit later, and his lordship shut himself away in his study at half past nine. Anyhow, Mr Charles said as how his lordship must have gone out, and they'd have to go and look for him.'

'In a blizzard?'

'Foolhardy, but Mr Charles is a tough sort of man, for all he works in an office. He said perhaps Lord Selchester had gone to the stables to check on the horses, and he'd see if he could get across the yard to see. Mr Dillon was all set to go with him, although Mr Tallis wasn't volunteering, but Mr Charles said that, given how dark it was, he'd need to tie a rope round his waist so he could find his way back, and Mr Dillon could hold on to the other end. I found Mr Charles a shooting jacket and some boots, and he had his own greatcoat on top. Ben found him a shovel from the furnace room, and out he went.'

'Intrepid, in conditions like that,' Hugo said.

'It wasn't no use either. He came back looking like a snowman and chilled to his bones. The stable lad was tucked up tight in his room above the stables, and there was no sign of his lordship. He'd been down to see to the three horses about an hour before, when the wind was getting up, and no, he hadn't seen his lordship, and there wasn't any call for him to come out to the horses; he'd know they'd be looked after. Which was true enough. Mr Charles said he'd checked the cars, which were parked under shelter in the other part of the stable yard, and Lord Selchester's Bentley was there.'

'Could anyone have driven in that weather?'

'Impossible. As you'll know, the drive's a mile long, downhill, and it's a terrible place for drifts at the bottom.'

'What did you do next?'

'Mr Charles was all set to telephone the police, but then it turned out the phone was off. Lines down, as might be expected in that kind of weather. Next thing, he said we should search the Castle, in case his lordship had come out of his study and been taken ill. But how could he come out with the door locked and the key on the inside? So there wasn't anything we could do but wait for the storm to blow itself out and then see if we could make our way to the town to get help. Only the snow laid and then it snowed again, so it was three days before one of the farmers got through with a tractor.'

# Chapter Ten

## Scene 1

Freya invited Hugo to accompany her to a meeting in Selchester. 'It's a perfect opportunity for you to meet the rest of the people who were at the Castle that night.'

'What kind of a meeting?' Hugo wasn't keen on meetings of any kind.

'A committee meeting. Plans for next summer. You'll see.'

Hugo gave her a wary look. Was this just the sort of thing that his friends had warned him about? They were on the upstairs landing, and Mrs Partridge's voice floated up from below. 'Telephone for you, Mr Hawksworth. Long distance.'

It was Valerie. Casting about for something to say, he told her he was becoming community-minded and going to a civic meeting. She was unimpressed. 'Hicks and bumpkins? Darling, don't let yourself be drawn into mixing with the yokels.'

Valerie's remark made up his mind for him; he would go.

Mrs Partridge, less vague than Freya, told him that the meeting was being held to discuss arrangements for celebrations next year. 'A thousand years since the foundation of the Cathedral. It's the sort of anniversary that gets those clergymen all worked up.'

Hugo and Freya drove into Selchester, and she told him more about it on the way. 'There'll be all the usual jollifications: bunting, street parties, a band, Morris dancing, bell peals and that kind of thing. There's talk of a royal visit as well, but the real business of this evening is to discuss putting on a big dramatic production in the Cathedral. That's why Vivian Witt will be there. She's the moving force behind the plan, together with the Dean, who is rather a sweetie and adores theatricals of any kind.'

'What about Lionel Tallis?'

'He'll come with his mother. Where Mrs Tallis goes, there goes Lionel, at least when he's in Selchester and not at his studio in London. She'll be doing costumes; she comes from a theatrical background.'

'Stanley Dillon?'

'He's the head Feoffee, which means he's really Mayor of Selchester, so he has a finger in every pie. Literally,' she added, 'seeing that his factory makes so many of them.'

'Feoffee?'

'Our local councillors are called Feoffees. We keep to the old ways here.'

The meeting was being held in the Masonic Hall, and as they went in, Hugo wondered if men in aprons were going to burst out of the cupboards with rolled up trouser legs, blindfolds and odd handshakes. In fact, it was a perfectly ordinary-looking hall, perhaps rather better polished and maintained than most municipal buildings. There was a table at one end and a few rows of chairs set out in the body of the hall.

Freya called out, 'Good evening, everyone. For those of you who don't know him, this is Mr Hawksworth. He works at the Hall—oh, hullo, Sir Bernard, I didn't see you—and I brought him with me because he's a whiz at lighting.'

Hugo opened his mouth to deny all knowledge of lighting and then shut it as Freya nudged him. He'd mentioned in passing that he had done some lighting for OUDS when he was at Oxford, but that hardly made him an expert.

Freya pushed him into a seat, and he whispered, 'What the hell are you playing at? I know nothing about lighting.'

Freya hissed back, 'Yes, you do. You told me about OUDS. It isn't until next year, so plenty of time to mug up on it. Find a friend who knows about it, and ask him.'

Hugo gave in to the inevitable, sat back in his chair and looked around.

'There's Charles, chatting to the Dean. You met him on Sunday.'

'I thought he was a Foreign Office man, so why is he here?'

'Representing the amateur dramatic society. He's a brilliant actor and always takes a part in local productions, if he can. He's on leave at the moment, just back from a posting in Washington. You know Sir Bernard, of course. His wife will be here, presiding over refreshments at the end. She was a stalwart of the WVS and misses it. The skinny young man in the dog collar is Larry. He's the Bishop's secretary, a palace spy in our midst.'

'I see you're very much part of the community.'

'Wrong,' Freya said. 'I'm Castle, and we've never really belonged. Poor dears, it'll alarm them when I'm turned out of the Castle and come to live among them. Then there won't be any Castle except the hotel people, and that will be quite different.' She went on, 'That's Lionel coming in. No, not the one who looks like a rugger player—he's the Cathedral surveyor. Lionel is the dapper man with an anxious expression. That's his mother with him, the one with her hair in an odd bun. Oh, and there's Vivian Witt.'

Hugo didn't need to ask which one she was. You would have to have been shut away in a lunatic asylum not to recognise that beautiful, wilful face with the pansy-smudged eyes and the exquisitely sensitive mouth. She was fortunate in that her looks worked well both on stage and in film, but Hugo did wonder what had brought her to Selchester and kept her here. He asked Freya, in an undertone.

She replied, 'Lots of London people like to have a hideaway in the country. And Selchester is far enough from town that her London friends aren't going to casually drop in. So it gives her a certain amount of privacy. She's here at the moment because she just finished a run in the West End. *St Joan.* She's due to begin filming soon, and she'll have come back to Selchester to recuperate her spirits, as she puts it.'

And to answer a few questions from the police.

'I think she really likes Selchester because she can sleep and drink and smoke without having some vicious member of the press take an unflattering photo of her. She can slouch around in ordinary clothes and pretend she's a normal human being.'

# Scene 2

Vivian Witt wasn't dressed this evening in the kind of clothes that she was normally photographed in, but it was hardly slouching. Her soft tweed skirt had Paris written all over it, and Hugo guessed that the twinset in a soft violet colour had probably cost more than most of the women's clothes in the room put together.

Mr Dillon pinged a glass of water with a pen to bring the meeting to order. The Dean sat on one side of him and Vivian Witt on the other, her elegant legs neatly crossed at the ankle.

A competent man, Dillon. And he had charm as well as authority. If he was behind this scheme, it would probably be a success.

Dillon began, 'We all know why we're here, and I'm very happy to see Mr Hawksworth joining us.' Everyone turned around and looked at Hugo, much to his embarrassment, and then, mercifully, Mr Dillon went on, 'We all know why we're here, and that is to decide on whether it will be possible to mount a theatrical production at the Cathedral to celebrate the anniversary. An ambitious production, not simply for the benefit of our own citizens, but to attract audiences from further afield and see whether we can put Selchester on the map.'

Murmurs from the floor.

'I know people have strong feelings about tourists and charabancs and all that kind of thing, but the fact remains that in these difficult times a certain number of the right kind of visitors to our town can do nothing but enhance our reputation and be good for business. I'll now hand you over to Miss Witt, who has some exciting news for us.'

Vivian Witt stood with a swift, graceful movement. Her voice was a marvel. Beautifully modulated, pitched exactly right. She was restraining the more flamboyant part of her nature, playing the role of thoughtful professional woman instead.

'I've spoken to Sir Desmond Winthrop about our plans.'

Another murmur, this time of excitement, ran around the hall. Sir Desmond was one of the great theatrical knights, a starry figure by anyone's standards.

'He is willing to take part if we decide to put on a play. Three evening performances and one afternoon performance. The play he would like us to do is T. S. Eliot's *Murder in the Cathedral*.'

Another murmur.

'It's a complex verse play, as I'm sure you all know, and our Cathedral will be a perfect setting for it. And you'll be pleased to learn that one of the reasons that Sir Desmond is willing to do this is that his grandfather lived in Selchester for several years.'

This time there was a little outbreak of applause.

'Sir Desmond is waiving his fee in this instance, but he stipulates that the other main parts are to be played by professional

103

actors, and they will have to be paid. The rest of the cast will be played by people from Selchester.'

She sat down amidst enthusiastic applause. Mr Dillon pinged his glass again and called on the Dean to say a few words.

The Dean, beaming all over his face, thanked Vivian Witt and added, 'Miss Witt didn't mention that Sir Desmond wants her to direct the play, and she has agreed to do this, also without a fee.'

This news wasn't received with the same rapture as the news about Sir Desmond.

Freya whispered, 'They're old-fashioned in Selchester about women. They'll come round to it. It's clear that Sir Desmond and Vivian Witt come as a package.'

Looking beyond her charming smile, Hugo came to the conclusion that the actress was more than capable of directing the play and ignoring any mutterings about women in charge. He whispered back, 'I fancy there's a rod of steel hidden in those tweeds and twinset.'

'Got it in one. And she has the Dean wrapped around her little finger, which will help to quell any misogynistic fuss and doubts from the clergy.'

This was all very well, but as the meeting moved on to cover the other delights that would be on offer, Hugo considered the question of the lighting. An amateur production would be bad enough; a professional one was impossible. How dare Freya co-opt him to do that? He had only the vaguest notion of stage lighting; he'd left all that to the enthusiasts in OUDS. And wouldn't it involve ladders? No way could he shin up and down ladders.

# Scene 3

One glance told Charles all he needed to know about Hugo Hawksworth. He had Service written all over him. Why was he at the Hall? That place was the graveyard of ambition—everyone knew that. Oh, but of course, the man was lame. He wondered how that had happened, but it didn't matter; it would be enough to chain him to a desk for the rest of his career. No different from Charles himself. Foreign Office, the Service—they were all government officials. Some more in the shadows than others, that was the only difference.

The Dean and Stanley Dillon had managed a good turn-out this evening. Nothing like the prospect of a big theatrical event to get the locals excited. He looked around the hall; this was quintessential England. Inward-looking, still licking the wounds of war, keeping the flag flying and hoping that Life Was Getting Better.

He liked the sound of what Vivian had planned. She was thinking big; Sir Desmond was a catch. He'd ask Vivian for the dates and make sure he could be in Selchester to take part. He should manage it; he would be spending the next two years at least in London after a long stint in embassies in various parts of the world.

It would make a change, living in London. Much more civilised than Washington; much better to be among Englishmen again, even if they were small-minded and obstinately had their backs turned to the future. Anything was better than Americans. And he could get down to his cottage here at weekends, do some fishing, read.

Freya looked a bit drawn. No doubt the discovery of Selchester's body had come as a shock. Town gossip said she knew more about the murder than she was letting on, but that was nonsense.

Hadn't Tom Arlingham quarrelled with his father, and weren't he and Freya always close? Not wise, first cousins . . .

Charles knew there was nothing in that. Tom and Freya had been like brother and sister. There'd never been a hint of a romantic attachment there. Good, time for a drink. God, look at Lionel. He wasn't taking this at all well, poor chap. A bundle of nerves, but he'd been questioned by the police and had come through that ordeal all right. He'd do.

# Scene 4

Lionel looked at Hugo with a professional eye. Good bones, and if he photographed men at all, he'd do a portrait of him. Half shadows, with the focus on those intelligent, wary eyes.

'*There's no art to find the mind's construction in the face.*' The words tumbled into his brain, and he gave a little gasp; unlucky to quote from the Scottish play. If he'd said it out loud, Vivian would have rebuked him. Or was it only bad luck in a theatre?

Shakespeare was wrong. One could read faces; at least, *he* could. This Hugo Hawksworth was a watcher and a listener, but not a bystander. There were whispers of violence in that face. Not irrational, unprovoked violence, but swift action and a coup de grâce in a tight spot. The man had been in more than one tight spot, he decided. You could see it in his face. During the war, no doubt, when violence came stalking even the mildest of men.

Not that it had stalked Lionel. Friends had urged him to become a war photographer, telling him the powers that be would snap him up, with his skill and reputation. Only what use was a war photographer who fainted at the sight of blood? So he'd been called up, sent for basic training with the great unwashed in a ghastly camp in Northumberland, where everyone from the Sergeant downwards had been beastly to him. His rescue had come in the shape of an officer who knew his work and sent him off to air reconnaissance, where he'd spent the rest of the war in comparative peace.

A play, here in Selchester, in the Cathedral. The T. S. Eliot play. With a murder at its heart—a pity they had to go for that. But wonderful for photos: knights and priests against the pillars, soaring arches . . .

His mother nudged him. 'You aren't paying attention, Lionel. Go and get me a drink. Gin and lime for me, since the Dean's providing.'

# Scene 5

The refreshments turned out to be of a superior kind; the Dean, a wealthy man, having supplied alcoholic drinks alongside the inevitable lemonade and tea.

'Now's our chance,' Freya said. 'Let's go and nab Lionel.' She guided Hugo across to where Lionel was standing with his mother. This was, Hugo quickly realised, not a good move. Mrs Tallis fixed him with a beady eye and wanted to know all about his experience in lighting.

Freya came to his rescue, saying airily, 'Oh, OUDS at Oxford and some things in London. Not a professional like you, of course, Mrs Tallis, but I'm sure quite able to deal with what we'll need in the Cathedral.'

Lionel seemed embarrassed by his mother's direct line of questioning, and he smiled at Hugo and said, 'Of course, we all know you're staying at the Castle. I do hope you're comfortable. It's such a great draughty place.'

'I'm not sure how I'll survive the winter, should I stay there that long, but I'm merely temporary.'

Lionel said, pursing his soft mouth, 'Everything is temporary at the Castle now, with Lady Sonia's plans.' This with a quick sidelong glance at Freya.

Freya said, 'Buck up, Lionel. It's hardly going to affect you very much.'

'On the contrary, it will affect all of us. It'll change the whole nature of Selchester. It won't be the same place at all. Look at Mr Dillon, wanting us to have coaches and trippers and things. It's all quite dreadful.'

Freya said, 'There'll never be many coaches coming here, and I can't imagine that a production of *Murder in the Cathedral* is going to attract hoodlums and undesirables to Selchester.'

Lionel said, 'Nonetheless, it won't be the same, mark my words. It was a bad omen your uncle's body being discovered like that. It would be better if he'd never been dug up.'

He said this with such anguish that Hugo was taken aback. Lionel reddened, and then burst out, his voice high-pitched, 'It's all too beastly for us. You wouldn't understand, Mr Hawksworth, since you're a stranger here, but now there's this dreadful suspicion hanging over all of us, and you, too, Freya.'

His mother, clearly not pleased at the turn the conversation had taken, smiled at them, nodded at Freya and Hugo, and bore her son away.

Freya said, 'Well?'

Hugo said, 'I never saw a more unlikely murderer, but who knows? Shall we go and talk to Mr Dillon?'

Mr Dillon was talking to Sir Bernard, who said to Hugo, 'Well done about the lighting, Hawksworth. I like to see you joining in.'

Mr Dillon said, 'Yes, it's good of you to volunteer your services.'

Just wait until Dillon found out how little he knew about stage lighting.

Sir Bernard nodded and moved away. Mr Dillon said, 'I gather your sister and my daughter have become good friends, and I'm grateful for it. Daisy hasn't always had an easy time of it at that school.' He went on, without a trace of self-consciousness, 'People mistrust me. You see, I'm a self-made man and not a local. I've only been here for twenty years. Some of the girls take a lead from their parents and don't behave quite as they ought, but your Georgia is a nice young lass, no side to her, and I dare say she'll be glad of a friend, too. It's not an easy thing for a girl to have lost her parents like that. I'm sorry for you both.'

It was said with simple sincerity, and were it not that a suspicion of being involved in murder hung about Mr Dillon, Hugo would have taken an immediate liking to him. He was on his guard. He didn't really want to like any of these people. He wasn't sure that he wanted to like Freya, but they were comrades in arms, and there was no help for it.

Casting around for a neutral subject, he asked about the Feoffees. Mr Dillon's face lit up. 'Ah, that's something I take a keen interest it. It's an unusual set-up, but one that goes back to medieval times.'

Hugo settled down to hear all about the Feoffees.

Meeting Vivian Witt was an altogether different experience. She didn't wait for Freya to introduce Hugo, but came over to them, skilfully drawing him away from Stanley Dillon. Waves of charm and sex appeal flowed over Hugo. Violet eyes appraised him, and her slightly husky voice made polite enquiries about how he was settling in at the Castle and Hall sound like a caress. She asked about his leg, 'Not a serious injury, I hope,' and thanked him for volunteering to help with the lighting.

He had an uneasy suspicion that she saw right through his lack of expertise on the lighting front. Then, miraculously, it seemed as though she might be going to throw him a lifeline as she said, with a lovely smile, 'Let me put you in touch with Simon Firbank. He's done a lot of work with lighting in venues like cathedrals and churches and stately homes and so on, and I'm sure he'll be able to give you some advice. About where to hire equipment and all that sort of thing.' There was a pause, a deliberate pause, and then she said, a hint of amusement in her eyes, 'Rather different from OUDS.' Another lovely smile for him; then she turned to talk to the Dean.

# Scene 6

Back at the Castle, Freya was about to open the kitchen door when Hugo put out a hand to stop her. He said, 'I'm pleased to have met them all now, and I dare say I shall get to know them socially, but I think there's little hope of my getting them in any way to open up or say to me what they haven't said to the police.'

Freya said, 'You're probably right, in which case we're just going to have to find out more about them. There has to be some reason why they were invited that weekend. How did they know my uncle, and why did he invite them together? The only one he knew well is Charles, who is his godson. Charles was based in London then, so was there some particular reason for him to be invited at that time, with those other guests?'

Hugo said, 'I thought nobody came from London on account of the snow.'

'Charles came the day before; he has a house here.'

'Three of them have strong London connections. I suppose it might be worth seeing what we can find out at that end.' He ran through names in his mind, people who moved in theatrical circles, people who would know about Lionel's work. And perhaps somebody on the business side, who might know about Mr Dillon.

He said this to Freya, and she gave him an approving pat on the shoulder. 'Good thinking. I'll see if I can come up with any contacts. Our enquiries have to be discreet, of course, but I have a feeling you're good at that, aren't you?'

'Enquiries, or discretion?'

'Oh, both, wouldn't you say?'

Then she pushed open the door, and they went into the welcoming warmth of the kitchen.

# Chapter Eleven

## Scene 1

H ugo decided to wait to phone Valerie until Georgia had gone grumbling to bed. He was grateful that the telephone was in Grace Hall rather than the Great Hall, a lofty chamber which made Hugo feel that the Sheriff of Nottingham was about to make an entrance. He sat down on the silk cushion placed on the stool beside the table with the telephone, picked up the receiver, jiggled the bar a few times and waited for the exchange to answer. He looked up at the inscription above the pointed door: '*Deo Gratias*'. That, no doubt, was why it was called Grace Hall.

Freya had warned him that the chances were that any of the girls at the exchange would listen in to his conversation. So when he was put through to Valerie, who greeted him with cries of joy and delight, he cut her off quite abruptly, saying cryptically, '*Pas devant les auditeurs*,' and then proceeded in a slow, dull voice to read her an imaginary list of books he would like her to find for him. After two minutes of this, he heard a tiny click on the line and guessed that the girl at the exchange had moved on to more entertaining fodder. Then he said to Valerie, 'Sorry about that, but I don't see why I should have people listening in to my conversations.'

Valerie said, 'I gathered that was what you meant. How frightful to be somewhere where you can't even have a private telephone conversation. I suppose things are so terribly dull there that they have to find whatever entertainment they can. Have they solved the mystery of the murdered Earl yet? After that first flurry it seems to have vanished almost entirely from the newspapers. I don't like to think of a homicidal maniac being loose in Selchester, especially when you're on the very spot where the crime was committed.' There was quite a long pause before she said in a slightly cooler voice, 'How are you getting on with Freya Wryton?'

Hugo, banishing the thought of the meeting from his mind, said more or less truthfully, 'We don't see much of her. She has her own tower in the Castle, and I don't know what she does in there all day. She's supposed to be writing some tome about the Selchester family.'

'Oh, Lord, is she a bluestocking? What a bore. Still, I suppose she has to find something to fill the time. Not married and not likely to be. I expect you know about that frightful affair when she ditched poor Roddy Halstrop virtually at the altar.'

Valerie was much given to gossip, a facet of her personality that Hugo had never cared for. But now he wanted her in a gossiping mood, and he also—although he hated to admit it to himself and felt guilty about it—wanted to hear about Freya.

'I thought you said you knew nothing about her.'

Valerie laughed. 'I didn't, but since you're cooped up in the Castle with her, I thought I'd better find out something. She was engaged to Roddy during the war. Frightfully suitable and all that, and I'm sure the family were delighted. And then, at the altar—I mean literally at the altar when she was standing there in her white frock, ancestral tiara on her head—she suddenly turned and fled from the church, casting off train and veil and leaping into a taxi. I gather it caused a tremendous rift between her and her uncle, but that was wartime, and everybody said that she was suffering from shock from the bombs and so on. I think they hoped that they would patch it up, but Roddy would have none of it. He'd been made a fool of, and then only a few months later he married Marigold Sint. Mind you, that didn't last. They split up after about a year and divorced. Quite a scandalous affair. She made all sorts of accusations about him, but it was all hushed up, and I think she just wanted to marry somebody else. She went to America.'

Hugo felt a familiar sense of distaste coming over him. When he was in London and in the presence of Valerie, with her glittering personality and vivacity, the full force of her gossip didn't have the impact it was having now.

She was still talking. 'Darling, when are you coming to London? You must already be dying to get away from that dreadful place.'

Hugo said, 'It's not so easy to get away. I'm learning the ropes at the new job, and I can't drive much until my leg gets better. Yes, it's better, but still a problem in the car. What am I doing for it? I'm taking exercise and having physiotherapy.'

'I don't see how anyone there will be as good as someone here in London.'

He didn't want to talk about the physiotherapist; the mere thought of the formidable Mrs Svensson made his leg ache. 'There are some interesting people here in Selchester, as it happens. Lionel Tallis for one. I suppose you must have come across him in your line of work.' Valerie was a fashion writer.

She said, 'Oh, Lionel, yes, a darling man. Wonderful, wonderful photographs, but he doesn't do fashion these days. And he won't photograph men any more, although he used to. Noel'—she meant Noel Coward; she loved to refer to celebrities by their first names as though she were on intimate terms with them—'begged Lionel to do a studio portrait of him, but he wouldn't have it. Only girls and women. Only portraits. With what he charges and his clientele, he must be making a good thing of it. I'd forgotten that he had a country hideaway. Oh, I remember now, he has a mother, doesn't he? He's the sort of man who would be attached to his mother. Who else? I'm intrigued to think of anyone who would choose to live in a place like Selchester. I mean Lionel and his mother are one thing, but why would anyone else want to?'

'Vivian Witt.'

There was another long pause. Valerie said, impressed, 'Well, she is a big fish. That would be her country place, because of course she has a flat in Chelsea.'

'I expect she likes to get away from London and the kind of publicity that surrounds her.'

Valerie said, 'Most people in her position would want to keep in front of the flashlights. But she doesn't. I suppose she's reached the point in her career when she doesn't have to. Do you remember my cousin, Ferdy Long?

'The actor?'

'Yes. By the strangest coincidence, I dined with Ferdy the other day. He was in this Shaw play that's just finished a run at the Adelphi, with Vivian Witt in the lead. He says that everybody in the business knows that Vivian's private life is exactly that: private with a capital P. The only man she spends any time with is Sir Desmond, and it's unlikely there's anything much to that. Ferdy said that a while back, maybe six or seven years ago, there was a rumour that she was having a hot affair with somebody tremendously important, something to do with money, but it was all utterly discreet, and she was never seen in public with anyone. Really, it is quite extraordinary that she is apparently so virtuous. An actress with a spotless reputation, I ask you.'

'Why shouldn't she be virtuous? I found her perfectly charming.'

Valerie was annoyed. 'Have you met her?'

'I was introduced to her. She's devastating. Amazing eyes.'

Valerie didn't want to hear about anybody else's amazing eyes. Then, remembering the existence of Hugo's sister, she asked, 'And how is Georgia settling down? Does she like her new school?'

'As much as any thirteen-year-old girl likes any school.'

'I still think it was a most tremendous mistake to take her away from Yorkshire Ladies. I was very happy there, and it really is a good school. I mean, no one's heard of Selchester High or whatever it's called.'

'I think she's happier at a day school,' was Hugo's diplomatic reply. He'd never told Valerie, out of a sense of solidarity with his sister, of the conversation he'd had with the headmistress of Yorkshire Ladies. Politely but firmly, she had made it clear that she would rather that Georgia didn't come back to the school for the new school year.

'Such a mistake not to get Georgia some sort of help. I know people don't believe in psychoanalysis for children, but Anna Freud is doing wonderful work, and if you were in London—'

Anna Freud, indeed. He said, 'There's not the slightest need for Georgia to see a psychoanalyst, however famous and distinguished. There's nothing wrong with her except being thirteen, an orphan, and finding herself in new surroundings.'

'Darling, it was so terrible for her. Traumatic, and these days we all understand how childhood events can warp the way you grow into adulthood.'

Hugo got off the subject of Georgia by making polite enquiries about Valerie's work.

'Frantically busy, darling.'

He listened patiently to her account of an article she'd had published, the viciousness of the magazine editor, her excitement over the new collections from Paris. He was dreading her inviting herself down to Selchester for a weekend. Why? Was it that he couldn't imagine Valerie in Selchester?

Fortunately, neither could she. 'It's a shame I'm so desperately busy because otherwise I would leap into the car and drive down to Selchester to see you and the Castle and even the spot where the body was found'—Valerie had always been a ghoul—'but it's simply impossible at the moment; you know how things are, and I'm having to work all the hours given.'

Hugo's ear caught another faint click on the line, and he reckoned that the girl at the exchange was back again, listening. Then the pips went, and so he was able to ring off, with a quick 'Goodnight.'

He put the phone down and frowned. Was there any useful information there? Perhaps.

# Chapter Twelve

## Scene 1

F reya and Mrs Partridge were looking over Freya's wardrobe. Sonia had telephoned while Freya was in the meeting, and Mrs Partridge passed on her message.

'Her ladyship told me to write it all down, as she was going out and wouldn't be able to call again. Very free with her language as per usual, and gave that Mabel at the exchange a right dressing-down for listening in. Which worked, as Mabel took a pet and unplugged herself. Anyway, Lady Sonia was ringing about the arrangements for his late lordship's funeral service.'

Sonia had been annoyed by Freya's absence. 'Make sure you get all the details, Mrs P. I don't want Freya turning up late or missing it altogether. Eleven o'clock Requiem Mass at Westminster Cathedral. She can come up the night before and go to Brown's, where her parents are staying. Breakfast for the whole family at the Savoy at nine. Then a private burial in Oxford at three that afternoon.'

'I wonder why Oxford and not here in Selchester,' Freya said as she held up a black wool dress.

'Lady Sonia said the people buying the Castle wouldn't like having him there.'

'Why ever not? Plenty of other Selchesters here.'

'Not recent ones.'

'I do hate wearing black. And where am I going to find a veil?'

'Do you have to wear one?' Mrs Partridge said, with a disapproving sniff.

'Yes, I do.'

'Here's the coat to go with that dress,' Mrs Partridge said as she shook it out. 'Bound to be chilly in a cathedral. You'd best see if Olive Simpkins has got a black hat with a veil.'

Olive Simpkins ran Selchester's only hat shop.

Freya pulled a face. 'And Mummy will take one look and lecture me about how provincial I look. Oh, well, it can't be helped.'

'Lady Sonia said the press will be out in force, taking pictures. She said a dead Earl's of no special interest, but a murdered one is.'

'I wonder why we're meeting at the Savoy.'

'That's because Lady Selchester is staying there.'

Freya and Mrs Partridge looked at one another.

'So Aunt Hermione's come over for the funeral?'

'Must have flown over, like your mum and dad.' Mrs Partridge spoke in awed tones; the idea of flying the Atlantic to attend a funeral impressed her, even if it was going to be a Popish affair, all incense and goodness knew what other wickednesses.

'I had a telegram from Daddy saying they'd be over, but he didn't say when. I'll telephone Brown's and see when they're expected. I wonder if my Aunt Priscilla is driving up. I could go with her.'

'Of course Lady Priscilla will be going. It would look odd if she didn't. Give me that dress, and I'll press it.'

Freya handed over the dress, wondering how many of the mourners would be that in other than name. She'd been fond of her uncle, and he'd shown her affection in his undemonstrative way. But his wife, who'd lived apart from him for years? His bitter daughter, now the possessor of all his wealth? His sister? It was difficult to know what Aunt Priscilla thought of him. Like her brother, she kept her feelings to herself. As for Freya's mother, there was no doubt about her opinion of her half-brother. How on earth had Daddy persuaded her to come over for the funeral?

# Scene 2

Freya asked her father that very question while they were waiting at the entrance of Brown's Hotel for her mother to join them.

'If it had just been a private burial, I dare say she needn't have come. At least, her absence wouldn't be remarked. But since there's the service at the Cathedral, which is entirely as it should be, we must be there and be seen to be there. It would be most inappropriate for his family not to attend.'

Freya gave her father's arm a squeeze. 'You are a conventional old thing.'

Edmund Wryton, correctly attired in black morning coat, his gleaming top hat in his hand, frowned down at her. 'It isn't just convention, Freya. Selchester was family, like it or not.'

'Did you have to bribe Mummy to come?'

He relented. 'There was a little difficulty at first. She insisted she wouldn't attend the requiem, that it would be hypocritical, she'd accepted for years that he was dead. All that kind of thing. It was my pointing out that Hermione would be glad to see her that made her finally agree to attend the services. That, and the chance to go to Fortnum's and Harrods; it seems you can't buy everything in America. Ah, here she is.'

Freya's mother didn't look as though she expected to enjoy the day ahead. 'Thankfully it will all be over by tea-time,' she said. 'Is the taxi here? Freya, darling, is that hat quite suitable?'

'Too bad if it isn't; it's all I've got,' Freya said cheerfully as she followed them into the cab and pulled down the seat.

She'd bought it after visiting her publisher, who had taken her out to lunch and handed over a large cheque. Wide-brimmed with a black feather curling around the crown, it was extremely dashing.

'You look like that portrait of that seventeenth-century Selchester Countess,' her mother said. 'And where's your veil?'

'In my handbag; I shan't put it on until the last moment.'

At the Savoy, Freya was pleased to see Aunt Hermione. She'd always been kind to Freya, and embraced her warmly.

It was amazing how well she looked. Certainly not a trace of grief there; indeed, she seemed much happier than she had ever been in those pre-war years at Selchester Castle. Would that arouse any comment? Should she be playing the sorrowful widow? No need; people would assume that her grieving and mourning had been done when Selchester vanished. The fact that she hadn't set her eyes on her husband for several years before he died was neither here nor there.

In that Freya was wrong. Her mother and aunt were talking about that. Lady Selchester said, 'I did see him, just the once. He was in Canada on some sort of government mission, and I suppose he felt obliged to look me up. He was angling for a reconciliation. He wanted me to come back to England, but I told him there was no question of that.'

Which confirmed what Freya had long suspected, but no one had ever said openly: Lady Selchester had stayed in Canada during the war from choice, not necessity. She was no coward. She hadn't remained there in order to escape the terrors of war, and had worked tirelessly for the war effort in Canada. No, she couldn't bear to live with her husband any more, and so had removed herself from him, from her life in the Castle—and from her children. Which must have been hard for her.

At a moment when Sonia, Aunt Hermione and Aunt Priscilla were gathered together at the other side of the room, and her father was fussing about removing a hair from his trousers, Freya said to her mother, 'I do wonder why they separated, because that's what it amounts to. When I was at the Castle in my holidays, they always seemed to get on perfectly well together.'

'Oh, well, marriages don't always work out, and of course there was no question of divorce, not with Selchester being so Catholic. People do drift apart, you know.'

Freya had the feeling that her Aunt Priscilla had overheard this remark. Sure enough, a few minutes later she said to Freya, 'At your age you shouldn't be so naive. That marriage was a disaster from the word go. I pitied Hermione, as I would pity any woman who married my brother. He would never change his ways.'

'Change his ways?' Freya looked at her aunt in astonishment. 'You mean he had mistresses and so on?'

Lady Priscilla's laugh had no mirth in it. 'Oh, your mind would run along those lines. There are worse things that can happen in a marriage than unfaithfulness.'

Freya said impulsively, 'Do you suppose Sonia knew what was amiss between her parents?'

Another snort of laughter from Lady Priscilla. 'Of course she did. Don't be a fool, Freya.'

# Scene 3

All of which left Freya puzzled, and she was still thinking about it as she sat in the Cathedral. She glanced along the line of her female relatives. Like a row of crows, emotions duly hidden behind black veils. Which concealed what? Relief? Probably. A question answered, a door finally closed. Grief? Perhaps she felt more sadness than Selchester's daughter, wife or sisters.

Would Tom have grieved for his father? Yes, surely he would. Or did he know whatever it was that Aunt Priscilla had hinted had driven a rift between his parents? Was that part of the reason why he'd been at loggerheads with his father?

If Tom had been here, the whole occasion would have had a different tone. The baton of the Earldom would have been handed on, and a sixteenth Earl would have led the mourners out of the Cathedral into the dusty London sunlight. She reached for a handkerchief to wipe away a tear, a black-edged handkerchief pressed on her by Mrs Partridge: 'You have to show respect at a funeral.'

Her father, next to her, frowned. She whispered, 'I was just thinking about Tom,' and he nodded.

The sonorous, solemn and often alarming liturgy of the Requiem Mass drifted in and out of her head. '*Dies irae, dies illa*'; no comfort there in the flames of hell and the terrors of Judgement Day. But at last it was over, and cardinal, priests, servers and choir processed down the aisle, with the Selchesters filing out to follow in their wake.

Behind them, the huge congregation began to stream out of the doors.

'Very well attended,' her father said approvingly as they went out into the grey daylight.

Freya recognised a Royal Duke, the Prime Minister, most of the Cabinet and phalanxes of those who were clearly among the great and the good.

'All very dignified, all very appropriate,' Freya's father said.

Freya gave his arm a squeeze, laughing at him. 'It didn't please your orderly mind that Selchester was never found.'

'No, it did not, and it doesn't please my orderly mind, as you put it in such unfilial words, that it now turns out that he was murdered. Just the sort of scandal we don't need, although it's not causing nearly so much of a stir as I expected.'

'Somebody put the stoppers on that.'

'My dear girl, what are you talking about?'

'Oh, Daddy, don't pretend. You know how it's done better than anyone. For some reason they don't want it to be spread all over the papers. They've decided Tom did it, with my assistance, so they aren't exactly falling over themselves to find out who really did murder him.'

Her father was appalled. 'Tom? And you a suspect? How can that be? You and Tom left halfway through dinner.'

'Superintendent MacLeod thinks we could have sneaked back and killed him. They don't know how he died—no marks on the body or anything—but they reckon Tom was trained to kill in various subtle ways and so pin the blame on him. And me.'

'We'll see about this.'

'I don't think you will. It's all going to be brushed under the carpet. Tom can't be brought to trial, which is convenient, and there's nothing but circumstantial evidence against me. And in fact there's a witness who can say I was back in Selchester in the flat before nine.'

'Then they can't suspect you.'

'They can, since the witness is Mrs Partridge, and as she says, Superintendent MacLeod wouldn't believe her if she told him what day of the week it was.'

'Even so, a witness is a witness. I take it you've consulted Vereker about all this?'

Vereker, of Vereker, Vereker and Fotheringay, was the Wrytons' family solicitor.

'No, I don't need legal advice. Not unless they actually charge me, and they won't. And Vereker can't do anything about all the rumours flying around in Selchester. No smoke without fire and all that.'

'You'll have to leave the Castle. We never were happy about you ruralising in Selchester. With no family there—'

'Don't forget Aunt Priscilla.'

'I'll have to have a word with Priscilla. Don't say anything to your mother. She'd be most concerned if she knew about this.'

'Do you imagine Aunt Priscilla won't have told her? And I'm not leaving Selchester, Daddy. I refuse to be hounded out by rumour and gossip, and besides, I need to be there for my writing.'

'Sonia's selling the Castle and disposing of all the contents, so she says. You won't even have a roof over your head.'

'I'll find a place in Selchester.'

'No young man on the horizon, I suppose?'

'No.'

He glanced at her, and changed the subject. 'How is that evil-tempered horse of yours?'

'Last Hurrah is fine. He's the real love of my life.'

# Scene 4

Stanley Dillon had taken a seat towards the rear of the Cathedral. What a gloomy interior it was, as though in perpetual mourning. Too many requiems, maybe. The whole place reeked of incense and impossible mysteries. It gave him the shudders. Still, he'd had to come. Not least from a sense of civic duty; it would have been extraordinary for the head Feoffee not to attend on such an occasion.

He sat through the unfamiliar sacrament, grateful for the Order of Service sheet and grateful that the plump man beside him knew exactly what was going on and nudged him on to his knees or up on his feet in the right places.

At last it was over, and he stood respectfully as the procession came down the aisle. After the clergy came the Selchester clan, led by the widowed Lady Selchester, arm in arm with Lady Sonia, both their faces concealed by their black veils.

It was years since he'd seen Hermione. The last time had been on a blustery autumn day when he'd been out riding and her car had purred to a halt beside him. She'd been on her way to Liverpool, to set sail for Canada. For a holiday, officially. In fact, to get away from her husband.

Behind them was Lady Priscilla. Stanley was a little afraid of her, although he'd never admit it. She caught his eye and gave him a nod of recognition. Was that a wink? No, it had to be a trick of the light. She was accompanied by her husband, Sir Archibald Veryan. Tall, distinguished, his face giving nothing away.

Neither of them would be grieving greatly for Lord Selchester. Nor would Selchester's other sister, Lady Veronica Wryton. And as for Lady Sonia . . .

What a family.

His plump neighbour gave him a little shove. It was time for him to move. He stepped out into the aisle, suddenly keen to be out in the fresh air.

# Scene 5

The Selchesters stood on the steps, waiting for the cars. To Freya's surprise, she saw the imposing figure of Mr Dillon coming towards them, impeccably dressed. He greeted first Lady Priscilla and then Lady Selchester with a kind of old-fashioned courtesy that suited him.

Her father and mother were buttonholed by a fellow diplomat. Aunt Hermione and Mr Dillon moved slightly apart, deep in conversation.

Why was Mr Dillon there? She supposed it must be as representative of the Feoffees of Selchester. Then she caught Aunt Priscilla's eye on the two of them, a knowing look on her face.

How odd.

Sonia came over to them. 'We need to make a move. The cars are here.'

Freya was in the same car as Sonia, with a distant cousin sitting in the front beside the chauffeur. 'Did your mother mind that he's to be buried in Oxford and not at Selchester?' she asked as the big black car set off through the London traffic.

'She left all the arrangements to me. And I don't know why you think it matters where he's buried.'

'Don't you think he might prefer to lie among his ancestors?'

Sonia gave her a chilling look. 'One might ask if the ancestors would want him there with them. Anyhow, I decided on Oxford. Why not? It was one of his places, after all.'

# Chapter Thirteen

## Scene 1

Back from the Hall, Hugo found Georgia in the kitchen. He was planning to retreat to his own room with a whisky and soda, but Georgia wasn't having that, instead bullying him into helping her with her maths homework.

She was contemptuous of his efforts. 'I'd have thought that someone who's supposed to be working in statistics could do better than that.'

'It's a long time since I've had to solve any differential equations,' Hugo said. Dredging up memories of distant problems, he managed to help Georgia finish her task.

She closed her books and stacked them neatly on top of one another. Mrs Partridge, who had been bustling around with pots and pans, announced that she was going out to feed the hens and bring the washing in.

'Good,' Georgia said. 'That gives us a good twenty minutes.'

Hugo eyed her suspiciously. 'Twenty minutes for what?'

'To get down to brass tacks. I know you're investigating this murder, and I think you need my help.'

Hugo said, 'I really don't know what you're talking about. Any investigations into Lord Selchester's death are best left to the police.'

'Rubbish. The police still want to pin it on Freya and her dead cousin, Tom, and you aren't keen on the idea.'

'Freya has an alibi.'

'Not one the police will take any notice of. That Superintendent doesn't trust Mrs Partridge.'

'How do you know that?'

'I keep my ears open and I hear things. It's looking bad for Freya; there are lots of dark mutterings about her.'

'Nonsense.'

Georgia went on remorselessly, 'And I heard you talking to Valerie, asking her to find out about people, people who were here the night Lord Selchester got done in, and you never do that. You always shut her up when she starts gossiping.'

Hugo was annoyed. There was a ruthlessness and a cunning to his sister that he hadn't suspected. Honesty compelled him to admit that it had been a certain streak of ruthlessness and cunning of his own that had enabled him to do his job and survive. So he said, rather weakly, 'I don't think you should get into the habit of eavesdropping. It isn't a pleasant habit.'

'No, but it's useful. Besides, it was accidental.'

'It's still eavesdropping.'

'Not in my book, it isn't. Eavesdropping is deliberate, when you creep up and open the door a crack or put yourself behind a curtain or in a cupboard to hear what people are saying. Given your line of work, I'm surprised you didn't notice that there's a kind of spy-hole in the stonework in the passage above Grace Hall. Your conversation came up like it was an echo chamber, and I was on the way to my room, so I couldn't help overhearing. Then it got interesting, so I stayed listening. Anyway,' she said with a dismissive wave of her hand, 'that doesn't matter. What matters is that I can help you. You want to find out which of those four people murdered his nibs.'

'If one of them did,' Hugo said.

'You need to find out more about them, let's just take that as read. It's the first thing you have to do: get to know your suspects. That's why you were asking Valerie for information, but I can tell you much more than Valerie.'

'Now you're being ridiculous.'

'No, I'm not. Because while you're up at the Hall doing your so-called statistics, I'm at school with all kinds of people who know all kinds of things about everybody in Selchester.'

There was some truth in what Georgia said; she did mingle with Selchester people far more than he did, and he supposed that even schoolgirls might have glimmerings of what was going on. In this Hugo showed his ignorance of just what thirteen-year-olds with keen intelligence and keen eyes were capable of gleaning, and how much more they knew about life than he and his contemporaries had done in a gentler pre-war world.

'Give me a piece of paper, you've got plenty of blank pages there,' he said, reaching out towards her pile and taking one of her exercise books.

Another scornful look from Georgia. 'One would think you'd never been at school yourself. That's my rough book, and they count the pages when you hand it in to get a new one. So there's no way I can tear a page out or use it for something like writing down a list of suspects.'

Hugo was momentarily distracted. 'They count the pages and check you haven't torn any out?'

'Yes, it's all to do with austerity and being careful about paper. That's what they say, but actually I think it's because they're anal obsessives.'

'They're *what?*'

'We've been discussing Freud—me and my friends. And that's what it is.'

'Freud?'

'Yes, Freud, sexy dreams and wanting to kill your father and all about the ego and libido and unconscious. It's all complete rot.'

Hugo was inclined to agree with her, but he was beginning to feel he'd underestimated Georgia.

'As it happens,' Georgia went, 'I have a new notebook. I bought it at the stationer's on the way home. If you're going to use it for your investigations, you'll have to pay me for it. It's a good one, and you owe me one and threepence for it.' She held out an expectant hand.

Hugo dug in his pocket and pulled out a selection of coins. 'I've only got a florin and a threepenny bit. Have you got a shilling?'

'No,' Georgia said. 'You can take it off my pocket money at the end of the week.'

Hugo knew that by the time he came to dole out her weekly pocket money, he would have forgotten that she owed him a shilling. He told her so, adding bitterly that she shouldn't be getting as much pocket money as she did. She'd upped the amount by deception—in fact, by downright lying. 'You told me Aunt Claire gave you half a crown a week, and it was actually two shillings.'

'You should have checked with her. You can't go back on it now because we came to an agreement.' She pushed the pad over to him, asked if he had anything to write with and helpfully supplied him with a pencil. 'We'll start with Vivian Witt. *Cherchez la femme* and all that.'

Hugo gave in to the inevitable, while Georgia steepled her fingers, narrowed her eyes and said, 'Everybody thinks they know quite a lot about Vivian Witt because her pictures are always in the papers and magazines and so on, but actually she's really secretive. Penny Dunlop—she's a girl in my class—is stage-struck. She wants to be an actress, although her parents are those kind of churchy people who think anything to do with the stage is really wicked, so she may have a problem. Some of the other girls are spiteful and say she isn't pretty enough to be an actress, but Daisy says that just because Vivian Witt's beautiful doesn't mean that all actresses have to be. There are also character roles.'

'True. And they tend to get more parts than the pretty ones. But what has this to do with Vivian Witt?'

'Everybody knows that Vivian Witt's got lots of sex appeal.' Georgia gave her brother a sly look from under her eyelashes. 'Did you find her attractive when you met her?'

Hugo was not going to discuss this. 'She is attractive, yes.'

'Well, people think somebody like that must have lots of affairs, lovers and so on,' Georgia said airily, 'but Penny says that's not the case. She thinks that there's some tragic love story in Vivian Witt's past, and that's why her name has never been linked to anyone. She goes out and about with Sir Desmond, but they aren't really a couple. Everyone knows that. So I don't believe it, that's all. I think she's a woman with a secret.'

'Do any of your friends happen to know why Vivian Witt came to Selchester in the first place?'

'To have a private life.'

'Here in Selchester, where people know if you've sneezed twice before breakfast?'

'Private as in away from theatre people and gossip columnists and so on.' Georgia heaved a loud sigh. 'Do sharpen your wits and concentrate.'

'What about why she was at the Castle that night?'

'Is there any special reason why Lord Selchester invited her, you mean? She's a star, and if he wanted to impress friends from London, then she'd be just the sort of person he would ask. Nobody says she knew him, although of course they might have met in London.'

'Or might not.'

'Okay, so that's something for you to work on. Leave a space, and we'll go on to Lionel Tallis.'

Hugo resignedly took up his pencil again. 'Go on. What do your sources have to say about him? I can't believe he interests them as much as Vivian Witt.'

Georgia said, 'If you're a student of psychology and human nature, then he's just as interesting.'

Hugo asked, 'Is gossip on the syllabus at your school?'

Georgia said, 'Talking about human nature, it's human nature to gossip and to be interested in your neighbours and what they're doing. In a place like Selchester, that's much easier than it is in London, and I expect people gossip there just the same, only it's lost because of all the other things going on. I suppose you know that people listen in to telephone conversations here. Yes, you do, because there was all that stuff when you were talking to Valerie. She must have thought you'd gone off your rocker, but I suppose she did catch on quite quickly for someone who's not all that bright.'

'Can we leave Valerie out of this, please.'

'Okay, let's return to our sheep.'

'Sheep? What have sheep to do with anything?'

'*Revenons à nos moutons*,' Georgia said in a not very creditable French accent. 'It's a French quotation from somewhere or other. The French teacher at school says it when we distract her from going on about things like irregular verbs. I thought you were supposed to be good at French; obviously not. In fact, I don't know what you are good at, seeing that your Latin is rusty, you're pretty hopeless at maths and now you don't even know French. Lionel Tallis is our sheep right now, and, as you know, he lives with his mother. She's a witch.'

Hugo put down his pencil, sat back in his seat and crossed his arms. This was going too far. 'I thought you were being sensible, but this is just fantasy.'

'I'm telling you what people say. They say she's a witch on account of her knowing all about herbs and things. They don't mean she goes round in a pointy hat, chanting spells. Although Selchester did used to have quite a lot of witchcraft. They had some trials here back when they burnt them.'

'That was in the seventeenth century,' said Hugo.

'Yes, a long time ago, and they still believe in witches, only they're different now. It doesn't matter because no one's suggesting Mrs Tallis put Lionel under a spell so that he murdered Lord Selchester or anything silly like that. In fact, nobody believes he could murder anyone because apparently he passes out at the sight of blood and if you say "Boo" to him, he jumps in the air. Except when he's working. A girl's sister did a London Season last year and was photographed by Lionel, and he knows exactly what he wants and is very bossy. Then the minute the photographs are finished, he turns back into being nervous again. And he has no sex life,' she added complacently.

Hugo shut his eyes. What did Georgia know about the sex lives of people like Lionel?

'Daisy says he's like a neutered cat. Some people are like that. So I don't think it's the same as Vivian Witt—that he's got a secret life that we don't know about. And as to why Lord Selchester invited him, well, Freya did say that her uncle used to have a varied bunch of people coming here, and I suppose he thought Lionel would fit in if they were an arty crowd. And even if he's not famous like Vivian Witt is, he's still quite well-known. Go on, write down that he's not the sort to be able to murder anyone.'

Hugo took up the pencil and obediently wrote, 'Unlikely to commit a violent crime.'

'Next comes Mr Guthrie, Charles Guthrie,' Georgia went on. 'No need to worry about why he was asked. He was Lord Selchester's godson and often used to come to the Castle. You know he's in the Foreign Office and all that, but I found out that he did some pretty adventurous things in the war. He ended up in Colditz, but escaped and made it back to England. He must have plenty of guts and gumption, don't you think?'

'Not many got out of Colditz and got safely home, that's true.'

'I wonder why he went into the Foreign Office,' Georgia said. 'If you're the kind of person he is, it must be awfully tame doing a desk job. Even if you do get sent abroad as a diplomat, it's all safe and cushy, isn't it? And a house in Selchester when you're on leave; it's not exactly exciting. Look at you. You wouldn't be at the Hall and hating it if you hadn't hurt your leg.'

How did she know how much his desk job irked him? He never spoke about his work. 'His kind of war can leave a man worn out. He may appreciate the quiet life here in Selchester; no bangs, no bodies.'

'There may not be any bangs, but there's a body. And country life being what it is, I bet there are all kinds of skeletons in cupboards that no one lets on about.'

'I suspect that's true everywhere.'

'Yes, but in London no one cares what their neighbours are up to. Here, everyone knows what's going on. Like Jason Filbert beating his wife.'

'Georgia! That's taking gossip too far. And who's Jason Filbert?'

Georgia shrugged. 'Dunno. Someone who lives in Selchester. Daisy says he gets a kick out of hurting his wife. Pleasure from pain.' She gave him a sideways glance. 'De Sade and all that. Sadism. You know.'

This was too much. 'Georgia, you have not been reading the Marquis de Sade.'

Georgia said, 'Calm down. No, I have not. It sounds absolutely ghastly, and anyway where would I get a copy from? It's banned.'

'Just as well. How do you know about de Sade? Surely they don't teach you about him at school?'

'Of course not. There was a girl in the top form at Yorkshire Ladies who had a copy of one of his books. In French. *Justine*, it was called. They found it in her locker, and there was the most tremendous stink.'

'I assume she was expelled.'

'You'd think so, when you remember how keen they were to get rid of me, and I never did anything like that. But actually, they didn't expel her. Her family were frightfully grand, and she was leaving at the end of the term anyway, so they let her stay. I wonder what happened to the book; I bet they've got it in the staff room.'

Mrs Partridge came back into the kitchen with a basket of eggs. 'You can wash these for me, Georgia, since you've finished your homework.' She nodded at Hugo. 'And you can bring me down the suit you're going to wear tomorrow, and I'll give it a brush. No, don't tell me you're going to wear those flannels and that old jacket you wear for work at the Hall, because I shan't believe you.'

Georgia turned off the tap and swung round, eyes full of suspicion. 'Suit? Why? Where are you going?'

'London,' Hugo said. 'I'll only be away for one night, and no, you won't have to board at your school because Mrs Partridge says she'll—' He'd been about to say 'Look after you,' but changed it to 'Keep an eye on you.'

'Why are you going to London? You didn't say you were going.'

'I have a doctor's appointment. I was going to postpone it, but I think I'd better go and get it over with. And I've a couple of other things I need to do in town. To do with work, before you ask.'

'Says you. When's Freya back, Mrs Partridge?'

'She's spending a couple of days in Oxford with her parents after the funeral. So it's just you and me, Georgia, and it'll be no good expecting me to help you with your sums.'

'No maths homework tomorrow,' Georgia said. She gave Hugo a knowing look. 'I suppose you're really rushing up to town to see Valerie.'

'As I said, I have a doctor's appointment.'

'Which lasts for two days.' Georgia finished the eggs and placed them carefully in the basket. 'Don't think we'll miss you here at the Castle. Stay away as long as you like.'

# Chapter Fourteen

## Scene 1

Since the Department had issued his ticket, Hugo was travelling first class, and he was grateful for it. Mr Godney, the station-master, greeted him with a gloomy face, touched his finger to his peaked cap and found him an empty compartment. 'It's not like it was in the old days, Mr Hawksworth. Not like when it truly was God's Wonderful Railway and everything spick and span, and comfortable travel for everyone, high and low.' He looked despairingly at the dirty carriages attached to a shabby locomotive, then looked a little more cheerful. 'Still, we have to look on the bright side. There are no reports of any delays, no trouble on the line, so you should have a good journey.'

Hugo grinned as he sat down in a corner seat and flipped open *The Times*. He'd been the recipient of Mrs Partridge's grim forebodings as to the dangers for anyone embarking on a railway journey to London. She'd tried to press sandwiches on Hugo, and when he pointed out that he would be in London by lunchtime and had had a substantial breakfast of bacon and eggs, she shook her head and said you never knew what might happen on the way.

Georgia was interested: 'What kind of thing?'

Mrs Partridge pursed her lips. 'The train could be derailed; there could be obstacles on the line.'

'And enemy attacks, no doubt,' Hugo said. 'The war is over, Mrs Partridge. I never heard that rail travel was dangerous these days.'

'There was an accident only last month, with several people injured; you never know what may be going to happen.'

As it was, Hugo had a perfectly uneventful journey. He finished his newspaper, and although he'd brought a book with him, he spent most of the rest of the journey looking out of the window. It wasn't a pleasant day; he'd left a blustery Selchester with scudding clouds, and as he drew nearer to London, the sky had become a solid grey miasma. When he alighted from the train into a dingy Paddington Station, the smell of fog wafted into his nostrils.

He'd been looking forward to London. Town was his real home, his milieu, and he expected it to be a haven and relief after Selchester. But no, he felt his heart sinking as he went out of the station into the grey streets and looked at the dispirited people walking with hunched shoulders along damp pavements. He took a bus to Baker Street and walked to Harley Street. A mere five minutes in the waiting room, with a copy of *Country Life*, and then a white-coated receptionist showed him into Mr Coulson's consulting room.

Edwin Coulson was the surgeon who'd looked after Hugo when he'd arrived from Berlin, and he took a proprietary interest in Hugo's leg. The doctor was pleased. He said that at the moment it looked as though there would be no need for further surgery, approved of what Dr Rogers had prescribed for the pain, and asked how often Hugo needed to take the painkillers.

'Never, if I can help it.'

Coulson tut-tutted. 'It's the same with all you men from your background. You think pain is something to be endured, and there's a virtue in suffering. If that leg troubles you—as it will while it's healing—take something to make it more comfortable. Otherwise, you won't sleep, and being tired won't help your leg or your career.'

Hugo went back into the waiting room, past the pile of *Country Life* magazines and a harassed-looking woman with a squirming child, and the receptionist let him out into the street. With his appointment behind him, and profoundly grateful that there was no likelihood of further surgery, his spirits rose. If he hadn't had an injured leg and a stick, he'd have walked with a spring in his step. Now he could look forward to lunch and the rest of the day. Even the murky atmosphere that was already beginning to catch at the back of his throat couldn't dampen his sense of well-being.

Hugo's light-heartedness had nothing to do with Valerie. He hadn't said so to Georgia, but he'd arranged his appointment with Edwin Coulson at a time when he knew that Valerie wouldn't be in London. He could simply have neglected to tell her of his visit, but that sort of thing always led to disaster; her best friend was bound to bump into him coming round a corner and report his presence in town.

Valerie had to be in Paris for the collections, and in response to her indignant, 'Darling, you must change the appointment and make it a week later,' he'd said apologetically that he couldn't change it. 'There's a question of another operation, so I really need to see Mr Coulson as soon as possible.'

That had sent Valerie off on a tirade about how he should have stayed in London, where there was no problem about getting to see his surgeon at any time and where he'd receive much better care and attention than he could possibly have in a provincial town.

Hugo, feeling the injustice of this, pointed out that the kind of exercise he was taking in Selchester had done his leg good. 'And the physiotherapy is helping, too.'

Valerie wasn't having any of that. 'We went over this before. Any physiotherapist in London is bound to be better than one who's chosen to practise in the sticks.'

It was exactly this attitude of Valerie's that had made Hugo arrange his appointment when he had. He didn't feel up to having yet another argument with Valerie about how he should leave the Service and come back to live in London. And, inevitably, marry her. She wasn't over-worried about the formalities; she was modern in her outlook and would be quite happy to live with him in sin, as it was so quaintly called, but he knew that would only be a temporary arrangement. Valerie was the kind of girl who wanted a ring on her finger and all the authority that being a wife would give her over her husband.

# Scene 2

Hugo could have used a private line from the Hall to call Henry Surcoat, a line that didn't go through the Selchester exchange, with its listening ears, but he chose not to. All calls to and from the Hall were logged; better not to broadcast what he was doing. So he'd written to Henry. He received no reply, which hadn't surprised him; Henry rarely answered letters. As he'd hoped, when he pushed open the door of the Dog and Fox, there was Henry sitting on the worn leather bench as if he'd not budged since the last time they met. This pub was a favourite haunt of theirs. It was in Bloomsbury, a good long way from where the Service had its offices, so no danger of their colleagues filling the place with their watchful eyes, keen ears and elliptic shop talk. The Dog and Fox was an old-fashioned pub, with high-backed seats, a sprinkling of sawdust on the floor and a strong smell of beer and the meat pies for which it was famous.

They ordered; Hugo enquired after Henry's wife and young son; they reminisced about old days in the field, complained about the evil weather and simply enjoyed each other's company with the ease of long friendship.

Like Hugo, Henry had been forced to give up field work. Not through any injury in his case. He'd lost his nerve after a difficult time in Prague, where Hugo, risking his own life, had managed to extricate his friend from a difficult and dangerous situation.

Hugo never mentioned that incident, nor did he feel that Henry owed him anything for saving his life; it was what you did for a colleague. He didn't need to twist Henry's arm, in any case. Henry, now presiding over the Records section of the Service, was possessed of an astonishing memory and a keen sense of curiosity. If Hugo wanted information on a Mr Charles Guthrie and wasn't requesting the file through the normal channels, then something unusual was afoot, and Henry thrived on unusual.

And Henry had another reason for taking an interest in digging out the details Hugo wanted. There was no problem in providing the known facts about Charles Guthrie. He'd been vetted when he applied to join the Foreign Office, and the Security Department had done a thorough job within the limits of what was required.

'What's a bit of a coincidence is that I know Charles Guthrie,' Henry said. 'Or used to. We were up at Cambridge together. That was before the war, of course.'

Hugo was interested. 'Were you indeed? Did you know him well?'

'We both rowed, although only the college second boat. We never aimed for the Blue Boat or anything like that. Charles fenced and got his Blue for that. Otherwise, we weren't reading the same subject, and he was brilliant. Way out of my league. Why are you asking about him? Has something come up?'

'Just background info for some stuff I'm looking into. So, brains and a good war, no trouble in passing the exams and boards for the FO, I take it?'

'Charles never failed an exam in his life. Sailed through, top of his entry. And he came with tip-top references, glowing reports from his tutor at Trinity, positively gushing encomiums from the Air Force bigwigs and so on and so forth.'

Henry had a tatty kind of satchel with him. He dived into it and pulled out a buff file. 'All there, all the official bumpf, anyhow. Have a look through while I buy us another beer. I can't leave it with you, of course, and in fact I don't see why you needed to come to me. Why the secretiveness, the subtle approach? Surely you could have requested it through the normal channels. Goodness knows, you've got the clearance to ask for almost anything.'

'I want to keep this low key. Won't there be a fuss about you taking the file off the premises? I thought that was a big no-no in these suspicious times. How did you manage it?'

Henry shrugged. 'Ways and means. I shall replace it quietly where it came from, and no one any the wiser. It's not flagged, there's nothing there to arouse anyone's interest. Except yours, it seems. You'll see there's really not much on him beyond what I've told you. Mostly the interviews and reports by the vetting team, written in their usual excruciating jargon. No doubtful connections, no naughty habits, no known political affiliation. See for yourself.'

When he came back with two brimming tankards, he went on as though there'd been no pause in the conversation, 'That did surprise me. We were all very left wing at Cambridge in those days. Not to the extent that Burgess and Maclean turned out to be, but it was the prevailing feeling that Communism was the answer to society's many ills and that the Soviets had the heart of the matter in what they were doing. I just went along to a few meetings, that kind of thing, but Guthrie was more intense about it. He was a member of the Thursday Club for a while. That was a kind of Socratic outfit that thrashed out the world's problems and wanted to swap democracy for something better. But he only belonged to it for a term or two. Just as well, seeing what became of some of the other members. One's now a fiery and very left-wing Labour MP. Another one writes all those books about how we ought to collectivise farming. However, Charles dropped out of the group and went back to the library and fencing salle and left politics to others.'

'Including you?'

'I lost any faith I ever had in the Soviet system before the war, during the show trials in Moscow. And none of us realised that a ghastly war would come along and blow away most of the unfairness and inequalities we hated.' He drank some more of his beer. 'Anyhow, there's nothing about any of his left-wing undergraduate interests on file. I dare say his tutor didn't think it worth mentioning. Besides, you'll see that one of his referees was Lord Selchester. That recommendation alone would have given Charles a clean bill of health.'

'Lord Selchester was his godfather.'

'Was he? Yes, it mentions that. Charles was something of a protégé of his. Wait a moment—Lord Selchester's the Earl who was found recently under the floorboards, isn't he? In your neck of the woods?'

Hugo was reading the file. He didn't look up, but said, 'Flagstones, not floorboards.'

'That's it. They just had his funeral service, sent him off in style. Not so dull in rural Selchester then, if there are bodies appearing all over the place. Bloodhounds on the trail, are they?'

Hugo said, 'It's a bit of a dead-end investigation after seven years. It will most likely lie on the books as an unsolved murder.'

Henry said, 'You'd think they'd make an effort, given what a nob Lord Selchester was.'

Hugo had finished looking through the file. 'You're right. Guthrie doesn't seem to be any kind of a political animal. Excellent war record, good officer, DSO . . . And that incredible escape from Colditz.'

'The Service had its eye on him after the war,' Henry said. 'Nothing came of it, since he was determined to go into the FO. He probably wasn't the right type for us. Too reckless. That kind of conspicuous courage is dangerous in the field.'

A waiter brought two steaming pies and a dish of vegetables. Henry reached for the mustard. 'Are you going to tell me why you want to know about him?'

'Do me a favour and don't ask why I'm interested in him,' Hugo said. 'It's a side issue to another case I'm working on. He's not important.'

Henry raised a disbelieving eyebrow and speared a chunk of meat. 'Just so. And how's Selchester suiting you? I always think of you as a Londoner through and through. I can't imagine you taking to country life. How do you get on with Sir Bernard?'

Hugo shrugged. 'I don't see that much of him. He seems to run a taut department, knows his stuff. Tell me, how did he get his K?'

Henry laughed. 'He was involved in some of the post-war mopping-up operations. United Nations, all that kind of thing. His real job was to keep an eye on what the Soviets were up to, but he had diplomatic cover, and when all the missions and meetings came to an end and gongs were being handed out, it was considered that it would look odd if he were omitted from the list. It's as simple as that. He was tremendously pleased; he's the kind of ass who thinks that actually adds distinction to him. I dare say he's convinced himself by now that he actually earned it. Does anyone ever earn a knighthood?'

Hugo said, 'I don't think he is as disingenuous as that, although he clearly likes being Sir Bernard. He's not a fool, and he certainly keeps a finger on the pulse.'

'He has a reputation for being wily. I know you didn't want to be posted to Selchester, and I'd have fought tooth and nail if they'd tried to move me, but actually it's one of our most important sections now. Not the archives—awful bore for you, being dumped there—but the section where they do interrogation training is highly thought of. So I suppose you're right and Sir Bernard is doing a good job. I expect he hopes to come back to London and take over from the Chief one day, and I dare say it could happen. Have you seen anything of him?'

'Sir Bernard?'

'No, you ass, the Chief.'

'I'm much too lowly a being for him to take any notice of me.'

# Scene 3

It was a kind of truth; he hadn't had any contact with the Chief since he'd seen him before he left London. But after he and Henry had parted, Hugo left a message for the Chief at his club and he met him that evening for a drink. The Chief was in a bad mood. 'Bloody fog. They've got to do something about it, bring in a chimney tax. But they won't; this government couldn't keep a goldfish in a bowl.'

Hugo knew this wasn't political prejudice. The Chief despised all politicians and all governments of whatever leaning and inclination. Then he turned a sharp eye on Hugo. 'You're caught up in this Selchester murder, I hear.'

'Sir Bernard asked me to keep a watching brief on the investigation, but there doesn't actually seem to be much investigating going on.'

'Open and shut business, so I hear. Wouldn't have thought it of young Arlingham, but he's where he won't be bothered by any accusations.'

'His cousin isn't, however.'

'Cousin?'

'Miss Wryton. Freya Wryton. Lord Selchester's niece. The police think she was involved.'

The Chief leant forward to tap his cigar ash into the heavy glass ashtray. 'Lady Veronica's girl. I wouldn't have her down as the murdering type. Unlike Lady Sonia, who's capable of anything.' He shrugged. 'Can't help but be casualties in this kind of business, and I dare say Miss Wryton can look after herself. All those Selchester women are tough.'

## Scene 4

Georgia was in Grace Hall on the telephone. With Hugo and Freya away and Mrs Partridge busy in the kitchen, she could settle down to a long chat with Daisy without being interrupted.

Daisy had rung up to ask about French homework, and after a detailed discussion of their day at school, remembered the reason for her call. She despised French, considering it a messy language, unlike Latin, which was logical and orderly. So she'd secretly read a book during the lesson and hadn't written down what the teacher had set for prep. 'Learning verbs? Hang on, I need to get another pencil, the lead's just broken on this one. I hate French verbs,' she went on when she came back to the phone. 'Go on.' There was silence at the Castle end of the line. 'Georgia, are you still there?'

'Yes. Hold on, I can hear a noise.'

'What kind of a noise?'

'Like someone moving around.'

'Mrs Partridge,' said practical Daisy. 'Or the wind blowing against the windows. You always say the Castle is full of creaks and groans.'

'This is different.'

'Don't tell me you think it's a ghost.'

Georgia wasn't going to admit a momentary fear that it might be just that. 'Of course not.'

'I expect it's Magnus the cat. Didn't you say he was there with you?'

Georgia peered around the dimly lit Grace Hall. No sign of Magnus, and he'd been there a few minutes ago. 'You're right; it must have been him.'

'Dad's calling me. He's complaining about how long I've been on the phone. I'll have to go. See you tomorrow.'

Georgia replaced the receiver and went off in search of the cat. The noise had come from where Lord Selchester's rooms were. Perhaps Magnus had caught a mouse.

No mouse, but there was a chirrup and Magnus came out of the gloom to wind himself round her ankles. She picked him up, ruffling his fur. 'You gave me a fright.'

Then she heard the noise again. And it wasn't Magnus, who was struggling in her arms. She put him down, and he vanished into the shadows.

Light-footed—why? Why did she feel the need to be quiet? She took a deep breath and followed the cat. What *was* that noise? Could it really be one of the Castle ghosts she half-believed in?

Fear fought with curiosity. Then she saw a line of light under the door of Lord Selchester's sitting room.

She relaxed.

Ghosts didn't switch on lights. Mrs Partridge must have inadvertently left a light on. She would switch it off and tell the frugal Mrs Partridge that she'd done so.

And the noise? Definitely the wind rattling at a window.

She pushed open the door.

And stood frozen to the spot.

There was a man in there, rummaging through a drawer of the big roll-top desk.

'Hey,' Georgia said, too surprised to be afraid.

The man started, and for one moment they locked eyes. Then he turned and headed for the door on to the terrace while Georgia took to her heels and ran in the opposite direction.

Panting, she arrived in the kitchen.

'An intruder?' Mrs Partridge said, darting into the scullery and emerging with a broom. 'We'll see about that.'

When they got back to the room, it was empty. The light was still on, the door to the terrace closed. Mrs Partridge stalked over to it and tried the handle. 'Locked,' she said. She looked around the room. Everything seemed to be just as she'd left it. 'Are you sure you saw a man in here?'

'I did. Truly, I did.'

Mrs Partridge gave her a long look, saw she was trembling and swept her out of the room. 'I'm going to call the police.'

They sat in the kitchen drinking hot, sweet tea and waited for the police to arrive, in the shape of Sergeant Camford. Bluff, matter-of-fact and unbelieving. He listened to Georgia's account in silence.

'Shouldn't you write it down in your notebook?' she said. 'Don't you want a description?'

'If I do that, it's an official report. And it seems like you didn't get a good look at the man. Medium height and quite thin. Wearing a dark coat. Could be anyone.'

'It needs to be official. Someone broke in. And I'm sure I'd recognise him if I saw him again.'

'So you say, miss. But I don't see any evidence of a break-in, and Mrs Partridge here says nothing seems to have been taken.'

'He was searching in a drawer, who knows what was in there?'

The Sergeant thought about that one. 'Nothing of importance. We'll have gone through his desk after his lordship went missing. With the trustees.'

'Then you'd best ask one of them to come and look,' Mrs Partridge said.

'I'll mention it to the Superintendent,' the Sergeant said stolidly. 'Meanwhile, there's nothing I can do here. It's a false alarm. Wasting police time isn't a good thing to do, young lady. So I'll take myself off and we'll say no more about it.'

He went away, his heavy boots sounding on the flagstones. Georgia looked defiantly at Mrs Partridge. 'I didn't imagine it. I didn't make it up. Why should I?'

'No reason, and I don't think you did. Police! Fred Camford always was a born fool. He's a man as couldn't find his own bootlaces.' She looked at Georgia. 'You won't want to be upstairs on your own. I'll make up a bed in the little dressing room. I can't say I fancy being down here, knowing there's someone must have a key. I'm going to get Ben to change that lock first thing in the morning.'

# Chapter Fifteen

## Scene 1

Freya sat on a bench at Oxford Station, waiting for the local train that would take her on the first part of the complicated journey back to Selchester. She didn't mind; she liked train journeys, although she hoped that it wouldn't be one of those ones where delays led to missed connections, and you arrived hours later than planned.

She'd said her goodbyes to her parents, who had steamed away on the London train. Thank goodness it was all over, both the family reunion and her uncle's obsequies.

Not that she hadn't been glad to spend some time with her parents, but her mother had been at her sharpest, teaming up with Lady Priscilla after the burial to try to organise Freya's life.

'You've been vegetating. Now that you'll have to leave the Castle, it's time to make some plans,' her mother said. 'It was never a good idea to shut yourself up in that tower with the family archives; that's no way for a young woman to spend her time. It's not even as though you're any kind of a scholar. Who is ever going to be remotely interested in a collection of facts about the family? The Castle has been convenient for you, I appreciate that, but now you'll have to find somewhere else to live. You won't be able to manage on your private income; with tax the way it is, it will hardly keep you in stockings. It's time to go back to London and get yourself a job. Your father will give you an allowance so you can pay the rent and so forth while you find something to do, meet new people, rejoin the world.'

'What would I do with Last Hurrah if I went to London?' Freya said, side-stepping the main thrust of their argument.

'You can't allow your life to revolve around a horse,' Aunt Priscilla said. 'I'll stable him, and you can ride him at weekends.'

'This whole business of the Selchester papers is absurd, and I can't think why you ever got into it,' her mother said.

'It's a way of shutting out the world,' Aunt Priscilla said decisively and brutally. 'An escape from reality.'

'I can recommend a good psychoanalyst,' her mother put in. 'That might be the best thing for you, darling. Sort yourself out.'

Lady Priscilla had no time for psychoanalysts. 'Priests for people who aren't Catholic and can't go to confession. At least priests are free; who's going to pay for Freya to go to some Freudian quack to learn about her phobias?'

'I will,' Lady Veronica said.

Freya lost her temper. 'It's my life, and I plan to live it to suit myself. I don't need a psychoanalyst, and I don't need any help from you or Daddy, thank you. And I'm not moving to London.'

# Scene 2

She heard a distant whistle, and the signal at the end of the platform dropped with a clang. Her train chugged in, two carriages drawn by a small, cheerful-looking locomotive. It came to a halt and let off steam in a burst of noise and vapour. A porter opened a door for Freya and put her suitcase on to the rack. She tipped him and settled in a corner seat, pleased to have a compartment to herself.

While her train waited at its platform, the train from London came in on the main line. She watched idly as it disgorged its passengers; not many at this time of the morning. Then she stiffened. That man in the light overcoat—she knew him. His back was turned to her, but he was unmistakable: his height, his carriage, the back of his neck.

It was Selchester. She jumped up to let down the window and call out to him, and then thumped back down in her seat, shocked.

How ridiculous. Lord Selchester was dead. The man was walking along the platform towards the guard's van and, as he looked round for a moment, she saw his face. There was a resemblance, but of course it wasn't her uncle. She wasn't seeing ghosts, and her mind wasn't playing tricks on her.

As her train began to move, she gazed out of the window, not taking in anything with her eyes, her mind elsewhere. Had the requiem and the burial of her uncle affected her more than she'd thought? It was always said that those left behind felt better after the funeral was over, but that would hardly be the case when you'd assumed the late lamented had been dead and gone these several years.

He'd passed on into the life beyond, if there was one, long before the earth had rattled down on to his coffin, tossed there by an expressionless Lady Selchester. If he had gone to judgement, it would have happened by now.

Or perhaps not. Theologians and philosophers said that time didn't really exist. She had been intrigued when she read Dunne's *Experiment with Time* and had grappled with his image of a train moving through time. How, if you were inside the train as she was now, you could only see things to either side, which was the present, a short way behind into the past and a short way ahead to what was to come. But if you were travelling on the roof of the carriage you would have an extended view. More past, more future and even be able to see further into the present on either side.

A completely different view.

She shook her head and made herself focus on the landscape passing slowly outside the window. The countryside was serene and lovely in its autumnal colours. Soon it would be winter, and those trees with green and golden leaves rustling in the breeze would lose their glory and become mute, bare bones.

She shivered. She didn't want to think about bones, about her uncle, lying in the graveyard. At least, she told herself, he was in a proper place and not at the Castle under the flagstones.

She set herself to think of him alive, not dead. To remember him as he was. Not as he was the last time she'd seen him, when he'd been in a towering temper, but as the kindly uncle of her childhood.

She'd been fond of him, but had she loved him?

No. Nor, it seemed, had anyone else.

Who, among all those black-clad people at the Cathedral or around his grave, had loved him? It was disturbing that a man with his vitality and intelligence and, yes, charm could pass from this life and leave so little sorrow behind him.

Not even his nearest and dearest had grieved.

Why? It was a question she didn't want to ask. She could pretend it was because after seven years it had become an old sorrow, an accustomed grief.

It wasn't. He hadn't been mourned by his family then; he wasn't mourned now.

Something in his life must have been out of joint, to earn him that much hostility. It was hostility, too, not mere indifference. Look at Sonia.

Perhaps if they found out what had been wrong with him, they'd also solve the mystery of his murder.

# Scene 3

The train stopped at a small country station, and she looked out on to the platform, almost expecting to see herself as she was twenty years ago in her grey school coat, hair tightly plaited under her pudding-basin hat, an overnight case clasped in a gloved hand, on her way to or from her boarding school.

She looked around her compartment. How different from the opulent travel of those pre-war days. When she went back to school from Selchester Castle, a footman would see her on to the train, hand her a hamper of food and, in winter, give her a stone hot-water bottle to put under her feet. She'd be entrusted to the care of some sensible woman passenger travelling north, until the guard saw her on to the school train at Crewe.

She'd always hated going back to school. She'd begged to be sent to the same school as Sonia, to the convent where the Selchester girls were traditionally educated, where her mother had gone. But her parents had refused. Her mother hadn't been happy there, and her Anglican father wasn't at all keen for her to go to a convent. So Freya had been educated according to a different family tradition and had gone to the school in Yorkshire, where her father's sisters and nieces had gone.

Even if she had gone to the convent, she wouldn't have had Sonia's company for very long, because Sonia, a couple of years older than her, had been expelled. At the time, no one used the word, but that's what it amounted to, despite the careful talk at the Castle of it being better for Sonia to be educated at home. A governess had appeared, a Frenchwoman with cynical eyes and the knack of keeping Sonia under control.

An older Sonia had been furious at the outbreak of war. 'Unless it's all over really quickly, there'll be no Season for either of us. Even if the Germans win and the war ends, there won't be a King and Queen, no Drawing Rooms—nothing. It's too bad. Why couldn't they have put it off for a year or two until I'd had my chance to be a deb?'

Freya had gone back to school, and Sonia had discontentedly taken herself to London, supposedly to do her bit for the war effort. Freya heard on the school grapevine—Lady Sonia Richmond's doings fascinated her friends—that her cousin was relishing the war: dining and dancing with officers and enjoying the freedom that having a mother in Canada and a father occupied all the hours of the day with government work gave her.

Sonia had another outburst of fury when it became obvious that single young women would be called up for war work. Freya couldn't wait; she longed to be in uniform and had at first been dismayed to find herself decanted into a dreary town halfway between Oxford and Cambridge, although once there she had found the work totally absorbing.

Sonia had no intention of spending her time in any such way, and had promptly found herself a rich husband. He was a Colonel in a Guards regiment, who obliged her by going overseas only days after their wedding. As Sonia candidly told Freya during one of her visits to London, 'Sinclair is the most terrific bore, but really, one had to do something. I might have been sent on to the land or the ATS. Imagine me in that ghastly uniform.' Her Colonel had even more obligingly been blown to bits in the desert, leaving Sonia an extremely wealthy and happy widow.

There had always been antagonism between Sonia and her father, perhaps because they were in some ways alike. When had antagonism become dislike and then hatred?

Freya shifted in her seat. Sonia. Sonia and Selchester. That row they'd had that afternoon of the day he vanished. What had it been about? Why had it brought on one of Sonia's worst migraines?

And what had been in those pills Freya had retrieved from Selchester's bedside table?

# Scene 4

Freya closed her eyes. Usually, she tried not to think about it, preferring to blot it out of her mind, but now she forced her mind back to that bitter night in January 1947.

The atmosphere in the drawing room was uneasy, with cross-currents she didn't understand. She went out and headed for the main staircase. On the first floor, she went along a wide landing and up another set of stairs that led to the part of the house where Sonia's room was. When Sonia had a migraine, she wanted to be left alone, but it would be a kindness to make sure that she had everything she needed.

She knocked lightly on the door, turned the handle and slipped in. The room was almost dark, only the light from the fire flickering and illuminating the four-poster bed in which Sonia lay. It was a large room, one that Freya had never liked, with its panelling and dark furniture and heavy curtains. Sonia looked drained and white, almost like a mediaeval painting, motionless under the rich brocade cover. Her eyes were closed, and her dark hair was spread out on the pillow.

As Freya tiptoed towards the bed, thinking that if her cousin was asleep, she would simply go away again, the pale lips moved, and Sonia said, 'Whoever you are, go away.'

'It's only me, Sonia. I came to see if there's anything I can do for you.'

'You know damn well you can't do anything for me.'

'Didn't Dr Rogers help?'

'He's given me new painkillers. Supposed to be stronger and they take away the nausea, but they make me so drowsy I can't stand up.'

Freya could believe that. 'Why would you want to stand up?'

'I must get the pills.' She spoke through teeth clenched with pain.

Next to the bed was a glass with two tablets beside it. 'Are they what the doctor left for you? They're right there, beside the bed—no need to try to get up.'

Sonia slowly turned her head and stretched out a thin hand, as though appealing for help. 'In Father's room, by his bed. You could do that for me.'

'Does he have some other tablets you want? Or a powder?'

Freya knew that her uncle, in most ways an austere and self-controlled man, was nonetheless a tremendous hypochondriac, much given to frequenting whatever fashionable doctor was held in esteem in London, quacking himself and, to the irritation of the local medical man who was often called in for imaginary complaints, wasting time, money and energy on curing non-existent ailments. 'I have rarely seen a healthier specimen. He will doubtless live to a great age like his grandfather did. Unless he doses himself to death, which is always a possibility.'

Among Selchester's extensive pharmacopoeia perhaps there was something that really would benefit Sonia, but should she take anything on top of what the doctor had given her? Freya said, 'Does he have something that would help you? Where would I find it? Shall I ask him?'

Sonia lifted her head, and a spasm of pain crossed over her face. She drew the back of her hand over her eyes and said in a thread of a voice, 'By his bed. The bottle shouldn't be . . .' and her voice tailed off. She sank back into the pillows. 'Please.' Tears trickled from under her closed lids. 'Please get them for me. I shouldn't have . . . If he takes them and the bottle is there . . . Blue bottle. For indigestion. Please.'

That last *please* was so desperate that Freya tiptoed out of the room. If the pills were working to stop the nausea, why would Sonia want indigestion tablets? Still, if it was fretting her, she'd get them.

In Selchester's room, beside the immense four-poster bed in which generations of Selchesters had been conceived, born and died, stood a small blue bottle. Freya took it back to Sonia, who put out a hand, grasped it, and with a groan thrust it under her pillow.

'Go away, Freya. Just go away.'

# Scene 5

Afterwards, Freya asked Sonia what the pills in the blue bottle were. Sonia had looked at her with those cold, brilliantly blue eyes and said, 'What pills? I don't know what you're talking about.'

She must have been too drugged to remember. Surely it had been some phantasm of a mind under the influence of pain and medication that made her so insistent about needing those tablets. Or had it?

That memory had opened the floodgates, and now Freya, listening with half an ear to the train rattling over the points, thought about Tom and her vehement conviction of his innocence. He couldn't have killed his father. *Couldn't* as in it would have been physically impossible? Or *couldn't* as in patricide was a crime too terrible for a man like Tom to commit?

As a boy, he'd got on better with his father than Sonia had, and there was never any doubt about Selchester's pride in his son and heir. Yet after the war, they hadn't seen much of one another.

Well, Tom's Army career was probably the reason for that. And it was inevitable that Selchester would object to Tom's marriage to a nobody, as he would see it, and that his father's contempt would annoy Tom.

Annoy—or infuriate?

And was that the sole reason for their estrangement?

Tom had a temper. A temper that had, when he was young, been uncontrollable on occasion. Freya had seen him in a blind rage, flying at that rogue Filbert when he'd tormented a half-dead creature instead of dispatching it swiftly and humanely. Hurling a croquet mallet at a visiting boy who'd cheated. Everyone did, after all, but this boy cheated and pretended he hadn't. And then there was the time he'd lashed out at Charles with the side of his sabre when Charles, angry at losing a fencing bout, had lunged at him after Tom had landed a fair hit.

Even when his reactions weren't so extreme, he deserved his nickname of Firecracker, apt as he was to flare up at an insult or an unkindness or a transgression of rules that he thought should be obeyed.

But to creep back into the Castle to seek out his father in his study, kill him and bury him? That wasn't an act of temper. That would have been a cold-blooded killing.

Which was what he was trained to do, and had done, during and since the war. Kill enemies.

Had his father become an enemy in his eyes?

Freya told herself, 'No.' Not Tom. Yet how could she know? How could any of them know while the events of that evening and of Selchester's death remained such a mystery?

The guard came into the compartment to clip her ticket. 'We'll be arriving in Grantley in a few minutes. We come in on the lower platform. You'll have to go to the upper level for the train to Thornhampton. Change there for Selchester.'

Freya walked along the platform and up the steps to the higher platform on the main line. There she sat on a bench, her suitcase at her feet, until the train drew in and a porter hurried forward to open a door for her. Good; she would again have a compartment to herself. She took out a book and began to read.

The door to the compartment slid open, and a man came in.

# Chapter Sixteen

## Scene 1

Freya gave the man a cold look, hoping he would go away. There were several empty compartments. Why did he have to come into this one?

He nodded at her and sat down in the corner nearest the corridor.

At least he didn't seem the chatty sort. Freya looked pointedly out of the window for a few minutes and then returned to her book.

'I think we've met,' the man said. 'Aren't you Freya Wryton?'

Freya laid her book on her knee and gave him a long, hard look. 'I am, but we've never met.'

'I'm sure you remember. At Lady Sonia's. A cocktail party.'

It was plausible enough. She had been to a few of Sonia's parties in her time, and they were usually crowded affairs, full of people Freya didn't know. People, she always had the feeling, she didn't much want to know. Easy to forget a brief introduction. Only she hadn't. She had a remarkable memory for faces, and she was quite certain she'd never met this man. He was ordinary-looking enough. A gent, by his clothes and accent, with pleasant, undistinguished features. But she'd have remembered those pale eyes. And she didn't.

So why was he pretending they had met? Was he trying to pick her up? She'd make it clear he was wasting his time. She gave him a polite, chilly smile and went back to her book.

'I saw you at Lord Selchester's requiem. You'll be on your way back from his funeral. Odd that Sonia was so insistent he should be buried there and not in Selchester. I dare say Lady Selchester wasn't much bothered one way or the other.'

Sonia? The requiem? Lady Selchester's indifference to her late husband's final resting place? Who was this man?

'Don't look so surprised. I worked for Lord Selchester.'

A government official of some kind, then. Although there was something about him that didn't fit her experience of civil servants.

'You were close to Tom Arlingham, of course. Very close at one time, so I heard. Sad, his falling out with his father so soon before he died. Before they both died, as it turned out. It always struck me as strange that they should be at loggerheads.'

'I hardly think my family affairs are any business of yours, whoever you may be.'

'Naturally the assumption was that Selchester disliked his engagement, but don't you think it was more than that? I suspect you're the one person Arlingham might have confided in.'

This echo of her reflections of just a little while ago was uncanny. But he was wrong on one thing. Sonia and Tom had never got on, but there was a sibling bond that some brothers and sisters had, however much at odds they might have been in daily life. If there had been some other reason for his anger with his father, apart from his wanting to marry Antonia, he would have shared it with Sonia.

She wasn't going to tell this man that.

The train steamed into another station and stopped with a shriek of brakes. The man stayed where he was and Freya gave a sigh of relief as the fellow passengers from hell in the shape of a harassed mother and three fractious children surged into the compartment.

A look of annoyance crossed the man's face as the two boys squabbled over a corner seat and the little girl began to whine.

Freya determinedly took up her book and steadfastly kept her head down until the train drew into Thornhampton. She hauled down her suitcase before the man, who had leapt to his feet, could offer to help her and whisked herself out of the compartment, into the corridor and out on to the platform. She hesitated for a moment. Then she headed for the siding where the Selchester train waited on the branch line. She walked briskly along the train, found an empty compartment, got in, crossed to the other door and jumped down on to the platform on the other side.

From a vantage spot beside an old and long-unused chocolate machine, she watched the man board the Selchester train just before the guard blew his whistle and the train began to move.

She'd have an hour to wait before the next train, but it was worth it to be shot of that man with the disconcerting eyes and his even more disconcerting questions.

## Scene 2

Hugo's train from London was late. They were holding the Selchester train, and the guard hurried him into a compartment, waving his flag and blowing his whistle even as he slammed the door. So it wasn't until they both alighted at Selchester that he saw Freya.

'Good,' she said. 'We can share a taxi. Have you been in London?'

'Yes, I had a doctor's appointment,' Hugo said. 'I left Georgia in Mrs Partridge's care. I hope she's behaved herself.'

They gave up their tickets, and as they came out into the station yard, were hailed by Stanley Dillon. He was sitting in the driving seat of a Jaguar, and he got out and came across to them. 'That's a bit of luck, seeing you here. I just dropped in to have a quick word with Mr Godney. I hope it all went well in Oxford, Miss Wryton. Let me drive you up to the Castle, you don't want to hang around waiting for a taxi. And I've something I need to tell you.'

They got into the car, but before he started the engine, Dillon said, 'Have you heard from Georgia or Mrs Partridge while you've been away?'

'No,' Hugo said, suddenly alert. 'Nothing's wrong, is it?'

'No, no. Georgia's fine. Don't worry. But something happened while you were away. She'll give you her side of the story, but I'm glad of the chance to tell you about it.'

Stanley Dillon had heard about the incident at the Castle from Daisy. 'That foul policeman thought Georgia had made it all up,' Daisy said indignantly. 'But she didn't. She wouldn't. If she were making something up, it wouldn't be that. And I was talking to her on the telephone when she heard the noise in Lord Selchester's room. She thought it was the cat. Or the wind.'

Now Dillon told Freya and Hugo what had, apparently, happened.

Hugo was impressed by the way Freya took the news. She didn't interrupt, exclaim or express dismay or disbelief. She listened, and when Dillon had finished, said, 'A shock for Georgia if she did disturb an intruder. And if the man had a key, we'll need to change the locks.'

'Mrs Partridge believes her,' Mr Dillon said. 'I dropped in at the Castle this morning. Ben's already changed the locks.'

'Why didn't Georgia ring me and tell me about this?' Hugo said. 'I'd have come straight back. She must have been scared out of her wits.'

'No, she seemed to take it all quite calmly. She said, sensibly enough, that she didn't want to bother you, and there was no point in you rushing back from London as there wasn't anything you could do about it. I suggested she come and spend last night with us, but she said that wasn't fair on Mrs Partridge, and Ben would sleep in the Castle until you came home. Bless the girl, thinking of Mrs Partridge, who's as able as anyone I know to look after herself. If that woman had come face-to-face with an intruder, she'd have walloped him.'

Bother him? As though he might have felt inconvenienced by her being in danger? Her stoicism might be admirable, but her reluctance to ask for him to come back troubled him. He shouldn't have gone to London and left her at the Castle like that.

Valerie. Georgia had probably supposed he was with Valerie and would be reluctant to cut short his time with her. Well, he wasn't going to leave his sister alone again. He was responsible for her, and he'd failed her. He felt hurt and guilty. New emotions for him, and he didn't care for them.

'I'm glad Georgia had the sense to turn tail and run,' he said. 'So the police aren't taking it seriously?'

'They are not,' Dillon said. 'I had to call in at the police station today, and I had a word with MacLeod. The Sergeant, who's a bit of a turnip-top, made a verbal report, and they'd decided there was nothing to go on. Mind you, MacLeod did say something a bit odd, about passing the news on to London as it was to do with the Castle. When I asked him why London would be interested—I suppose he meant the Yard—he said I must have misheard him. Georgia will be home from school by now, so you can talk to her yourself. You're the one who's closest to her, Hawksworth. She's your sister; you'll know if she made it up or not.'

Would he? Hugo would have said he'd got to know Georgia better since they'd come to the Castle, but how well was better? Why would she make up such a tale? Attention seeking? Heaven forbid. He could imagine Valerie instantly on the telephone to Anna Freud if she got wind of such behaviour.

'Trust her,' Freya said, reading his thoughts.

Dillon dropped them at the Castle, and Hugo headed for the kitchen. Georgia was sitting at the table, Magnus purring on her lap. She was surreptitiously feeding him pieces of cake while she ate a large slice of bread and jam. Her face lit up when she saw Hugo, but all she said was, 'Oh, the travellers return, do they?'

Freya had gone upstairs to her rooms with her suitcase, but she was back down and in the kitchen almost immediately, her face flushed. 'Someone's been in the Tower,' she said. 'Disturbing my papers. Mrs Partridge, have you—'

'I have not. I was up there to dust the day you went off and not since then. I didn't touch your desk; I never do, since you like to do that yourself.'

'It was the burglar,' Georgia said triumphantly. 'Before you ask, Freya, I haven't been near the Tower. Why should I? And if I were snooping about, which I wasn't, I'd take jolly good care to leave everything exactly as it was. I bet that man was looking in your room for whatever it was he was searching Lord Selchester's desk for. I wonder what it was? Maybe a map or a secret document. Anyway, now that policeman will have to believe me.'

'I don't think he will,' Freya said. 'Move along, and give me some of that cake. If it's Sergeant Camford, he'll just say I'm mistaken about my papers. He thinks all women are witless.'

Mrs Partridge, on her way in from seeing to the hens, heard this last remark. 'Fred Camford is the witless one. Gormless as they come, and there's no point trying to change his mind, what there is of it. Let's be thankful nothing's missing and no harm done. If the man who broke in here is a regular burglar, he'll mostly likely break into someone else's place, like they do. Then the police will have to sit up and take notice.'

Georgia sighed, and then her face brightened. 'Oh, it isn't all gloom and doom and the criminal classes stamping in and out. Something good happened as well. There's a postcard from Uncle

Leo, asking if he can come to stay. He says there are some papers you have to sign, Hugo.'

Freya, intrigued by what her aunt had told her about Leo Hawksworth, said they had plenty of room and she'd like to meet him. 'I'll tell Aunt Priscilla, and I bet she'll come over to see him. When does he want to come?'

'Thursday,' Georgia said complacently. 'I know the postcard is addressed to you, Hugo, but postcards are fair game, everyone knows that. You and Freya were away, so I asked Mrs Partridge, and she said to ring him up, because that was what Freya would want, and he'll be here on the 4.05 train. I said you'd leave work early and meet him, Hugo. You don't seem to work regular hours, so that should be okay.'

Hugo looked speechlessly at his sister and then felt obliged to apologise to Freya.

'Don't worry. Georgia is quite right. I approve of people being decisive.'

'I'm glad he's coming,' Georgia said. Then she gave her brother one of her direct looks. 'And I'm glad you're back. It feels safer with you here.'

# Chapter Seventeen

## Scene 1

Caleb Plinth was beginning to wish he'd caught the bus instead of taking a short cut through the West Wood. Dusk at the end of a cloudy day had brought a mist swirling up from the river, and the half-light, the damp mossy earth underfoot, and the thick canopy of branches overhead made for a cheerless atmosphere.

There was an eerie stillness in the wood; no sounds of birds or creatures in the undergrowth.

He crossed the stream, stepping on the flat rock in the middle, and it was then he heard the footsteps. He stopped and listened, uncertain where they were coming from. As he walked on, he decided that the footsteps were in front of him. If he quickened his pace, he might catch up with whoever it was and have company for the rest of the walk through the darkening woods.

But were the footsteps in front? He had a feeling that something was moving behind him. And moving carefully, stealthily.

A forest creature? No, a person, probably someone out with a gun, intending to take a pot shot at a rabbit or two.

He was becoming uneasy and found himself looking round, as though expecting to see someone following him. He quickened his pace, fighting a growing sense of alarm.

He couldn't bear it any longer. He turned quickly off the path and retreated into a small circle of trees. They towered above him, but the crinkled solidity of the big trunks was strangely comforting.

With the only other sound a soft rustle of wind in the leaves above his head, he could hear the footsteps coming closer. He held his breath as a man, indistinguishable in the shadowy light, drew level with the clump of trees and moved on without pausing.

Mr Plinth waited. Let whoever it was go ahead. Finally, relieved to be alone, he stepped out from the safety of the trees. As he regained the path, a shot rang out.

## Scene 2

Superintendent MacLeod drove out to where Mr Plinth was waiting for him by the gate that led into the woods.

'I don't often come this way,' Mr Plinth said, as he climbed into the police car and it jolted its way along the track. 'It's a lonely place. You get the odd walker at weekends in the summer, but it's not a path many people take.'

'You're sure it's Jason?'

Mr Plinth swallowed. 'I reckon so. Whoever it is had red hair and is wearing that old jacket of his.'

'A poacher's jacket.'

Both men knew all about Jason Filbert. At one time, he'd worked for Lord Selchester in the Estates Office. He had some knowledge of old buildings and would advise whether a surveyor needed to be called if anything was amiss with the Castle. Otherwise, he mostly did odd jobs around the place, fixing a door, mending walls, rehanging a tapestry.

Honest, he was not. Lord Selchester had sacked him for having his hand in the cash box, and he'd been up in front of the magistrates for poaching more than once. He made a living of a kind, helping with building work, and was generally known as a wife-beater.

'I hear that Polly finally walked out on him,' MacLeod said as they walked the short distance to the path where Mr Plinth had found the body.

'Surprised she put up with him that long,' Mr Plinth said. 'He's been uttering some pretty vicious threats about what he'd do to her when he found where she was.'

'Well,' said MacLeod, looking down at the shattered body. 'He won't be coming after her now.' He'd crouched down beside the body and stood up, looking at the papers he'd taken from the blood-stained jacket. 'Not much doubt it's him. Here's his ration book, along with a couple of others. We'll have to do a formal identification. And find Polly. She'll need to be told.'

'She'll be dancing on his grave when he's safely six foot under, I dare say.'

'Don't touch that gun,' MacLeod said, putting out a hand to stop Mr Plinth, who had bent down to pick up the rifle that lay to one side of the body. 'We'll need to check it for prints, just in case there's any question of foul play.'

Foul play. The words hung in the air.

'There's a lot of folk didn't much care for Filbert,' MacLeod said, 'but none of them likely to shoot his head off. Either he did it himself, deliberately, or more likely he didn't take the trouble to break his gun before he climbed over the stile.'

Mr Plinth opened his mouth to say something about the footsteps. About the footsteps he'd heard both ahead of him and behind him. Then he shut it. He must have imagined them.

# Scene 3

Mr Bunbury toiled up the hill with the afternoon post. 'Late, I'm afraid,' he said. 'Couple of letters for you, Miss Wryton, and one for you, Mr Hawksworth. And I brought a copy of the *Gazette*. I thought you'd like to see it, as maybe you hadn't heard the news.'

'What news?' said Mrs Partridge, annoyed that there should be any news that she hadn't known about before it was ever in the paper.

'There's a body been found in the West Wood. Jason Filbert.'

'Jason Filbert? Dead?' Mrs Partridge said. 'That's the devil claiming his own. How did he die? I'd have said he was hale and hearty and set to plague the world for a good few years yet.'

'Shot himself. Climbing over a stile, they say. An accident. Thank you, Mrs Partridge, a cup of tea would be much appreciated.'

Georgia fell on the newspaper. There was a photo of the dead man on the front page, and she stared at it before letting out a yell that made them all jump.

'That's him! That's the man who was in Lord Selchester's room.'

'I heard you'd had a break-in,' Mr Bunbury said. 'Two sugars in my tea, please, if you can spare it. Doesn't surprise me if your intruder was Jason Filbert. Sneaky sort, he was, and there won't be anyone grieving for him, that's for sure.'

Hugo wrenched the paper away from Georgia. 'It doesn't really say much. Just where he was found and that the police aren't treating it as a suspicious death.'

Mr Bunbury blew on his tea to cool it. 'I don't see Jason Filbert making a silly mistake with his gun like that. Cautious is what he was. A good shot, mind you, but not the careless or reckless sort when it came to guns. He'd never go over a stile without breaking his gun. Just shows you how little the police know about anything.

It's suicide or foul play, that's what it is, and if Polly Filbert hadn't taken herself off to her sister's place in Cornwall a couple of weeks ago, with no intention of coming back, they'd be wondering if she hadn't decided to take a pot shot at him.'

# Scene 4

Freya was looking after the bookshop for Dinah the next morning, and she found the town abuzz with the excitement of a second body. Jamie had rushed over to the bookshop as soon as Freya opened up.

'My dear! Such drama in tranquil Selchester. Who would have thought it? And in the Castle grounds, too.'

Freya went on unpacking a box of books, methodically taking out each volume and checking it against the invoice.

'Freya, don't be so irritating. How can you not be interested in another body on your doorstep!'

'One body is quite enough, thank you. Besides, the West Wood is not on my doorstep; I don't have seven league boots. And I have to get on with this.'

'There'll be a third,' Jamie prophesied. 'Things always go in threes, don't they?'

'Do they?'

Jamie wasn't going to give up. 'And have you heard about the mysterious stranger who just happened to be in town and just happened to have been seen talking to Jason the night before he was found dead?'

'What has that to do with anything? The police aren't treating it as murder. Accidental death, they say.'

'It's what they say, but one always wonders . . . They claim they know all about the stranger. He came into the tearooms. Quiet man, not the sort you'd think would know Jason. Strange pale eyes, made me feel quite odd.'

Freya stopped unpacking the books and stared at Jamie. 'Pale eyes? What did he look like?'

'Not the kind of man you'd notice in a crowd. Nondescript, really. Wearing a smart mac. Well-spoken.'

Freya didn't like the sound of this. 'You say the police know who he is?'

'Yes.' Jamie sounded regretful. 'Apparently he's some kind of private investigator. All above board. I dare say he's an ex-policeman. They stick together, don't they, these detectives? Of course they wouldn't say why he was in Selchester. I expect it's something to do with Nightingale Cottage. Although I suppose Mrs Filbert might have employed him to investigate Jason and his ill-doings, but why would she? Everyone knows what he got up to, and Polly Filbert most of all. But that would account for Mr Graham seeing him with Jason.'

'Were they having an argument? Are two men talking grounds for suspicion?'

'Don't bite me, duckie—I'm only keeping you up to date with the news. No, nothing hostile, so Mr Graham says. Simply deep in conversation.'

It was a coincidence, nothing more, but the mention of pale eyes worried Freya. 'Is this stranger still here?'

'No,' Jamie said regretfully. 'He's gone. Mr Godney says he bought a ticket to Scotland and caught the early train to Thornhampton.'

It must have been the same man. Freya had never met a private investigator, and so she didn't know whether his conversation in the train was normal for people of his ilk. He'd worked for Selchester, he'd said. That was odd; why would Selchester need the services of a private detective?

Divorce? Wasn't that what those sort of people were mostly employed for? Was it something to do with Aunt Hermione? No, any investigation into her private life—and that was an unpleasant notion—would need to be carried out in Canada.

What then? It was a pity he'd left Selchester, or she could have asked him. He might have told her. Or not, if he was a man with a sense of discretion about his clients. Even dead ones.

She put him out of her mind and went back to unpacking the books.

# Chapter Eighteen

## Scene 1

H ugo got to the station just after the 4.05 had come in. He bought a platform ticket, went through the barrier and stood looking up and down the platform. There was Leo at the far end, dressed in clerical black, helping a woman with a child and a lot of parcels down from the train.

His uncle set the child on its feet, handed the woman a final parcel and came striding down the platform towards Hugo. He was a tall, lean man with a high-arched nose and a vast deal of energy about him.

He reached Hugo and embraced him warmly, much to the horror and embarrassment of Mr Godney. He didn't hold with Papists, and here was a man in a Roman collar hugging Mr Hawksworth.

Hugo saw the disapproval on the station-master's face and said, 'This is my uncle, Mr Godney. He's come to pay us a visit at the Castle.'

The station-master's eyes narrowed. Then he said, unexpectedly, 'You've been here before, sir. I don't often forget a face. It would have been before the war, you were visiting the Castle then, too. It was when they had that ball for Lady Priscilla's youngest.'

Leo smiled. 'You certainly have a remarkable memory for faces.'
'That would have been, let me see, 1934?'
'1935.'

Somewhat mollified, Mr Godney took Leo's ticket and saw the Hawksworths through the barrier and out to where Hugo had parked his car.

Leo's eyes lit up. 'It can't be good for you to drive with that leg of yours. Let me take the wheel.'

Hugo went round and got into the passenger seat. 'It's nothing to do with my leg. It's simply that you like driving fast cars, and you don't have any opportunity for it these days.'

Leo let the clutch in with a sigh of satisfaction. 'No, indeed. What a beauty she is. I quite envy you.'

Hugo said, 'Rather than going straight to the Castle, I thought we might pick Georgia up from her school. It's on our way, and she'll be delighted not to have to take the bus. And to see you, of course.'

Leo drove at nerve-wracking speed and pulled up with a flourish outside the gates of the High School as hordes of identically uniformed girls were pouring out. Leo said, 'What a peculiarly unbecoming uniform. I suppose that's the purpose of it, to stop them being individuals and mark them off limits.'

'It's done nothing to quell Georgia's individuality, I assure you.'

'No, not all the grey flannel in the world can diminish an ardent spirit. I can see that several of these young ladies have plenty of personality,' he added, as one of the younger girls, her hair coming adrift from its plaits, came skidding through the gate, whacked another girl across the legs with her satchel and ran off towards the waiting bus.

'There's Georgia,' Hugo said, waving.

A girl standing beside Georgia was staring at Leo. She said something, and Georgia gave her a hefty shove before loping over to the car. She clambered into the back and leaned forward to kiss her uncle. 'Hello, Uncle Leo. Why are you driving?'

'To save Hugo's leg. Tell me, why did you push that girl?'

'No reason, except she said you looked odd. She's foul anyhow, and needs teaching some manners. Step on it, Uncle Leo—I'm longing to show you the Castle.'

'It turns out that this isn't your uncle's first visit to the Castle,' Hugo said. 'He was here for a ball.'

'Nearly twenty years ago,' Leo said.

'Which room did they put you in?'

'I don't remember. Perhaps I'll recognise it when I get there.'

'I shouldn't think so. Most of the rooms are shut up, and nothing looks the same when it's all covered in dust sheets.'

They reached the Castle gates, jolted their way up the drive and through into the stable yard. Last Hurrah put his head inquisitively over the half-door, and Georgia went over to stroke his nose. As usual, he tried to nip her, but she moved smartly away. Leo joined her and blew into the horse's nostrils.

'He seems to like you,' Georgia said. 'You'd think your black suit would frighten him. Still, Brother Horse and all that.'

'I am not a Franciscan,' Leo said, wrenching his suitcase out of Hugo's grasp. 'No, let me; I have two good legs.'

'Since one doesn't carry a suitcase with one's legs I don't think it makes any difference,' Georgia said. 'We go in the back way, Uncle Leo. None of the state you'll have had on your last visit. We live in the kitchen these days.'

## Scene 2

Mrs Partridge's opinion of priests was that they carried religion too far, but within minutes she had succumbed to Leo's charm, made tea for him and put a generous slice of cake on his plate.

'Where's Freya?' Georgia asked in an attempt to distract Mrs Partridge while she helped herself to a second slice of cake.

Mrs Partridge whisked the cake out of her reach. 'There's bread and butter if you're hungry, Georgia. No more cake, or you'll not want your supper.'

'No danger of that,' Freya said as she came into the kitchen.

Hugo and Leo rose to their feet, and Leo, giving her a long look, said, 'But I remember you. You were peering down through the banisters, watching the guests come and go. It was at a ball given here at the Castle for Helena Veryan—she must be your cousin.'

Freya looked at him just as intently. 'Yes, and I remember you, because you brought up ices for Sonia and me.'

Almost before he'd finished his cup of tea, Georgia was urging Leo to go on a tour of the Castle. He gave in to the inevitable, stood up, thanked Mrs Partridge for her excellent cake and said, 'I'd certainly like to see the picture gallery again.'

'That's as good a place to start as any,' Freya said.

The little group lingered in the picture gallery, despite Georgia's efforts to move her uncle along. 'I hate it here,' she said. 'All these faces of dead people looking out at you. I feel they're just waiting until it's dark, and they'll step down from their frames to rustle up and down and rattle doorknobs and whisper.'

Leo said mildly, 'Selchester Castle does have a reputation for being haunted, but let me assure you, Georgia, people long in their graves can never affect the living in any way.'

'I don't know that you're right about that,' Georgia said. 'People do all sorts of things that have an effect after they're dead. Legacies and hidden secrets—that kind of thing. Why, look at Lord Selchester. Dead for seven years, and now we're all jumping about because of him.'

Leo had come to a gap on the wall, an outline of dust showing that there had been a framed picture there. His eyebrows rose and he turned to Freya. 'What happened to the portrait that hung here? It was a remarkable portrait. Of a seventeenth-century Countess, if I remember rightly. You resemble her; you have the same eyes.'

'You're talking about the seventh Earl's Countess,' Freya said. 'I love that portrait, and so I borrowed her, and she hangs in the Tower where I have my rooms. I'll miss her when she has to go.'

Leo said, 'Hugo told me that Lady Sonia plans to sell the Castle.'

'Yes, it's to become some kind of grand hotel. The contents will be cleared out and sold separately; my cousin's calling in one of the auction houses to do a catalogue. I'd like to buy my Countess, but Sonia wants the whole collection of portraits to go up for sale together, and so I'd have to go to the auction and bid for her if I want her.'

Leo said, 'She was a redoubtable lady, judging by her portrait.'

'Like Freya,' Hugo muttered under his breath. Leo heard and his mouth twitched.

Georgia asked, 'Oh, was she the one who held the Castle against Oliver Cromwell's Army?'

'That's the one,' Freya said.

'Anyway, it doesn't matter, since the picture isn't here. Do come on, Uncle Leo. All these ruffs and long dresses and wigs and strange hats aren't like real people. Why would anyone want to look at them?'

Leo stopped in front of a more recent portrait. 'Your uncle,' he said to Freya. 'It's a good likeness, from what I remember of him.'

Freya said, 'Did you know him well?'

'I only met him the once, at Helena's ball.'

Georgia wanted Leo to see the Old Chapel.

Freya said, 'Ghoul. I'm afraid I shan't come with you. I can't bear to go near it. Besides, I need to take Last Hurrah out for some exercise.'

Hugo said, 'I'm with Freya, it's not my favourite place. I'll be in our sitting room. Georgia will show you where it is.'

Georgia led her uncle to the Old Chapel, hurrying him along the stone passages and finally pushing open the Chapel doors with a triumphant flourish. 'There, this is where they found the body. They've put the flagstones back, so it's as though he was never buried here. Just think, if the pipes hadn't leaked, he could have been here forever.' She watched Leo with interest, her head on one side. 'Are you praying?'

'I am.'

'For Lord Selchester?'

'For his soul.'

'Doesn't it get awfully tiresome, praying all the time?'

'You get used to it,' Leo said. He frowned as he stood and looked around the Chapel.

'Do you think it will be haunted after all this?' Georgia asked.

'I do not.'

'He may not clank about in chains, but he's certainly a presence in a lot of people's minds. Hugo's obsessed with finding out what happened to him. He's angry because the police think Freya had something to do with it, and he doesn't think so. And I think he's bored with all the stuff he does at the Hall, and a murder is much more up his street. I reckon he was a spy in the war, but he won't say so. Clam is his middle name, and that's so suspicious, don't you agree? Everyone else goes on about the war and what they did, and you'd think Hugo spent all that time sitting in an office doing nothing. Which isn't very likely. And he's just as cagey about what he's been doing since the war. Not to mention how he hurt his leg. So either he's a master criminal, running some international gang, or it's espionage.'

'I hope you don't share these thoughts with your friends, Georgia.'

She cast him a scornful look. 'As if I would. I'm not stupid, Uncle Leo. But I don't believe all this numbers stuff, and nor would you.'

'Numbers?' Leo said.

'Statistics?' She grinned at her uncle. 'The Hall, where Hugo works, is supposed to be a government department of statistics. Big sign on the gatepost and all that. Funny how they have to have a guarded gate with soldiers, just to watch over a lot of figures.'

## Scene 3

Georgia deposited Leo outside their sitting room and went off to do her homework, extracting a promise from her uncle to help her with some maths later.

Hugo was sitting at his desk, but got up as his uncle came in. 'Have a chair. Whisky?'

Leo sat down by the fire. 'I gather from what Georgia let slip that you're taking an interest in this investigation, Hugo. Rather outside your normal line of duty, is it not?'

Hugo stiffened. There was more than a hint of the inquisition in his uncle's calm tone and shrewd eyes. 'I was asked to keep what my Chief at the Hall calls a "watching brief". Because of Lord Selchester's position, he had quite a lot to do with the kind of work that's done at the Hall.' He knew he sounded defensive, and it irritated him.

'I do know something about what goes on at the Hall,' Leo said.

Hugo supposed he shouldn't be surprised. Leo might no longer be in the Army, and he'd accepted a vocation that inevitably cut him off from his former life, but it didn't mean he didn't still have friends who knew what was going on. 'It's the charmed circle,' he said.

'You could call it that.'

They both knew exactly what Hugo was talking about. His own recruitment into the Service had come from a casual conversation his father had had with a man at dinner, a man whose son had been at school with Hugo. Hugo's father had mentioned Hugo to the man, saying that he would make a good Intelligence Officer.

Strings were pulled, a transfer arranged—all utterly civilised. Hugo had the right background; he was 'one of us', and an interview, which turned out to be with the father of another friend, was an amicable chat over a drink at a London club. The Chief knew Hugo's father, and his daughter was married to a cousin of Hugo's.

The Service was a web of such relationships. No one ever doubted the patriotism and loyalty of 'us'; that was taken for granted.

'The charmed circle has rather fallen apart now, since Burgess and Maclean defected,' Hugo said.

'I imagine that ruffled a few feathers.'

'To put it mildly.'

It was unbelievable—unimaginable—that those two, with their impeccable backgrounds and connections, could have so comprehensively betrayed their country, and the Service had been aghast. Burgess was an Old Etonian, Maclean the son of a former government minister; who would have ever for a moment thought they could be traitors?

'That's why I'm here in Selchester,' Hugo said. He flexed his injured leg. 'And this, of course. I'm going through old records, following long-ago trails, matching A with B, trying to find even a hint that we might have other traitors.'

'And have you?'

'I'm sure we have. And if they were recruited before the war, contemporaries of those two, then they could by now be high up in the Service.'

Leo nodded.

Hugo knew his uncle understood the anger he'd felt—still felt—at that treachery. In a world where you had to trust your colleagues, that trust had been shattered when the defectors appeared at the press conference in Moscow, traitors to their country and their friends. Hugo was outraged when he thought of those who had died because of what these men had been up to.

'I dare say I shouldn't be telling you this. But I'm sure the Russians know exactly what I'm up to. That's the name of the game.'

'And I shan't be telling anyone about what you do. Why should I? Georgia doesn't believe you're an ordinary civil servant, by the way. She thinks you're in espionage.'

'How the devil—sorry—why on earth does she think that?'

'I expect everyone in Selchester knows that whatever goes on at the Hall, it isn't statistics. So tell me why the police suspect Freya.'

Hugo had spent that morning at the Hall, his proper work thrust to one side, writing out everything he'd found out about Lord Selchester's death. He handed the folder to his uncle. 'Read that, and then you'll know as much as I do. I'd welcome a fresh view, and I'm sure Freya will as well.'

# Scene 4

Freya was amazed at how comfortable a guest Leo was; it was as though she'd known him for years. She watched with amusement as he skilfully took Georgia through some tricky maths problems.

'Wish you taught at my school, Uncle Leo. I understand it when I do it with you.'

Hugo said, 'I thought you physicists didn't bother with anything as basic as algebra.'

'On the contrary, I tell all my undergraduates that algebra is key to everything. They don't believe me, of course, but I still make them do it.'

Now, after an excellent dinner, they were sitting in the library. The red-shaded lamps gave off a soft glow, the heavy curtains were drawn and they sat companionably together in leather armchairs drawn up round a crackling fire.

Leo had Hugo's folder on his lap. 'We come to an inescapable conclusion. The police might not believe Freya's alibi, but I do, and so do you, Hugo. Perhaps Lord Arlingham wasn't the man Freya thought he was, and perhaps he did return to the Castle and kill his father, but it's out of character and far-fetched. He is, however, a convenient scapegoat. If you leave him out of the equation, you are therefore faced with some kind of a conspiracy. There are two possibilities. The first and, it seems to me, the more unlikely one is a conspiracy of the four members of staff: Mr Plinth, Mrs Hardwick, Ben and the girl Hattie. By the way, Hugo, you need to talk to the girl and find out what her story is. She was the only one of those four to have left the servants' hall during that time.'

Hugo said, 'She only went to the lavatory.'

Leo said, 'Even so, she's worth talking to. I can't believe that she was quite as stupid and hapless as Mr Plinth and the Superintendent have made out. I'd say fanciful and frightened, and I think you should find out what frightened her.'

'You said two possible conspiracies,' Freya said. 'The other one being the four guests.'

Leo said, 'Yes. It's exactly the same situation for them as for those behind the baize door. They all vouch for one another, so either they were all in it together, or none of them had anything to do with it. But I think you're looking in the wrong place, if I may say so, Hugo. You've considered motives for the four guests and found none. It's a key question: Why were those people invited to the Castle for that weekend?' He looked at Freya. 'Do you know who any of the other invited guests were? The six who didn't come because of the bad weather?'

Freya said, 'No, I never asked. I should think Plinth might remember. They can't have had anything to do with it, though, since none of them were here. They can't have been involved in the murder.'

Leo said, 'It might throw some light on why any of them were invited. And why none of those who made it that evening seemed happy to be here.'

'What do you mean when you say I'm looking in the wrong place?' Hugo asked.

'You're like the man who lost his key. When asked why he was looking in that particular spot for it and was he sure he'd dropped it there, he said, no, he hadn't dropped it there, but that was where the light was. You're looking under the light, and you need to investigate the shadows. Begin with the victim. Begin with Lord Selchester. There has to be something in his character or his actions or his life that led to his becoming a murder victim.'

They sat in silence, looking into the fire. Freya could tell Hugo was annoyed with himself; of course Leo was right. Start with the victim, that's where you'd find a motive for murder.

The library door opened, startling them. Magnus stalked across the floor, his tail held high, eyes gleaming in the firelight. He surveyed them for a moment and then jumped on to Leo's lap. Leo smiled, dropped the folder on to the floor and tickled the cat under its chin with long fingers.

'I hope you don't mind,' Freya said.

'On the contrary, I like cats.'

Hugo said, 'You're quite right. We've made the mistake of focusing on suspects and not on the victim.'

'So, Freya,' Leo said. 'You knew Lord Selchester, which we didn't. Tell us about him. My brief encounter with him told me nothing more than that he was exactly what you'd expect of a man of his background and position.'

Freya got up and thrust another log on to the flames. She knelt down on the hearth, prodded the embers with a poker and then said, 'I've been thinking about him a lot since . . . since they found his body and since the requiem. I'm not sure how well I did know him. He was kind to me, but he was a reserved and self-contained man. Stiff upper lip and all that. And I was a child at the time I stayed here at the Castle, so Sonia and I didn't see much of him. He spent most of his time in London, but even when he was home, Sonia and I lived almost separate lives up in the nurseries and then the schoolroom.'

Leo said, 'You surely got to know him better during and after the war.'

'I hardly saw anything of him during the war. He was busy and so was I. You know what it was like.' She gave Leo a quizzical look. 'Maybe you didn't, shut away in your Oxford college.'

'Word did reach us. We weren't as isolated as all that.'

'I lived in London immediately after the war, and I lunched with my uncle once or twice in the House of Lords, but that was usually to discuss money matters. He was my trustee. When I came to Selchester, he would invite me to the Castle, as he did that night, to make up numbers or if he wanted me to act as hostess when Sonia wasn't there.'

'Plinth disapproved of some of his guests, said they weren't the kind of people an Earl should know,' Hugo said.

'Selchester had a wide circle of friends, that's perfectly true. The sort of people you'd expect him to entertain: local nobs, the grander county, colleagues from the House of Lords, other politicians, government officials, Army types, distinguished academics from Oxford and Cambridge—all very Establishment. The ones Plinth didn't like were the writers and artists and people who led a more Bohemian way of life. Quite different.'

'People like Lionel Tallis and Vivian Witt, in fact,' Hugo said.

'So one couldn't accuse him of snobbery?' Leo said.

'Oh, one could. He was the most terrific snob,' Freya said. 'Think how he reacted to Tom's engagement.'

' A man with two personae?'

'I suppose he was. I never thought of that, because to me he was always just Selchester.'

A daydreamer, Freya knew that in those days she'd taken people as she found them, never bothering to wonder about them or suspect them of being anything other than they appeared.

'How did he get on with the rest of the family?' Leo asked.

'My mother, who's his half-sister, always disliked him. And Aunt Priscilla—oh, she wouldn't come out and say it, but I think she saw a side to him that I never did.'

'And then there was the estrangement from his wife.'

Freya could have said but didn't, out of a sense of family loyalty, that even his daughter hated him. She wondered again what was in those pills that Sonia had left on Selchester's bedside table.

They were interrupted by Mrs Partridge. 'Just to let you know, Miss Freya, that Lady Sonia's been on the telephone. I said I'd come and get you, but she was in a hurry and asked me to give you a message. Seems she'll be here tomorrow, late afternoon, and she's bringing some man with her. I didn't catch his name. Rupert somebody. She says it's to do with the pictures and all that.'

# Chapter Nineteen

## Scene 1

People in the town knew about Lady Sonia's impending arrival before Freya did, thanks to Mabel's eager work. Within seconds of Lady Sonia cutting the connection, and while Mrs Partridge was making her way from Grace Hall to the library, Mabel was passing on the news from the telephone exchange. A couple of phone calls, and it spread like wildfire, unwelcome news to nearly everyone.

'It means she's had the go-ahead from the lawyers to do what she likes with the Castle,' said Mr Bunbury, who was playing darts at the Red Lion. 'That'll be you out of a job, Ben.'

'Some of these smart hotels have stables,' Mr Wandsworth said. He poised his dart, narrowed his eyes and then cursed when he just missed a double eighteen.

'I've got my pension and that'll come to me now his lordship's safely tucked away six foot under.' Ben finished his beer and stood up. 'Time for me to get back to the Castle.'

Two doors down from the Red Lion, Martha Radley was busy reading the tea leaves for Dinah and Mrs Svensson, who'd dropped in to discuss the news. She tipped the cup up and peered into the black dregs. A look of surprise came over her face. 'Lady Sonia shouldn't be too quick to take possession. I see a disputed inheritance in the leaves.'

'Get on with you,' said Mrs Svensson. 'Who's to dispute it with her ladyship? There was only her and her brother, and he's gone, God rest his soul. Her ladyship will get everything, and as for the title, there's no disputing about that. Everyone knows there aren't any male relatives close enough to inherit.'

Mr Graham had to be up with the lark to drive to market for supplies of fruit and veg, so he was already in bed and asleep when the rest of Selchester was talking about Lady Sonia. He heard the news early the next morning, when the lad who helped him came bleary-eyed to work.

'Late as usual,' Mr Graham said.

'I was up late, at the Red Lion. I won my match and had a pint or two to celebrate. Did you hear the news about that Lady Sonia?'

Mr Graham listened and shook his head. 'It's the end of an era. Things won't ever be the same again here in Selchester without an Earl up at the Castle.'

The lad was a fervent Socialist. 'That's all nonsense. That's all stuff from the history books. What did the old codger ever do for you?'

'He was a good landlord. And he died before his time, taken out of this world unnaturally. You should show some respect.'

'Come the revolution, there won't be any Earls.'

'Come the revolution, you'll likely be hanging from the nearest lamppost for being such a darn fool.'

# Scene 2

Sonia's car pulled up outside the great front door with a squeal of brakes. Her passenger, a pale young man made paler by her driving, got out and went round to open her door.

Sonia didn't get out, but hooted her horn loudly and impatiently. 'Where is everyone?'

Freya, writing in the Tower, heard the horn, sighed and got up, to the annoyance of Magnus, who'd been snoozing on her typescript. He stalked out of the room after her.

Mrs Partridge was in the kitchen, peeling potatoes. Father Leo had insisted on helping with the other vegetables, and although she was shocked at his offer, she gave in when he said he was quite accustomed to it and reached out for the beans.

They heard the horn, and Mrs Partridge put down her knife with an exclamation of dismay. 'That'll be her ladyship.' She glanced at the kitchen clock. 'I don't call twenty to four late afternoon.' She wiped her hand on her apron and made for the door, followed by Leo, who was curious to meet Lady Sonia.

'Good heavens,' Sonia said. 'A priest! Who are you?'

Mrs Partridge said, 'It's Father Leo Hawksworth, Mr Hawksworth's uncle. Mr Hawksworth is lodging here, as you very well know. Father Leo is visiting us, and he's a friend of Lady Priscilla's.'

Freya came down the steps, with Magnus still following her. She saw Sonia, at the mention of Aunt Priscilla, restrain the remark that was on the tip of her tongue and instead give Father Leo a wary look.

Sonia air-kissed Freya, 'How are you, darling?' and introduced the pale young man. 'This is Rupert Olivier. He's from Mansville's, the auctioneers. Off you go, Rupert. Mrs Partridge will show you to your room.' She turned to Mrs Partridge. 'When he's left his things, Mrs P, you can show him where to go. He can start in the state rooms and then do the gallery. Then he can work his way round the rest of the rooms.'

She swept contemptuous eyes over what she could see of the Castle. 'God, I shall be glad to be rid of this place. Freya, come with me. Not the cat; you know I can't stand cats.'

# Scene 3

Freya had things of her own to do, but she sensed that Sonia wanted company. The childhood closeness when they had spent their holidays together in the Castle had formed a bond between them; a bond that had in its essence survived into adulthood and their divergent lives. So she didn't object when Sonia demanded she go with her to Selchester's rooms.

They walked into the Great Hall, full of shadows and silence. Glum, antlered beasts looked down on them with lifeless eyes, and Sonia, pausing in front of the vast fireplace in which their ancestors had roasted oxen, remarked that the shields and lances hanging above it were dusty.

'You can hardly expect Mrs P to get up there on a ladder and clean the wretched things,' Freya said.

'She could get someone in to help. Still, it won't be long before I never have to look at them again.'

'Won't you leave them at the Castle? They've been here for quite a few centuries.'

Sonia shrugged. 'If the buyers want anything so ghastly and are prepared to pay me for them, they can stay.'

Once again, Sonia's indifference to her family and her heritage worried Freya, but she knew better than to say so.

They went down the long corridor to where Lord Selchester had his study and his sitting room. They had to go past the entrance to the Old Chapel, and Freya felt a chill run down her spine; she didn't think she'd ever get used to the thought of her uncle's body lying there all this time.

Sonia didn't give the Old Chapel a second glance.

She threw open the door to Lord Selchester's sitting room, not used since his disappearance, and went through to his study, similarly undisturbed. The room still seemed to contain something of Lord Selchester's presence, and even Sonia, insensitive as she was, felt it. She gestured towards the large roll-top desk. 'It's odd not to see him sitting there.'

Freya watched as her cousin went over to the desk and took out a key. 'Isn't that supposed to stay locked, for the executors?'

'Yes, but that doesn't bother me.'

'Are you looking for something?'

'Yes, of course I am. He had a black notebook that I want.' She opened each drawer in turn and finally dived down into the desk's kneehole. After a moment there was a click and a slim drawer slid out at the other side of the desk.

'I never noticed that drawer,' Freya said.

'No, you aren't supposed to. It's a secret drawer, and it's hidden by that panel.' Sonia had come round to the other side of the desk and was riffling through the contents. 'All old stuff, nothing of any use.'

'Where did you get the key from?'

Sonia said, not looking up, 'A friend.'

Freya frowned. Why should a friend of Sonia's have a key to Selchester's desk?

Her cousin got up and pushed the drawer back in. 'Not here. Where on earth is it?' She swung round and glared at Freya. 'You haven't seen it, have you? You've spent all this time at the Castle, so you might have come across it.'

Freya was annoyed by Sonia's peremptory tone. 'No need to snap. I haven't seen any black notebook, as it happens.'

'About this size.' Sonia flicked her hands to indicate something about five inches by three.

'Quite small,' Freya said. 'Easy to miss.'

'I know he kept it in here. What can he have done with it?'

'Maybe it was among the papers that the trustees took away.'

Sonia shook her head. 'No. I insisted on looking through all those, as I was entitled to do, although they're such a bunch of stuffy men that it's difficult to get them to see sense. But it wasn't there. It was all financial papers and leases and so on. That notebook should be here and it isn't. I have to know what's happened to it. I need to find it.'

'Why is it so important?'

Sonia said, 'None of your business,' and then relented and said more mildly, 'There are some addresses and things in there that I want. Private things.'

Freya said, 'Private is what Selchester was. He was a most private man.'

'Private and full of secrets. "Reserved" is the word people used to describe him; it sounds so perfectly English and stiff upper lip. Secretive would be a better word. There was a whole side to Father that you never saw. Or you may have seen it, but never took any notice of it; you were always lost in a world of your own.'

That was true.

'I know exactly what he was like, and what he was up to. I hated him for it then and I hate him for it now,' Sonia said with chilly vehemence. 'Which is why I shall have such satisfaction in selling all the things that he loved so much. Everything that stands for him and the whole damn Selchester family—all gone for good.'

'Why did you hate him so much?'

Freya might have asked, 'Why do you still hate him so much?' because it didn't seem that the intervening years since her father's disappearance had mellowed Sonia's feelings towards him at all.

Sonia looked at her with cold, unemotional eyes. It was a look that had perturbed Freya when she was a girl, and she didn't like it now.

'I don't need to pretend to you, do I? After all, you know how much your mother disliked him. Don't worry,' Sonia went on. 'I'll go through the motions and behave beautifully and dutifully, just as I did at his beastly funeral. I was able to hide my lack of grief behind a veil, thank God. So hypocritical, all the fuss and ceremonial. As though he had really been a good man and a worthy citizen.'

'Oh, come on, Sonia. You make him sound a monster. He was always perfectly kind to me, and he was an excellent landlord, did a lot of work for charity. Altogether one of the good people.'

'He was pleasant to people until they crossed him. That was just pride—he didn't care about anyone except himself. He wasn't nice to you when you ditched Roddy at the altar; I remember him being extremely unpleasant.'

'He wasn't the only one. You were pretty decent about it, but—'

'Because I knew what kind of man Roddy was. No good being mealy-mouthed; he was the sort of man who liked roughing women up. Fortunately, you went to bed with him before you'd tied the knot at the altar, and realised just what a brute you were going to marry. Lucky you to have had the guts to run away, although the Lord knows why it took you so long to ditch him. You really did leave it until the last minute, didn't you?'

'You know how it was in the war, everything topsy-turvy. I wanted to have at least some kind of an ordinary life. Getting married was an ordinary sort of thing to do.'

Why was she saying this? Why did she feel obliged to justify herself?

'Ordinary life in the time you could spare from your typing job? You never talked about your war work. I suppose it was something utterly secret, and that's why you never mention it.'

'Utterly secret? Why would they employ someone like me on secret work? I never talk about it because it was so boring.' Freya

195

had lied fluently so often about what she'd done in the war that the words tripped neatly off her tongue.

Sonia went on, 'Father was beastly to you over Roddy, and he was beastly to Mummy. I don't mean that he ignored her or had mistresses, although he did. It's because he never really loved her, or, rather, that his way of loving her wasn't normal.'

'Not normal?'

'Oh, for heaven's sake, Freya, come out of the clouds and face facts. Father had a touch of the Roddys about him. You must have noticed. You can imagine what kind of a marriage it was. Mummy didn't like it, and so after she produced an heir—poor them; what a disappointment that they had me first. Thank goodness Tom came along and she could feel she'd done her duty. After that, Selchester took his pleasures elsewhere.'

Sonia stood with her hands on her hips and surveyed the shelves. 'All these damn books. I suppose the notebook could be tucked in among them. Well, I haven't got time to go through them, so you'll have to do it. And if you find the notebook, don't go prying into it.' She gave Freya a long hard look. 'You won't, will you? Now that I've asked you not to?'

'Of course not. Nor would you.'

'Oh, but I would, darling, I would. That's the difference between you and me. You have a sense of honour, and your word given is just that. Not so with me.' She looked at the shelves and shrugged. 'I was going to take all the books off the shelves, just to check that the notebook wasn't anywhere there. But you can do it for me, and then I'll sell them. They'd better go to Dinah. You box them up for me and take them to her, see what she'll give me for them. Just the ones in here; Rupert will arrange for the ones in the library.'

'I don't think she'll buy all these from you. She might put them up on the second-hand shelves and give you a percentage for any she sells.'

'I suppose I'll have to be content with that.'

'It'll be peanuts. These aren't first editions or anything, and they're not worth a lot. Second-hand books don't have much value these days.'

'What else can I do with them?' Sonia said.

'You could give them to the vicar for the church fête. There's a bookstall there, and they usually do quite well out of it.'

'The vicar can go hang. They're to go to Dinah. Tell her to put the money aside for me, and I'll collect it in due course.'

Could she really care about such a small sum of money? 'Is it really worth it?'

'Every penny counts.'

'Look at everything you're going to inherit.'

'Yes.' Sonia sat back on her heels with a sigh of satisfaction. 'Lots and lots of lovely money. Such luck that Tom didn't marry that girl, and that he'd made a will in my favour when he went off to war. Otherwise, I'd only have what Selchester left me and not scooped the pool.'

'Death duties will be hefty,' Freya said. 'Won't they be double, now they assume Selchester died before Tom?'

Sonia's face darkened. 'The tax man's greed is outrageous. Lucky me that there are some valuable pieces that the nation apparently wants to own. There are the Titians, those Bellini bronzes and the Shakespeare folio, for instance; the lawyers think we should be able to settle the death duties with those.'

Freya knew it was inevitable that the collection would be broken up, and no doubt it was right that some of the great works of art which the Earls of Selchester had collected over the centuries should belong to the nation. Even so, the prospect gave her a pang. 'And the family portraits? Do you still intend you'll sell them?'

'Heavens, yes, I'll get rid of all of those; off to the salerooms as soon as it can be arranged. They aren't that valuable; people don't want to buy portraits these days. Wondering about your Countess? If you'd had any sense, you'd have had that copied a while ago. Who would ever have noticed? Or tucked it away in the attics. When the trustees did the formal inventory, they didn't include some of the stuff that Father kept stacked up in the attics. I'll sell that privately and keep the proceeds out of the hands of the tax people.'

Freya said, 'Should you be telling me this?'

Sonia gave her an appraising look. 'You may disapprove, but you won't say anything to anybody about it. Family's family after all.'

'So the hotel will get an empty castle.'

'I don't mind selling them some of the stuff, if we can make a deal, but anything valuable will go to the salerooms.'

'What about the land? The farms, all the property on the estate and in Selchester? Local people are worried about what kind of landlords they may end up with.'

Sonia waved a dismissive hand. 'Welcome to the new world. A lot of them have had it very cushy, and if they can't make enough to pay the rents, then they should move out and leave make room for people who can.'

'Don't you care at all about them?'

Another shrug from Sonia. 'Not in the least. I can't pretend my childhood here was happy. I have no affection for the Castle or the town, and I'm just relieved that now it's all going to be settled, and I can enjoy my rightful inheritance.'

Freya shook her head. Could Sonia really be that hard-hearted? 'I thought Sinclair left you very well off.'

'Something you don't understand, Freya, situated as you are, is that however rich you are, it's always good to be even richer. Yes, Sinclair left me well provided for—I only married him because he was so wealthy—but now I shall be extremely rich, and I intend to enjoy every penny.'

She went on, as though the thought had only just occurred to her, 'Mummy was asking what will become of you when the Castle is sold. I told her I didn't know.'

'I'll be fine, thank you. Don't worry about me.'

'I never do worry about anyone else—haven't you noticed? And what about these lodgers of yours? This Hawksworth man, and isn't there a schoolgirl sister?'

'It was only ever a temporary arrangement. Bernard will have to find somewhere else for them.'

Sonia said carelessly, 'They can stay for the time being. They aren't doing any harm, and I suppose it's company for you. It must be a frightful bore having no one but Mrs P and Ben to talk to. Although I'm not too keen on the uncle. He's not staying long, is he?'

Freya said, 'No. He teaches in Oxford.'

'Good. It gave me rather a shock seeing a priest sitting here.'

'Don't tell me you have a guilty conscience.'

Sonia shot her a scornful glance. 'Of course not. Unlike you, I'm not a heretic. Whatever sins I commit, I simply nip along to Farm Street and confess to the Jesuits. The fathers give me absolution and so I don't have to worry about my conscience at all.'

## Scene 4

Georgia was in the kitchen, helping Mrs Partridge make scones. Her keen ears caught the sound of hooves, and she looked up. 'I thought Freya was upstairs in her room, writing. But that must be Last Hurrah.'

It wasn't. Firm footsteps came along the passageway, and the door opened. There stood a woman who, Georgia knew at once, must be a Selchester; she closely resembled many of the more formidable portraits in the gallery. The newcomer looked her up and down. She had piercing eyes that made Georgia feel she should get up and curtsey or something. She stayed put.

'Who are you?' the woman said. 'Oh, I know—you must be one of Bernard's lodgers, the Hawksworth girl. Afternoon, Partridge. Where's Freya? And did I see Lady Sonia driving away?'

Mrs Partridge put down her rolling pin and said, 'You did, my lady, and yes, this is Miss Georgia.'

'Leo's niece, are you?' Lady Priscilla didn't wait for a reply, but turned back to Mrs Partridge. 'I waved at Sonia, but she took no notice. Of course she saw me, tiresome girl. Is she staying here?'

Georgia said, 'No, she's gone back to London.'

'Never mind. It's not her I've come to see. Where's your uncle, young lady?'

'Somewhere with my brother. I think they're in the library. They were going to look at some books.'

Lady Priscilla nodded briskly and said to Mrs Partridge, 'Tea in the library then.'

The door closed behind her, and she could be heard striding off. There was a silence in the kitchen, and then Georgia said, awed, 'Gosh. Is that Freya's auntie? She's rather alarming.'

Mrs Partridge said, 'She is that. Never mind her, we need to get these scones into the oven if they're to have anything with their tea. You can help me lay up the tray.'

# Scene 5

Hugo was as startled as Georgia had been to see a strange woman advance into the library. Leo looked up from a small, leather-bound volume, recognised her at once, stood up and went towards her, his hand held out. 'Lady Priscilla. It's been a long time.'

'It has indeed, Leo. And this is your nephew, Hugo Hawksworth, I suppose.' Her eyes raked him from head to toe, and she asked abruptly, 'What happened to your leg?'

'I injured it.'

Lady Priscilla wasn't letting him get away with that. 'That's no kind of an answer. How did you injure it? Fall off a horse? Cracked it playing cricket?'

Hugo longed to say, 'No, I took a bullet from a member of the East German secret police.' Instead he murmured, 'A bicycle accident.'

Lady Priscilla wasn't interested in cycling accidents. She weighed him up and gave a snort of laughter.

She clearly didn't believe him, but why was it so unlikely? Hugo suspected she knew a good deal about what went on at the Hall and why a man like him might end up behind a desk there.

Leo, who knew exactly how Hugo had hurt his leg, changed the subject. 'Are you looking for Freya?'

'I wanted to see you, Leo. Where's Freya?'

'In the Tower, writing, I believe,' Hugo said. 'Shall I go and fetch her? She probably doesn't know you're here.'

He was glad to escape from Lady Priscilla's bracing presence, and he took his time going up to the Tower room. He knocked on the door and went in as soon as Freya called out, 'Come in.' She was at her desk, and as he came in, she thrust some pages under an exercise book. She looked, he thought, slightly self-conscious. Was she writing a love letter to someone? What did she write, all those hours she spent in here, toiling away at that typewriter. He'd heard her clacking at the keys past midnight on some days. Was she really writing a history of the Selchester family? He noticed a pile of books and papers that might have been to do with her work; he also noticed a film of dust on top of them.

He wasn't the only one with a secret life.

He didn't comment on it, but said, 'We have a visitor. Your aunt's here.'

'Aunt Priscilla? Oh, heavens, when did she arrive? I didn't hear a car.'

'I think she rode over, since she's wearing breeches and boots.'

'I'd better go and make sure that Ben is there.' She paused at the turn of the stairs to peer out of a landing window that looked down on to the stable yard and said, 'It's all right. Ben's down there taking care of her horse.'

Hugo joined her by the window. 'It may be the angle, but that looks to be a big horse.'

Freya said, 'It is. That's Jupiter, one of her hunters. Eighteen hands, but he has a peaceful temperament.'

'Unlike Last Hurrah.'

Freya laughed. 'Aunt Priscilla can ride almost anything, but it was definitely a tussle when she was up on Last Hurrah, and I wouldn't say she came out best from the encounter.'

They clattered on down the staircase through Grace Hall into the Great Hall and along the passages and doors that led to the library. Lady Priscilla and Uncle Leo seemed to be getting on famously. Anecdotes, recollections, information about common friends were passing to and fro. Leo had been asking after Lady Priscilla's three daughters and laughing at the account of the doings of one of her older grandchildren.

Freya went across to her aunt and greeted her with a dutiful kiss.

'Still shutting yourself away in the Tower and writing?' Lady Priscilla said. 'Your parents are quite right, it's time to put all that on one side and start a new life. I dare say Sonia wants you out of here as soon as may be.'

Freya said, 'I've still a lot of research to be done. And although Sonia doesn't have to wait for Selchester to be declared dead now, there's still heaps of stuff for the lawyers and trustees to do, death duties and all that. Shall I go down to the kitchen and ask Mrs Partridge to make some tea?'

Lady Priscilla said, 'I've already done that.'

Freya sat down and Hugo leaned against the window frame, watching this strange trio. Freya didn't look like her aunt, yet they were clearly blood relatives. Their voices, the way they had of looking so directly at you when they were speaking. And their hands; both of them had elegant hands.

Freya was asking her aunt why she'd ridden over. 'Was it to see Sonia? She left a little while ago to drive back to London.'

'No, I saw Sonia at the funeral, and I have nothing to say to her. Nothing that she'd care to hear, at any rate. No, word reached me that Leo Hawksworth was staying at the Castle. Jupiter needed exercise, so I rode over.'

As was her way, she changed the subject abruptly and looking at Hugo, said, 'I hear you were present when they uncovered my brother's body.'

Hugo's heart sank. He didn't really want to have to give a blow-by-blow account of the grisly discovery in the Old Chapel. She didn't seem the kind of woman to find it upsetting, but Lord Selchester was her brother. 'Yes, I was there just after the workmen found his body.'

He started to offer his condolences on her loss, but she cut him short. 'Let's not have any false sentiment. I've assumed any time in seven years that he was dead. But of course it's different now; it's a murder enquiry. It's high time the police stopped all that nonsense about Tom and you, Freya. What are you doing to quell the ridiculous rumours?'

Leo joined his fingers together and sat back, as though prepared to enjoy himself. Hugo was about to come to Freya's defence when he was saved by Mrs Partridge with the tea tray. She was followed by Georgia, who was carrying another tray piled high with scones and jam and cream.

A quick look at her brother, another at Lady Priscilla's firm, interrogatory expression, and she raised her eyes to heaven. Vamping the part of a stage maid, she carefully laid the things out on the table according to Mrs Partridge's instructions. Hugo could see that she was about to drop a curtsey and frowned at her. She grinned at him and bounced out of the library in Mrs Partridge's wake.

'Lanky kind of a girl,' Lady Priscilla said. 'I hope she's getting enough to eat. Girls that age need a lot of food when they're growing. She takes after you, Leo. I expect she's going to be tall, which isn't necessarily a blessing for a woman, not with so many short men in the world.'

Tea was poured and handed round; scones sliced, buttered, jammed and creamed. Then a relentless Lady Priscilla returned to the attack. 'All this rubbish about Tom being the murderer because of his Army background. Trained killer and all that. If everybody who'd been in the Army was automatically a murder suspect, we'd be living in a most strange country.' She turned to Hugo. 'What did you do in the war?'

Hugo said carefully, 'I was in the Army. Intelligence Corps.'

If he thought this would shut her up, disappointed that he hadn't mentioned some crack Guards regiment, he was wrong.

'Were you, indeed? No doubt that involved quite a lot of cloak-and-dagger stuff. You people learned to kill just as much as those in the SAS. No one suspects you of murder whenever a corpse turns up.' She bit into a scone. 'And so Selchester continues to cause trouble for his family and everyone else even after he's dead and buried. Typical. He would be pleased to know that's what he's doing, exerting power from beyond the grave.'

Leo said, 'Aren't you being uncharitable? Weren't you fond of your brother?'

'Don't be sentimental, Leo. I was several years older than Selchester, and we never got on. We more or less rubbed along. Certainly better than he and Freya's mother did; Veronica always mistrusted and disliked him. He was a man who needed to dominate others, and he liked to have them in his power.

Hugo said, 'Do you mean he was the kind of person who kicked his dogs and beat his horses?'

Lady Priscilla looked at him with scorn in her eyes. 'Don't be a fool. I don't mean anything of the kind. You've lived long enough to know the kind of personality I'm talking about. He was a meticulous man, and he was never cruel to animals or deliberately unkind to children. He may not have shown them much warmth, but he'd never have harmed them. No, it was his fellow men—and women— he wanted to have at his mercy. He wasn't a pervert or a maniac. It was hard for Hermione, I always felt sorry for her. Did you know her, Leo?'

Leo said, 'The only time I met her was when I came to Helena's ball.'

'She's a nice woman and a good one. I hope she can find the kind of happiness with her second husband that she couldn't with the first. I wouldn't care to be married to a man like Selchester.'

Leo said, 'Priscilla, I do wonder why—'

'Why am I saying this in front of you and in front of a stranger like your nephew? Because I trust you, Leo, and know you have plenty of common sense, which is unusual in a man. As for Hugo, Sir Bernard—who gets more tedious and pompous by the year—told me that Hugo's involved with the murder investigation in a semi-official capacity and liaising with the police on behalf of his department. You have a misguided view of what your uncle was like, Freya, as I told you in London. You're anxious to clear your name and Tom's, and Hugo Hawksworth is trying to help. And by great good fortune, Leo is here at the Castle, so for goodness sake, make use of his intellect and experience. If the three of you can't do better than the police, then I despair.'

## Scene 6

'I'll come with you to the stables,' Freya said to her aunt.

As soon as they were outside the library, Lady Priscilla closed the door and said, 'A private word with you, Freya, before I leave. We'll go into the Countess's Morning Room.'

It was a pretty room, with linen-fold panelling and ornate plasterwork on the ceiling. Freya sat in the window seat while her aunt took an upright wooden chair, first dusting the seat with her handkerchief.

She came straight to the point. 'There's something you need to know about your uncle. I'm not sure whether it will be any use to you, and I trust you to be discreet with the information. It mustn't ever become generally known. I like the look of young Mr Hawksworth. He seems to me to be a man who has his wits about him. You're quite right; he would fit in perfectly at a Tudor court or Renaissance palace. If he can help to sort all this out, I shall be grateful to him. You can tell him what I'm going to say to you. And that goes for Leo, too; quite apart from his calling, he was always a man of the utmost discretion. He helped me get Helena out of a very difficult situation. Trust him.' She went on abruptly, 'Do you know the real reason why Hermione went to Canada?'

'Sonia was talking about her mother only this morning. She said that Selchester didn't behave very well towards her.' Freya hesitated. There were things she didn't really care to mention to her aunt.

'Did you never wonder why they led such separate lives? Selchester in London, Hermione at the Castle, and no more children after Tom? Selchester wanted an heir and a spare, and it's surprising he didn't get his way, but Hermione wouldn't let him near her once she'd had Tom. You'd think that a man like Selchester wouldn't put up with that, but Hermione had some kind of hold over him. So they lived in a state of truce, presenting a good face to the world as people of our sort do in an unhappy, unsuccessful marriage. Hermione also wanted to make a good home for Tom and Sonia, with some semblance of normal family life. You helped with that. An outsider, as you were to some extent, can prevent a family turning on itself. That's why Hermione was always so keen for you to spend your holidays here, and why your mother agreed.' She paused, eyes on the panelling, her mind in the past. 'I don't insult her by pitying her, because she chose to keep the status quo. For the sake of appearances. She was hardly the first Countess of Selchester to have a difficult husband and a difficult life. Selchester women have coped with adversity over the centuries.'

Freya was silent, waiting to see where this was leading.

Lady Priscilla got up, strode over to the other window and said, 'The south lawn's in a shocking state. Doubtless once the hotel takes over, everything will be immaculate—and probably in ghastly taste.' Then turning round again to Freya, she went on, 'Hermione had an affair. A passionate affair, with a local man. With Stanley Dillon, in fact.'

Freya looked at her aunt, dumbfounded. Whatever she'd expected, it wasn't this.

'Hermione was left to herself a good deal, and, as you know, she loved hunting. The intensity of the chase and the exercise gave her at least a physical release from her stifling existence. Dillon also hunted. It was one of the things that got him accepted into the neighbourhood. He had first-rate horses, rode well, had excellent manners and was good in the field. And so . . .'

'And so my uncle found out about the affair?'

'Yes. He was furious. It was all right for him to have his amours, but unforgiveable for Hermione to find consolation elsewhere. There wasn't any question of divorce; Selchester would never have agreed. Quite apart from his religious scruples, he'd see it as scandalous and a public admission of failure. But the knowledge of it gave him power over Hermione, and it was then that Hermione decided she couldn't stand it any more and went off to Canada. I don't think she intended to stay there. I think if war hadn't broken out, she might have come back and tried to lead a separate life in England. As things turned out, there she was. It was hard on Tom, but he was away at school. Sonia bore the brunt of her father's anger. She was too like her mother, and she always took her mother's part. He hated her for it.'

So there was a connection between Selchester and Stanley Dillon. An old enmity, but one Freya knew would have lasted, at least on Selchester's part. He wasn't a forgiving man. In which case, why had he invited Dillon there for that weekend? And more to the point, why had Dillon accepted?

'I'm sure that when the affair ended with Hermione going abroad, Selchester would have gone to some lengths to find something to give him a hold over Dillon,' Lady Priscilla said. 'He'd have been prepared to wait for revenge. Even as a boy, he'd let things lie for a long time before he took action to restore something to the way he thought it ought to be. It could be to do with some activity of Mr Dillon's during the war. He was involved in all kinds of food processing, supplying stuff to the Army and so on. Maybe there were deals that weren't entirely correct. Selchester would have been on to that very swiftly.'

Freya said, 'You mean he would have exposed him, reported him to the authorities?'

'No. To Selchester, information meant power, and he wouldn't do anything obvious with what he knew. That wasn't his way. Cat and mouse, that was what he liked. Playing with a creature that thought it could get away, allowing it to escape and then batting it back, knowing that any moment he could move in for the kill. Much more satisfying than a swift, clean end.'

Freya's heart sank at what she'd heard. There was no question of challenging what her aunt had said, or considering it might be embroidered half-truths. 'I had no idea. Poor Aunt Hermione. Poor Sonia.'

'Yes,' Lady Priscilla said. She got up and headed for the door. 'I'm afraid Sonia is the one who suffered most in the end. However, she's a considerable heiress, and money matters so much to her. And perhaps now that Selchester is dead and buried, she can start to live a life that's no longer dominated by him.'

They went out to the stables without saying any more, each of them wrapped in her own thoughts. Ben led Lady Priscilla's big bay hunter out of the box, saddled him, then brought up his knee into the horse's belly. Jupiter gave a snort of indignation as Ben tightened the girth a couple of notches.

Lady Priscilla laughed. 'Ben knows Jupiter's little ways. Puffs himself out from sheer contrariness. Just like some people I know.' She looped the reins over the horse's head and mounted. She looked down at Freya and said, 'Do what you can, Freya. You and Hugo. Find out who murdered Selchester.'

'Even if the murderer does turn out to be Tom?'

'It's always better to know the truth. If you have any doubts about Tom, then all the more reason to find out for sure. I don't believe he did it—not for a moment. In which case, his name has to be cleared. He may no longer be with us, but his reputation and honour still matter.'

# Chapter Twenty

## Scene 1

Hugo caught the bus back from work. It dropped him at one of the entrances to the Castle grounds and from there he could take a path up to the stable yard. By the end of the day, his leg ached, but the daily walks were doing it good—or so he told himself. This evening, his leg was cramping when he got off the bus, and he sat down on a boulder to massage the damaged muscles back to some sense of their duty.

It was a lonely stretch of road where he seldom met anyone, and so he was surprised to hear someone say his name.

'Good evening, Mr Hawksworth.'

He looked round, and there was Superintendent MacLeod, solid and professional looking.

'I heard you came this way and thought I'd catch you.'

Hugo was wary. What did the Superintendent want with him? And why here? Why not at the police station or up at the Hall? Neutral territory, perhaps.

'I thought it best not to let folks see me having a chat with you. We try to be discreet.'

'Is it about the Selchester case?' Hugo felt at a disadvantage sitting on the boulder, with the Superintendent looming over him, so he stood up, leaning on his stick. 'Do you mind if we walk? I find it uncomfortable to stand for long.'

'You're going up that way?' MacLeod gestured in the direction of the Castle. 'I'll walk along with you, if you don't mind.'

Hugo unlooped the rope that fastened the battered gate and pushed it open. The path was wide at this point, wide enough to take the two of them side by side.

'I just wanted to bring you up to date on the investigation,' MacLeod said. 'It's more or less sewn up, and there'll be the formal report coming through, but I thought you'd like to know how things stand.'

'Have you new evidence?'

'It's all circumstantial, but it's enough to satisfy me. We interviewed those who were at the Castle that night, the ones who were the last to see him alive. Mostly, their statements tally with what they said before, although of course the questions weren't exactly the same; they wouldn't be once it became a case of murder. This time, we needed to find out about possible motives and so on.'

'And you found them?'

'No. We never suspected any of the staff. They had no reason to want his lordship dead, nothing to gain by it. And in the case of Mrs Hardwick and that daft Hattie girl, who doesn't seem to have all her wits about her—sullen creature, she is—they'd not have the strength to go taking up flagstones. As for the four guests, they're in the clear. Mr Tallis, Mr Dillon and Miss Witt hardly knew his lordship. They were invited as an act of courtesy, as locals of some standing, so Mr Guthrie told us. He, of course, was well-acquainted with Lord Selchester, being his godson and having known him all his life. And he's no motive, none at all. He didn't stand to gain in any way through his lordship's death; on the contrary, his godfather had been useful to him in his career and would no doubt have been in the future, had he lived.'

'Which brings us back to Lord Arlingham.'

'It does indeed. And what we've found out about him confirms what we suspected all along. History of a violent temper since boyhood, Mr Guthrie told us. And—key information that didn't come out previously—Lord Arlingham threatened his father only ten days before the night of the crime. Mr Guthrie was at the Castle that afternoon; he'd gone up to play a round of croquet with Lord Selchester. Father and son were in the study, and Mr Guthrie was on the terrace. He heard Arlingham shouting at his father, "It makes me want to kill you. You don't deserve to live." Then a door slammed and a few minutes later, Mr Guthrie saw Arlingham going off in his car, driving like the clappers.'

'Did Guthrie have any idea what they were arguing about?'

'According to him, it was a ferocious row—raised voices, passions running high. Not what I'd call an argument. And no, he didn't know what it was about, although he assumed it was to do with Arlingham's relationship with the young lady who was also the subject of the row when he stormed out of dinner.'

'Hearsay,' Hugo said. He swished a bramble out of his way with his stick, noticing that the blackberries were ripening fast. 'Not evidence that would last a minute in court with a good lawyer on the case.'

'It isn't a matter of court, though, is it? Lord Arlingham can't be brought to trial, as we know. But the likelihood is that he did it, and we'll be telling the coroner that's what our conclusion is.'

'Our?'

'The police.'

'Here? Or in London?'

'We've been in charge of the investigation here in Selchester. We just keep London informed in case there are any political or security implications. Which there aren't.'

Was MacLeod a decent but misguided copper, doing his duty as he saw it? Or was he obeying orders? Orders from whom? 'The coroner can't direct a jury to find Lord Arlingham murdered his father, not on what you've got.'

MacLeod's chin went up. 'That's not for you to say, sir, is it? He may go for naming names, or decide that the verdict will stand as murder by person or persons unknown. But the police won't be making any further enquiries, and that carries a lot of weight with the coroner.'

# Scene 2

The path narrowed and the two men parted. Hugo walked on to the Castle, impatient to talk to Freya, angry that he couldn't walk any faster, even more angry at his encounter with MacLeod.

Last Hurrah was in his box, looking out over the half-door as Hugo walked across the yard. Good; Freya was probably in. He walked down the passage to the kitchen and looked in. Mrs Partridge was there.

'I'll just put the kettle on, Mr Hugo. Or would you like a beer? You look hot.'

'Not yet, thank you. Do you know where Freya is?'

'Up in the Tower, as far as I know. Writing.'

'I'll be back for the beer in a minute.'

The spiral staircase up to Freya's Tower was hard on his leg, and he was glad to get to the top and pause to catch his breath before knocking on the door. Freya was at her typewriter, keys clacking busily. Her hair looked as though she'd dragged hasty fingers through it. Looking for inspiration? Tearing her hair out at the antics of her ancestors?

She stopped abruptly as he came in, instinctively sliding an exercise book over the pile of typewritten papers beside the machine.

Family history? Really? What was she actually writing?

'Come in,' she said. She pulled out a chair for him. 'Stairs hard on the leg?'

For the first time, he saw the portrait that she had hung on the wall opposite her desk. It took away what breath he had left. The woman in the portrait would have been remarkable looking in any age. She had the elongated nose, high forehead and unnaturally sloping shoulders of a Restoration beauty, but the curl of her mouth, the tip-tilted end to that nose and the humour in her eyes had an eternal charm. And Freya was astonishingly like her. He looked from then to now and said, 'Anyone would know you for a descendant.'

'Yes, odd, isn't it, that genes should survive for all those generations? She had a much more interesting life than I do and was far more redoubtable than I'll ever be,' she said, sounding regretful.

'You don't know. If you were plunged into the middle of a civil war, who can say what you could or couldn't do?'

Freya smiled. 'What brings you up here? I assume you haven't come to say Mrs P is brewing a pot of tea. Although'—she glanced at her watch—'she probably is.'

'I've just had a conversation with Superintendent MacLeod.'

The smile faded, and Freya, looking at him intently, said, 'And it's not good news, I can tell. Oh, well, spit it out.'

Hugo told her what the Superintendent had said.

'He's wrong about one thing, anyhow,' Freya said. 'Mr Dillon and Selchester weren't the strangers he thinks they were. We know that. Did you tell him so?'

'I did not. We can make use of the information, but it's hardly the kind of thing to pass around. Not at the moment, anyhow. And I don't suppose it would make any difference to MacLeod. After all, the injured party was Selchester; any revenge would be on his side, not the other way round. Besides, it was hardly current. It all happened ten years before that evening.'

'So we're right about a stitch-up,' Freya said. 'Tom did it and that's that, as far as they're concerned.'

'Are you really convinced, deep down, that your cousin Tom couldn't have killed his father? Or do you just not want to believe it?'

'I was sure he wouldn't have done such a thing.'

'Was?'

'Gut instinct. Knowledge of Tom. Yet anyone can do anything if pushed hard enough. Like her.' She nodded at the Countess on the wall. 'She killed men while defending the Castle. Would she have dreamt she could do that? Did her husband ever think she would have had that much toughness and courage? Same with Tom. It's so very, very unlikely, but . . .'

'You can't know for certain.'

'No.' She fell silent, looking out of the window across the misty evening landscape. 'I can't know. I wish,' she said, suddenly vehement, 'oh, how I wish there were some evidence on his side, something that would make it impossible for him to have killed Selchester.'

# Scene 3

When Freya came into the yard the next morning for Last Hurrah, she found Ben polishing Hugo's car.

'The Reverend gent is going to take it out later,' he said. Ben was suspicious of all clergymen, and Catholic priests were definitely outside his scheme of things. He put down his leather and was going towards Last Hurrah's loose box, but Freya stopped him.

'I'll saddle him. You get on with the car.' She peered in to look at the dashboard. 'Very fancy.'

'This is a good car. You don't see many of them on the road.' Ben leaned over and tapped the fuel gauge. 'Have to tell the Rev to put some petrol in, or he won't get far. It's to be hoped Mr Hawksworth gave him some petrol coupons.'

Freya stood stock still, Ben's words unheeded.

Fuel gauge.

Tom, that night, in the car, as they'd driven away from the Castle. He'd tapped the fuel gauge in just that way: 'Have to fill her up. Won't get ten miles out of Selchester on this, damn it, let alone to London. Hope there's a garage open.'

She saddled Last Hurrah, mounted and was trotting out of the yard in a matter of minutes. Ben stared after her, scratching his forehead as she reached the drive and put her horse into a canter along the grass verge. 'She's in a fair old hurry,' he said to the car. He shrugged and went back to polishing the windscreen.

Abandoning her earlier intention of taking the path that led to the woods, Freya headed down the drive and towards Selchester. She rode past the livery stables and turned into Wilf's garage.

Wilf came out to greet her. 'Thought for a moment one of those pesky ponies from the stables had got out again,' he said. 'What can I do for you? Does Last Hurrah need his brakes checking?'

'Information. I know there's a garage with petrol pumps about three miles out of town if you're heading for London, but isn't it quite new?'

Wilf thought for a moment. 'Been there three or four years, I'd say.' He looked across the yard and nodded to where Stefan was talking to an AA patrol man clad in regulation Automobile Association jodhpurs and boots, his goggles dangling from the handlebar of his bright yellow motorbike. 'Ask Brian—he'll know.' He went over to the two men. 'This is Miss Wryton, Brian, from up at the Castle. Wants to know when Laycock's Garage started business.'

Brian was a sandy-haired man with alert eyes in a sunburnt face. 'Late fifty-one.'

'I thought so,' Freya said. 'What about before then? On the same road, heading for the main London road. Was there a garage? Within a few miles of Selchester, not far along the road?'

'There used to be one, past Wilkins Farm. Old Mr Fibbins's garage. He had just the one pump. He didn't need more; there weren't the cars on the road then that there are now.'

'Would his garage have been there in 1947?'

'Lord, yes; he started up back in the 1920s, went on until 1948.'

'Is it still there?'

'Not as a garage, no. When young Joe Fibbins took over from his dad, he gave up petrol and cars and went in for tractor repairs. And all kinds of farm machinery. Done well with it.'

'How far is it from here?'

'Five or six miles.'

'Not a good road for a horse,' Wilf said, 'if you were thinking of riding. No verges to speak of and too many blind corners.'

He was right. Freya sighed. She'd have to ride back to the Castle and come back on her bike, or borrow Hugo's car if Leo hadn't already gone off in it. 'Bother.'

'Is it something urgent, miss?' Brian said. 'If you can leave the horse here, I could take you. I'm not strictly supposed to take any-one on the pillion, but I don't think any of my superiors are in the area at the moment.'

'Stefan will look after Last Hurrah, Miss Freya,' Wilf said. 'He was in the Polish Cavalry before he went into aeroplanes, and he understands horses.'

Stefan looked pleased, and as Freya dismounted, he reached for the bridle, speaking to Last Hurrah in what Freya thought must be Polish.

'I'm not sure he'll understand you,' she said.

'I promised him an apple. He understands that in any language.'

'If you'd like to get on the bike, miss, I've got a spare pair of goggles in the box,' Brian said.

Freya settled herself on the pillion and put on the goggles. Brian pulled on his long leather gauntlets and kicked the motorbike into life. He went out of the garage, swerved to the left and headed for the bridge.

The journey brought back wartime memories of lifts on motor-bikes; Freya would have enjoyed it more if she hadn't been so intensely hoping this wasn't a wild goose chase. She found herself praying that this might be the answer to where Tom had been when Selchester was killed.

Ten minutes up hill and down dale and a series of alarming bends later, Brian slowed down and pulled off the road on to a pot-holed area in front of a ramshackle workshop with three tractors drawn up in front of it. As he turned off his engine, a young man, thin and snub-nosed, came out from behind one of the tractors, wiping greasy hands on a rag.

'Morning, Brian.' He looked enquiringly at Freya. 'This your young lady? You better not let Mr Farquhar see you, or you'll be in trouble.'

Brian reddened under his tan. 'This is Miss Wryton, from up at the Castle. Got a question about when this was a petrol station.'

Freya didn't have any time for niceties. She said urgently to Joe Fibbins, 'It's a strange question to ask now, because it's about something that happened nearly seven years ago. January 1947. You might remember it because it was the first night of the really bad snow. Brian said your father would have been in charge of the garage then.'

'He was, but if it was the night when it started to snow, then he was out. What do you want to know?'

'If anyone here sold petrol to a friend of mine. He'd have come past at about half-past eight. You wouldn't have been open then, would you?'

'No, we closed at five in those days. But if it's the night I'm thinking of, there was a chap ran out of fuel a couple of miles down the road. He came tramping along with a can to get some petrol.'

Freya's heart lurched. 'What did he look like?

'He must have been fit, because otherwise he wouldn't have been able to tramp the two miles; the snow was coming down quite heavy by then. Army, I'd say. He had that kind of toughness about him. Dark, with a scar on his chin.'

Scar on his chin? It had to be Tom.

'He drove a Lagonda, if that's any help.' His face brightened and he said, 'Beautiful job, you don't see many of those on the road. Not now, nor back then.'

'If he was stranded two miles away, how did you see his car?'

'He walked into the garage and found me in the office. I was finishing the week's accounts. I was quite happy to sell him a can of petrol, even out of hours, and he had the coupons. It was a dirty night, though, with all the snow and wind, and I had Dad's old truck outside. I told him to hop in and I drove him back to his car with the can of petrol. That's how I know it was a Lagonda.'

'Did you notice the number plate?'

'I was going to mention that. It was a funny one: RUN 123.'

Freya closed her eyes, relief flooding over her. Tom's Lagonda, Tom's number plate. Then a thought occurred to her, and the joy went out of her. Tom could still have turned round. He could have put the petrol in the car and driven back to the Castle. 'Did you see him drive past the garage?'

'It was snowing that hard and starting to drift, so I drove ahead of him as far as the turning on to the London road. That wasn't so bad; it's on the other side of Copse Hill and so doesn't get hit quite so hard by the weather. And it's a better road than this one. The banks are high here, and so it gets snowed up fast in conditions like that. Six weeks that snow lay, and they had a job to help get a tractor through to the animals from the farm.'

'Could he have come back along the road?'

'That evening? No. I had a time of it getting back to the garage in the truck; he'd never have made it in that car. Even with chains, and he told me he didn't have any. No way could he have got even halfway up Copse Hill.'

Freya thanked Joe so effusively that he eyed her doubtfully. 'What's this all about?'

'It's tremendously important. It will clear an innocent man's name.'

'A police matter, is it? Lawyers? Or is it a private detective case?'

'The police will want a statement, and there might be a lawyer, too.'

'Court case?'

'No.'

Joe Fibbins looked disappointed. 'Well, you tell the police to come and talk to me, and I'll tell them just what I told you. They know where to find me.'

Freya climbed back on the pillion of the bike and waved to Joe as Brian swung on to the road and headed for Selchester. She clung on as the motorbike roared up Copse Hill, wondering why she'd said that about a lawyer.

'Because,' Hugo said later, when they were all gathered in the kitchen to hear her news, 'you don't entirely trust the police.'

'Not after they scorned Mrs P's alibi for me, no.'

'Besides,' said Georgia, 'they're awfully keen to pin it on your cousin Tom. Now they can't, and that's going to annoy them.'

# Chapter Twenty-One

## Scene 1

On Saturday, it poured with rain. Games at Georgia's school were cancelled, much to her delight, and Freya roped her in to help sort out and box the books in Lord Selchester's study and sitting room. Leo volunteered his services, and Georgia gave him a cynical look. 'That's only because there might be some books there you want to read.'

'Sonia says your uncle is to have any of the books he wants,' Freya said.

'Golly, you're in favour, Uncle Leo. You must have charmed her. Or perhaps she considers it an offering to the Church, like buying indulgences in Chaucer.'

Leo, who'd plucked a copy of *Heavy Weather* off a shelf, was too busy laughing at some antic in the busy life of the Empress of Blandings to correct Georgia's view of indulgences. 'I don't think of Lord Selchester being a Wodehouse man,' he said.

'He wasn't. That book must have belonged to Aunt Hermione,' Freya said. 'He said Wodehouse was an irredeemably middle-class writer whose view of the upper classes was entirely bourgeois. My uncle had no sense of humour.'

'Does the person at the bookshop really want all these?' Georgia said, scanning the shelves. 'Is it a second-hand bookshop?'

'No, but she sells some second-hand books, and she's happy to take any of them she thinks might sell.'

'What will she do with the ones that no one wants?'

'Don't tell my cousin, but anything Dinah doesn't have room for or can't sell, she'll pass on to the vicar for the fête.' Which was, after all, Freya told herself, where they should have gone in the first place.

Georgia plucked the books off the shelves, calling out the titles to Leo, who was making a list of the books. She passed them to Freya, who flicked them with a feather duster and stacked them in boxes provided by Mrs Partridge.

'I won't offer to help,' Mrs Partridge had said. 'There are too many books in this house, and I'm glad to see them go, but I don't care to linger in his lordship's rooms. It doesn't seem right.'

Georgia finished the shelves in the study and wandered into the sitting room. There were floor-to-ceiling shelves against one wall, and she looked at them without enthusiasm. Still, there was one of those little curved stepladders with a pole that she liked the look of, and so she climbed up to the top shelf to start taking down books from there. Most of the books on the top shelf were larger ones, and she called through to Freya to come and see if they would be any use to Dinah. 'These are art books, atlases, that sort of thing.'

Leo came to the door and said, 'I should think those would do well in a second-hand bookshop. Rather than climbing up and down those steps all the time, why don't you hand them down to me, and then we'll stack them on the floor to list and pack.'

Georgia sneezed. 'It's really dusty. Cobwebs, too. I bet there's an army of spiders living up here.' She opened a book to bang the dust off it, and found a brown envelope inside it. She came down the steps with the book in one hand and the envelope in the other. She passed the book to Leo and looked inside the envelope. 'There are photos in here.' Her voice tailed off in a startled, 'Oh!'

Leo was at her side in an instant, took one look and removed them from her hand. He said in a calm voice, 'Back up the steps, and let's have some more art books.'

Georgia said, 'But—'

'Do as you're told, Georgia.'

'But those are photos of—'

'Studies for sculptures. You can pass down that *Times* atlas at the end of the shelf next, and I'll start a new box.' The normality of his deep voice chased the worry and shock out of Georgia's mind, and she obediently went back up the stepladder and reached for the atlas.

Freya picked up the envelope, slid the pictures out and exchanged a horrified look with Leo. He shook his head. She put them back in and gave the envelope to him, and he tucked it inside his jacket.

After another hour, Georgia felt she'd had enough. 'I might go for a walk with Daisy,' she said plaintively. 'I suppose I could ask her to come and do the books, but I don't think she'd want to. The rain's stopped and the sun's coming out.'

Hugo had come looking for them and heard what she said. 'Much better for you to go and have a walk.'

As soon as the door closed behind Georgia, Freya said to Leo, 'Those photographs!'

'What photographs?' Hugo said. 'Don't tell me Lord Selchester had naughty pictures stowed away.'

Leo took out the envelope and handed it to Hugo. 'Not naughty, no. That isn't the right word for them.' Then he said to Freya, 'Did Lord Selchester have any inclination that way?'

Freya said, 'You mean, was he a queer? No, I'm sure he wasn't.'

Hugo was blinking as he looked at the photographs. There was one in particular, of three men, and he turned the photograph over. 'There are names written on the back.'

Freya put out a hand for the photograph. Hugo hesitated.

'Be protective about Georgia, but don't you dare try to protect me.'

Hugo gave her the photograph. She gave it a brief look, pulled a face and turned it over. 'That's Selchester's handwriting.' She looked at the photograph again and said, 'I think Lionel Tallis took these.'

Hugo said, 'Why?'

'It's his style, somehow. And look here.' She tapped the bottom left-hand corner of the photo, where 'FT 1945' was inscribed in the same hand.

Hugo took the photo back and read out one of the names. 'Nicholas Lantern. Why does that name ring a bell?'

Freya said, 'Nicholas Lantern was a Member of Parliament, a Labour MP. He was elected after the war in the Labour landslide.'

'Was an MP?' Hugo said. 'Not now? Did he lose his seat in the next election?'

'No, he didn't lose his seat,' Leo said. 'He committed suicide while he was still an MP. It was in all the newspapers.'

Hugo said, 'When was that?'

'1946. November 1946.'

Hugo thought for a moment. 'I was abroad then, which I suppose is why I didn't know about it.'

'What about the other two names?' Freya asked. 'I don't recognise them.'

'John Jones. Not as distinctive a name as Nicholas Lantern. And the third one, Arseny Kravtsov, must be a Russian.'

'A Russian,' Leo said with a sigh. 'A Labour MP, an unknown Mr Jones and a Russian.'

'Not good,' Hugo said.

'Good for us,' Freya said. 'Whoever they are, this is a link between Lionel Tallis and Selchester. That's three of the guests accounted for: Dillon, Lionel and Charles.'

'I'll see what information I can dig up on these nude gentlemen,' Hugo said.

'Which leaves us to discover the connection between Vivian Witt and Lord Selchester,' Leo said.

Freya said, 'You think there is one?'

'I do. And I think we need to clarify why Charles Guthrie was here in that company. If there was an underlying purpose to the invitations to three of those four, we should find out if there was also one for the fourth person present.'

Hugo waved the envelope to and fro, thinking aloud. 'That's not all we want to find out. If the four of them were responsible for Lord Selchester's murder—'

'Or complicit in it,' Leo said.

'Or complicit, then there's a link between them as well. One forged in the heat of the moment—or some prior friendship?'

'Conspiracies aren't usually spontaneous, are they?' Freya said. 'Surely they involve plotting and planning in advance.'

'A conspiracy to murder, yes. If it's a conspiracy to cover up a murder, not necessarily.' Leo smiled at Freya. 'I think we should leave Miss Witt to you. She won't be able to charm you as easily as she would a mere male.'

# Scene 2

Charles took the early train up to London. He wanted to visit his tailor in Savile Row, and with that accomplished, he took a cab to South Kensington. He told the taxi driver to wait. 'I'll only be a few minutes.'

He strode into the dim depths of the Brompton Oratory, and there, in one of the numerous side chapels, he lit a candle in front of the image of a saint and stood for a moment, his head bowed in prayer. Then he walked out as swiftly as he had come in.

He climbed back into the taxi. 'Whitehall, the Foreign Office.'

The taxi driver swung his cab round. 'Been saying your prayers? My old woman does that—she's a Roman Catholic. I never took to it myself. Got a patron saint, have you?'

'Oh, I think so,' Charles said. 'Joshua.'

'Is he a saint? I thought he was just one of them blokes in the Bible.'

Andrew Painswick's secretary looked up as Charles came in, and smiled at him. She liked Charles. Everyone did. 'Go straight in. He's expecting you.'

Painswick was a tall, thin man who wore elegant tweeds and a monocle, an affectation that often led unwary people to underestimate him. His languid air was deceptive, as Charles knew full well; his boss was as tough as they came.

Painswick wanted Charles's take on a report that had come in from Washington. 'Good of you to come in person. It wasn't necessary.'

'I had a couple of things to do in town.'

Painswick opened a file on the desk in front of him. 'Dull stuff, trade, but you handled it when you were there, and I thought it was quicker to ask you than to request a briefing from America.'

The matter was dealt with quickly, and Painswick thanked Charles courteously as he placed the file in his out tray.

'Enjoying your leave? You've been in Selchester, I take it? Quite a lively place just at the moment. I was at Selchester's requiem; sad affair, that. I suppose the police are on the case? Difficult, after all this time. I used to work with him, you know. An able man. Keen brain. Took the long view.'

'He was my godfather.'

'Of course, I'd forgotten. Did he leave you anything? Lady Sonia inherits the Castle and estate, does she not? She'll be even richer than she is already.'

'I suppose Lord Selchester was as rich as everyone assumes? I mean, with the war and so on. A lot of people in his situation have had a struggle.'

Painswick moved in the same circles as Selchester had done, and if there'd been any rumours of financial troubles, he'd have heard them. Charles waited as Painswick inspected the heavy signet on his little finger.

This was why he'd come to London instead of settling the Washington business by phone. It had occurred to him, as he read the newspaper reports of the requiem, that none of the three there that night had said what Selchester would gain from blackmailing them. Blackmailers usually wanted money. But if Selchester was as rich as Charles thought him to be, then he couldn't have had any need of pecuniary gain. Dillon was a rich man, certainly, but Tallis and Vivian? Hardly.

So what had he been up to? And how had he come by the information that enabled him to blackmail his victims?

'Oh, Selchester had no worries of that kind, none at all. He'd made some excellent investments and did very well out of property in London at the end of the war. I think one can say he died an extremely wealthy man.'

# Chapter Twenty-Two

## Scene 1

Freya on Last Hurrah trotted down the alley that ran behind the Daffodil Tearooms. When they reached the back gate, she reined in, slid down from the horse's back, drew the reins over his head and hung them over the gatepost.

The gate was locked, but Richard had heard the hooves and he came out in his whites to open the gate for Freya. He nodded at her and addressed the horse with a friendly, 'Hello, you bad-tempered beast.' He had a quartered apple in his hand, and he held it out for Last Hurrah, who was tugging at the few tufts of grass that ran alongside the alleyway. The horse raised his head, rolled his eyes at Richard and then grudgingly dropped his nose to take the apple from the palm of his hand. He crunched it up, gave a vigorous toss of his head and went back to cropping the grass.

Freya followed Richard across the yard, spick and span and business-like as always, and through the back door into the kitchen. As the door closed behind them, a whinny from Last Hurrah was followed by a curse, and a voice yelled, 'It's a menace that horse; shouldn't be allowed out.'

Richard grinned. 'That's Bobby Sackbut. I hope Last Hurrah took a hefty bite out of him, or at least trod on his feet. He's a varmint, that lad. Go on in—Jamie's there. Don't worry about Last Hurrah. I never knew a creature more able to look after himself than that horse.'

The local bad boy went whistling on his insouciant way, and Freya went through the swing doors into the tearooms.

Only two tables were occupied. One near the window held a coven of Selchester women inspecting a stand of cakes and talking nineteen to the dozen.

Vivian Witt sat at the other table, at an inside corner. Alone. She was motionless, staring down at a newspaper that lay open on the table, but she looked up as Freya approached. Her eyes were swimming with tears; huge eyes in an unnaturally pale face.

Freya, after one look, sat down opposite her and reached out for her hand. It was icy cold. 'Whatever is the matter? You look as though you've just had the most terrible shock. Or are you ill?'

Vivian brushed the newspaper with a violent, uncontrolled movement of her other hand, and it slid to the floor. Freya bent down to retrieve it. It was a copy of *The Times*.

'No,' Vivian said. 'I'm not ill. And I have had a shock. Someone—someone I knew rather well has died. I read it in the paper. I wasn't expecting it.'

'I am sorry. Not a close relative, I hope. Not a member of your family?' Freya said. It couldn't be, or Vivian would have learned of it in a personal way, not through the obituary columns of *The Times*.

Vivian shook her head. 'No. It was someone I haven't seen for several years. It's still shaken me.' She pulled herself together with a visible effort. 'You know how it is, when a name from the past leaps out at you like that.'

Jamie was hovering, eyes bright with sympathy and curiosity.

'Not bad news, dear?' he said hopefully.

'Vivian's a bit upset,' Freya said. 'Tea, I think.'

'That's right. You should have a cup of strong tea with lots of sugar. It saw us all through the Blitz. Nothing like it if you've had a bit of a shock.'

Vivian said, ' Thank you, Jamie. Some Earl Grey—'

'That won't do you any good. You need a strong cup of tea. I'll go and make it right away.'

Freya watched Vivian gather herself together, forcing a smile, smoothing her hair. The Vivian that Freya had seen when she came in was the real woman; now she was back in the presence of a woman behind a mask. This was Vivian Witt the actress, putting on a performance.

Freya wasn't sure whether to enquire further about who had died. You never knew whether people wanted to talk about a loss or couldn't bear to. Better stick to neutral topics. 'I'm glad you're here,' she said. 'I wanted to have a word with you about volunteers for the play in the Cathedral. I'm in charge of arranging all that. There's no problem with finding people to sell programmes and show people to their seats and so on, but as far as getting help goes—carpenters and so forth—I'll need your advice.'

'Front of house and backstage,' Vivian said, her voice and manner now completely under control. She took a gold compact out of her bag and patted powder on her nose and under her eyes. 'Quite different requirements. Don't worry, though. Stanley— Mr Dillon—has offered the services of as many of his craftsmen as we may need. Talk to him. He's the man you want in a crisis.'

'Crisis?'

'I'm sorry; I don't know why I said that. I'm not thinking clearly. You have to forgive me.'

'I'll talk to Mr Dillon about it.'

'How are you getting on at the Castle with your lodgers? I thought Hugo Hawksworth a charming man.'

'Charming?' It wasn't the adjective Freya would have used.

Vivian went on, 'But it must be odd to have a priest staying with you.'

Freya said nothing. She didn't need to; Vivian was talking to herself.

'Of course, Lord Selchester was a Catholic. It's odd, isn't it, how we talk about having something on our conscience? As though it sat there like a sack on one's back. A kind of incubus.'

Where did Lord Selchester come into these reflections on conscience? And how odd that Vivian was talking about such things to someone who was hardly more than an acquaintance.

Vivian frowned, looking as though she regretted her words. Jamie bustled up with a tray. 'Tea for you, Vivian, and I've brought you a cup, too, Freya. Now, you're to eat some of this delicious cake. It's exactly the thing to soothe troubled nerves.'

Vivian looked at the slice of sponge cake on her plate as if it might poison her.

Freya took a forkful of hers. 'You'll have to try to eat it, or Jamie and Richard will be offended.'

Vivian took a small mouthful.

Very well, Vivian had mentioned Selchester. So why not risk it? 'There was something else I wanted to talk to you about,' Freya said. 'To do with Lord Selchester's death.'

The shutters came down on Vivian's face. 'Really? I don't see why. It's hard for you, the whole business.' She paused and went on as though she were speaking from a script. 'I understand that the police suspect your cousin, Lord Arlingham, of killing his father. You were close to him. It must be distressing for you.'

'I was close to Tom, although not in the way town gossip suspects. He didn't do it.'

'You sound very definite. Has new evidence come to light?'

'Tom has an alibi. So do I, if it comes to that, but I was never going to be more than an accessory. Although you can hang for that in a murder case.'

Her words were deliberately brutal and Vivian winced. 'There was never a question of that, was there? Not with Tom dead.' And then recalling herself, she said, 'I'm sorry, that was tactless of me. I met him for the first and only time that evening, but he seemed a good man. I am truly glad if he's no longer a suspect.'

Her words were heartfelt, which surprised Freya. She said, 'So now the police will have to find a new suspect, or they may just close the case and label it "Unsolved". I don't want that.'

'Take my advice and leave that to the professionals.'

Freya persisted, 'For instance, why were you invited to the Castle? Did you know my uncle?'

Vivian shrugged. 'As I told the police, I have no idea. I suppose it was because of my name and reputation. If he was having guests of what you might call an artistic kind, he no doubt thought I would add glamour to the proceedings. It happens when you're famous. I didn't like to refuse, what with Lord Selchester being a power in the land here and my being a new arrival in the town. He sent me a very civil letter.'

'So you'd never met him before?'

Just the slightest flicker in Vivian's eye told Freya that she was lying. 'No. Look, what is this about? If you and Tom are in the clear, why don't you just put the whole thing behind you? Let the dead past bury its dead.' Realisation dawned in her eyes. 'I know why you're asking these questions. How stupid of me; how very stupid. Your Mr Hawksworth works at the Hall, for Sir Bernard. And Lord Selchester spent the war doing hush-hush stuff. So Mr Hawksworth is helping the police with their enquiries, although not in the usual sense. He's put you up to this, hasn't he?'

'Hugo hasn't put me up to anything. He's taking an interest and I'm glad of it, because I want to know who killed my uncle and how and why, and I don't think the police are going to come up with any answers.'

Vivian went on, her voice acid, 'Do tell me, in your efforts to be detectives, are you going to question Charles Guthrie? Though of course you can easily talk to him since you know him so well. Or perhaps you're intending to play the inquisitor to Mr Dillon or poor Lionel, who's already so shattered by this whole affair that he'd probably have a nervous breakdown?'

'Did you know Lionel before you came to Selchester?'

'No, as it happens, I didn't. I never sat for him, and I only know him at all because of that dreadful party at the Castle. Now his mother's doing the costumes for the Cathedral play, I see something of him. Enough to know what a sensitive soul he is.'

'Had you met Mr Dillon before that evening?'

Now Vivian wasn't lying. She said with perfect confidence, 'No, that was the first time I'd met him.'

She gulped down her tea, rummaged in her bag for her purse, put some coins on the table and stood up. 'I'm going. I resent being interrogated like this. Just let me tell you how unpleasant it appears to an outsider, you lot at the Castle playing Sherlock Holmes.'

'One last thing,' Freya said, also standing up and putting a restraining hand on Vivian's arm. She spoke in a whisper, although the buzz of gossip from the other table would drown out anything she said. 'Was Lord Selchester blackmailing you?'

Vivian froze. 'How can you possibly know that? Has one of the others . . .' Her voice tailed off. Then she rallied and said, 'I don't know what you're talking about.'

'Lord Selchester was blackmailing other people. Blackmailers tend to make a habit of it.'

Vivian managed a laugh. A professional stage laugh, low and musical. 'I'm a successful enough actress, but why would a man as rich as Lord Selchester blackmail me? He was an extraordinarily wealthy man, surprisingly so when you consider how many of these old families have suffered from taxes and death duties and dividends drying up. Anything I could scrape together would hardly keep him in brandy and cigars.'

'Perhaps he demanded payment of a different kind.'

'Perhaps you should mind your own business.' Her eyes fell on the newspaper, and she stooped to pick it up before drawing herself up, taking a deep breath, and smiling radiantly at Freya. 'Nice to talk, Freya,' she said into the silence that had fallen. With a further smile at the table of gossips as she went past, she made her exit.

Freya looked after her, admiration mingled with pity. She finished her coffee, told Jamie she'd be back in a minute and went out to the newsagent, where she bought a copy of *The Times*. Then she went back through the tearooms and out into the alley to Last Hurrah.

# Scene 2

Leo was helping Ben in the vegetable garden, busy with a hoe. He looked at Freya. 'Do you have some news?'

'I've been with Vivian Witt,' Freya said. 'There's something in the newspaper I want to show you. When you've finished weeding.'

'I'm sure the weeds can wait,' Leo said. 'Let me put the hoe back in the shed, and I'll come inside.'

'I'll be in the library,' Freya said.

Hugo arrived home from the Hall just as Leo came in to wash his hands.

They joined Freya in the library, where they found her in a fret of impatience. She thrust the newspaper at them, folded back on the obituary page.

Hugo said, 'Has someone died?'

'Quite a few people, looking at all the names. But if you mean has anyone I know died, the answer is no. However, there is someone on that list that Vivian knew, and the news of his death was unexpected, she said. And it's really upset her. She was in quite a state.'

Hugo ran his finger down the announcements, then noticed a photograph above one of the longer obituaries at the side. 'I bet it's one of these. Dame Sylvia Simpson . . . Nurse in the First World War, charities, wife of . . . Doesn't sound likely, and she was ninety-two, so her death can't have been that unexpected.'

'Sharpen up, Hugo. I did say *his* death. It must be one of the men there.'

'Three of them get full obits. Another ancient—oh, old Lord Luffley. That wouldn't be a surprise. He had a heart attack in the House of Lords a few days ago. It was in all the papers: "Peer collapses on floor of chamber in mid-speech". Wait a minute. Now, this is interesting. Sir Alistair Mackenzie, financier. Died in a climbing accident in Scotland. Aged fifty-three. Poor chap; his climbing partner lost his footing, and he fell while trying to help him. That's our man.'

'How can you be so sure?'

'All the others in the paper seem to have lived to a ripe old age. And they're all county and country types. Tweedies, Georgia would call them. How likely is it that Vivian would be upset to hear about any of them? And Valerie—a friend of mine in London—mentioned that she'd heard a rumour about an affair with a money man. That's how she put it.'

'Vulgar,' Freya muttered. 'Money man, indeed.'

'Sir Alistair was a great deal more than that,' Hugo said. 'Hugely wealthy, but more to the point, he was the man they brought in during delicate negotiations over treaties and so on with foreign governments. He advised whichever government was in power, breakfasted with the Director of the Bank of England and knew more about public finances than the Treasury.'

'How do you know all this?' Leo asked.

Hugo said, 'I've read about him.'

He could have replied, more truthfully, 'Because I saw his file just the other day; the Service keeps an eye on men like him.' Any involvement with an actress would surely have been noted and watched. If there had been an affair, the two parties had been very, very careful. It was odd, though, that such a liaison had been overlooked.

Leo was reading the obituary. '"A man much in the public eye. He leaves a wife . . . married in 1935, no children. A staunch Presbyterian, Elder of his Church . . ." Dear me. A man of his standing and reputation must have been very smitten to risk an illicit liaison.'

Freya said, surprising herself, 'A man might well fall deeply in love with Vivian Witt. One always supposes actresses are shallow, but she isn't.'

# Chapter Twenty-Three

## Scene 1

T alk to Ben before you go off to see that Hattie,' Mrs Partridge said. 'From what I hear, she's none too keen on anyone or anything to do with the Castle.'

Hugo couldn't think why Leo was so insistent they talk to Hattie. 'MacLeod took her statement again, along with all the others. Just the same as before. She was in the kitchen with the rest of the staff, left for five minutes to go to the lavatory, heard nothing, knew nothing and didn't ever want to hear about Lord Selchester ever again. I quote, "The orphanage had no right to send girls out to places like the Castle where there were ghosts and people got done in." What can she possibly tell us that we don't already know?'

Ben didn't think Hattie was daft. 'She's one of those who keeps her mouth buttoned, that's all. Keen eyes and ears, knew what was going on. Nothing amiss with her wits. All right, she did go on about ghosts, but then there have always been ghosts at the Castle, and some people see them and some don't. She was one of them that does. But she won't talk to you, sir, with your being a Reverend. She doesn't hold with Papists; no, nor vicars or any clerical gents. That I do know. Her and Jim, who's a good man, go to chapel. And no point you trying to talk to her neither, Miss Freya, what with being his lordship's niece. She didn't care for his lordship—not one bit—and she'll clam up if you go ringing on her doorbell.'

'Which leaves me,' Hugo said. 'Very well, Leo, I'll go and see if she has anything to say that's the slightest use. I'll leave work early tomorrow and drive over.'

'Best have a reason for calling,' Ben said. 'I'll give you a jar of my special leather lotion to take for Jim. He's drayman at the brewery there. He looks after and drives their big horses, and he'll appreciate my sending a jar. The stuff they give him to use isn't half as good.'

So, with Ben's offering on the seat beside him, Hugo set off for Yarnley. It was some five miles from Selchester, a picture postcard village with a Norman church and stone houses grouped charmingly around the green and along the sloping main street.

Hattie, now Mrs Miller, was at home. She opened the door to him with a baby balanced on one hip and her face rather flushed. She had an interesting face; slanting hazel eyes and high cheekbones gave her an exotic look quite unlike that of most of the locals.

'Yes?'

'My name is Hugo Hawksworth. Ben asked me to drop off this leather lotion for your husband.'

She seemed taken aback. 'Oh.' Then her eyes narrowed. 'How do you know Ben?'

He might as well tell the truth. 'I'm lodging at the Castle. I work at the Hall.'

'But you aren't one of the family?'

'No, no connection at all.'

'You'd better come in. Jim will be back in a few minutes, and he'll want you to take his thanks back to Ben.'

Hugo ducked his head and went in. It was one of those cottages where the door opened directly into the front room. Hattie deposited the infant in a playpen in the corner. 'Would you like a cup of tea? I'll be making one anyway, to have ready for Jim as soon as he comes in.'

'Thank you.'

She disappeared to put the kettle on. Ben was right and MacLeod was wrong. Whatever Hattie was, she wasn't daft.

'For a moment I thought you were from the police,' she said as she came back in. 'If you were, you wouldn't be sitting there, I can tell you that. How long have you been at the Castle?'

'Not long.'

'Sooner you than me. It's a terrible place. I worked there—did Ben tell you that?'

'He did.'

'I hated it there. It wasn't what I wanted to do at all. It was the orphanage that sent me there. They said it was a good position and I was lucky to get it. I didn't really want to go into domestic service at all. I'd far rather have found work in a shop or something, but they like to place you somewhere where they thought you were being looked after, and Mrs Hardwick was kind enough. She'd taken people from the orphanage before and had a good reputation. But who would want to be stuck away in that Castle? It was like something out of one of those horror films, what with the cold and all those ghosts. Don't they bother you?'

'No.' Feeling he should elaborate, he said, 'I'm not one of those people who see ghosts.'

'I suppose not. I do, and have done ever since I was a little girl. Not everywhere, but when they're there, I see them. And there were ghosts at the Castle. Frightened me out of my wits, that place.'

She wasn't making that up. Some people did see the unseen, and she was one of them.

'Was it only the ghosts that frightened you?' Hugo said.

She got up and went back into the kitchen, returning with a pot of tea and three cups on a tray. 'I didn't like Lord Selchester. He was almost more scary than the ghosts. I dare say he's one now; they say an uneasy spirit always walks.'

Hugo took the cup of tea she held out to him, and refused her offer of sugar. 'Hattie—may I call you Hattie?'

She nodded. She was sitting on the edge of her chair, wary.

'I'd better come clean. I'm not the police and I'm not one of the Selchester family, but I am helping to find out the truth of what happened on the night Lord Selchester died.'

Wariness turned to defensiveness. 'I've had the police here, that Superintendent as he calls himself, Mr High and Mighty with his, "Now listen, my girl . . ." I told him what I told him last time.'

Hugo's senses were tingling. Hattie knew much more than she'd told the police. She had a secret, and it was a secret she was longing to tell someone. He needed to make her happy to confide in him. His voice and posture were relaxed. He smiled at her, willing her to trust him.

'Sensible of you,' Hugo said. 'You need to be careful what you say to the police. They can twist something perfectly innocent so it sounds as though you've done something wrong.'

Hattie nodded. 'I haven't done anything wrong. Leastways, not *done* anything. I didn't murder his lordship.'

'Of course you didn't, and I don't suppose for a moment the police think you had anything to do with it.'

'If that Superintendent asked me what day of the week it was, I wouldn't tell him.'

'What if I asked you about that night? Would you tell me the same as you told the police? Because that was the truth, as far as it went, but you saw or heard more than you told them, didn't you?'

Hattie burst out, 'I didn't tell them because they didn't ask me. They just wanted to know why I went to the lavatory—well, that shows you how stupid they are. Why does anyone go to the lavatory? And whether I met anyone while I was out of the kitchen. And the answer's no.'

'What didn't they ask?'

'They didn't ask me which lavatory I went to.'

Hugo decided to leave that for the moment and said, 'And they didn't ask why you seemed upset and frightened when you came back into the kitchen?'

'He thought that was comic, did the Superintendent. Mr Plinth had told him I thought I saw a ghost. He said I was always imagining there were ghosts about the place. It's easy enough to laugh at ghosts and presences when you don't see or hear them.'

'Did you see a ghost?'

There was a long pause before she gave a kind of sigh and then took a deep breath.

'I did see a ghost, but that's not why I kept quiet all these years.' It was all coming out in a rush. 'We were supposed to use the lavatory along from the kitchen, but it was ever so cold. Freezing, that night. Anyway, there was a dark patch between the kitchen and that lavatory which always made me feel afraid.'

'So what did you do?'

'I did what I'd done before. I don't hold with all this not being allowed out of the servants' quarters, locked away like we were animals after nine o'clock. So I used to go to the lavatory that's tucked

242

away on a landing. I reckoned that nobody would see me, as all the guests were downstairs and there was only Lady Sonia upstairs, lying poorly in bed.'

'Go on,' Hugo said when Hattie hesitated.

'You can go straight up what they call the attic stairs, but that way there are more dark places I didn't like. So I went round the other way. You know, along the passageway with that funny little window that you can look down from into Grace Hall. That's when I heard voices. I was really worried because I thought maybe they'd noticed me, and then I thought maybe it wasn't people at all; maybe it was ghosts again. So I kind of froze. I didn't know what to do, and I just stood there looking down, and then the voices got louder, and there were two of them standing right underneath me.'

People, not ghosts, Hugo hoped. 'Who were they? Could you see?'

'His lordship and that actress, Miss Witt. I hadn't seen any of the guests, because of course I was below stairs, but I'd seen her on the pictures. And even if I hadn't seen her, I'd have known her by her voice. It's low and kind of full of what they call "come-hither". She looks lovely in the films and I peered down to see if she really is as lovely as that. Which she wasn't, because she was in a right fluster, her face all screwed up. She was in an evening frock, all slinky with no back and low at the front, showing most of her chest.'

'And she was talking to Lord Selchester?'

Hattie swallowed. She reached out for her tea and drank it. 'Not talking, shouting. You could see she was scared—and angry, too. His lordship was just standing there with that look on his face he had, like a cat that's got its paw on a mouse.' She shivered. 'Looked like the devil was in him, and intent, somehow, like he wanted to gobble her up but was going to play with her first. He had this knife in his hand—'

Every cell in Hugo's body was alert, but he mustn't seem eager or surprised. He must be calm, unthreatening, sympathetic. 'What kind of a knife?'

'It was the silver paper knife from his study. At least, it wasn't a real paper knife. Mr Plinth told me it was called a stiletto, and it was very old, from Italy. His lordship kept it sharpened; I once cut myself on it when I picked it up to dust his desk. He was feeling it with his thumb, like he was telling her how sharp it was. She was saying there was something she couldn't do, and then he had his hands round her throat, and he was kind of stroking her. It made me feel strange. I mean I thought at first it was going to be a romantic thing and, like on the pictures, there was going to be a kiss and everything. But it wasn't like that at all.'

Hattie grimaced. 'It makes me feel funny now just to think of it. He caught her dress in front and he drew a sort of line down her chest with the point of the knife, like he was writing on her. It left a line of blood. He had her hands twisted behind her back in his other hand and she cried out, "You're hurting me," and he said, "Yes." Just that: "Yes." His voice had gone all husky. I didn't know what to do, whether to shout for help or what. Miss Witt was panicking, I could see it in her eyes, but she broke free and called out for help herself. He came at her again and said, "No one will hear you. They're all too far away." She snatched the knife from him, and then he lunged at her and—and the knife went into him. He sort of crumpled, and I think he hit his head as he went down. That's all I know because then I felt a presence loom over me, and everything went blank.'

'A presence? You mean someone came and found you?'

She gave him a scornful look. 'No. Like I said, a presence. A dark presence.'

Best not to enquire further about the presence. 'Did you faint?'

'I dunno. The next thing I knew, I was back outside the kitchen door, so I must have come to and then scarpered. I was all trembling and freezing cold, but I knew I couldn't say what I'd seen. So I got a drink of water at the tap in the sink by the wall there, and then I went in. They noticed I was in a bit of a state, so I said I'd been frightened by a ghost. They just went on talking like nothing had happened.'

So that was it. Self-defence; no one would call it murder. Or would they? An actress and a dead peer? Not good. 'Why didn't you tell the police what you saw and heard?'

Hattie was defiant. 'Why should I? Next thing I knew, there wasn't a body, and his lordship had vanished. How could I be sure he was dead, even though I'd seen him lying there? How did I know he wasn't going to come back and take it out on me for telling on him? You didn't know his lordship, but he wasn't a man to get on the wrong side of.'

'Once his body was found, and the police came to question you again, you could have told them the truth, couldn't you? When there was no danger from Lord Selchester?'

'Yes, and get put away in jail for perjury because I kept my mouth shut back then? No, thank you. I won't tell them anything more than I already did. You can't make me—it's just your word against mine, and I'll say you made it all up. No one will believe you because those four won't tell anyone what happened. They didn't then, and they won't now.'

## Scene 2

Freya and Leo were alone in the kitchen when Hugo came in. He propped up his stick in the corner, limped over to the table and said, 'Leo, you were quite right. Hattie had a story to tell.'

He described what Hattie had done and seen that night, and because he had trained himself over the years to remember conversations verbatim, her personality shone out. When he finished, Freya let out a long whistle as though she'd been holding her breath.

'Poor Hattie, keeping this a secret all that time,' Leo said.

'Is she trustworthy? Is she telling the truth?' Freya asked. 'A secret kept for all this time or a story made up and embroidered over the years?'

Georgia erupted into the kitchen from the scullery, a dripping boot in her hand. 'It sounds true to me.'

Hugo stared at his sister. 'Georgia, have you been eavesdropping again?'

'You've got a fixation about eavesdropping. I happened to be in the scullery, washing the mud off my lacrosse boots'—she held up a damp boot—'since we've got kit inspection tomorrow. You three are in here, talking about Hattie and Lord Selchester's murder at the tops of your voices, and that's eavesdropping? Move along, Freya.' She sat down on the bench, dropped the boot on the floor and planted her elbows on the table. 'Hattie would have to have a pretty vivid imagination to make all that up. Especially if she didn't know anything about the guests except that Vivian Witt is a film star.'

Hugo opened his mouth to tell Georgia to remove herself, but Leo, a smile hovering on his lips, shook his head.

Sensible Leo, Freya thought. Any attempt to dislodge Georgia now would end in a battle of wills and a scene. Hugo was getting better at handling Georgia, but still hadn't learned to avoid confrontations.

'I know what you're thinking,' Georgia told her brother. 'You want to order me out of here. Forget about it. I bet I can supply helpful insights. I understand all about motivations and repressed desires and all that. It's in Freud.'

Leo said to Freya, 'You're in the business of making up stories, if I can be permitted to describe your writing in those terms. Does Hattie's story read as fact or fiction?'

Freya stared at him in astonishment. What did he know about her writing? No one except her publisher knew what she wrote. Combined with astonishment was shock. Shock at these further revelations about Lord Selchester.

Despite what they'd found out about him, she still remembered him as the kindly if distant uncle of her childhood. The man described by Hattie was a monster; she couldn't—wouldn't—believe Selchester could have behaved like that.

She tried to keep her voice steady. 'If Hattie saw what she says she did, then Vivian was being physically threatened and she fought him off as best she could. I can't blame her for that. And the whole business with the knife—that was clearly an accident. Hattie could be making it all up, but there's a kind of messy reality to the details that rings true. Of course, she could simply be a habitual and accomplished liar.'

'She could, but I don't think she is,' Hugo said. 'I'm good at spotting liars.'

'So much for blackmail,' Georgia said. 'It was a crime of passion.'

'It was not,' Leo said. 'Self-defence against an attack of that kind cannot be described as a crime of passion. Freya, did Lord Selchester have such a knife?'

'Yes. It's in his study, still on his desk. Slightly tarnished, but probably still as sharp as ever.' Freya swallowed hard, her gorge rising at the thought of what it might have been used for.

'Hattie's evidence may answer the question of how and why Lord Selchester died,' Hugo said. 'It doesn't tell us why those four went on to hide the killing, bury the body and lie, steadily and consistently, to the police.'

'To protect Vivian?' Freya said.

'Apparently, none of them knew Vivian. Why risk criminal charges for a stranger? They could be accused of aiding and abetting a murderer, being accessories after the fact and perjury. Serious charges that would land them all in court and probably in jail. It makes no sense.'

# Chapter Twenty-Four

## Scene 1

Freya was barely awake when she heard the sound of the telephone. She reached for her dressing gown and, yawning, went down the spiral stairs and along the passage to Grace Hall, half hoping whoever it was would give up and ring off before she got there.

'Why does it take you so long to answer?' said an impatient voice at the other end.

'Sonia?' What was Sonia doing up at this hour? Freya knew her cousin rarely saw her bed before three or four in the morning. 'Is something the matter?'

'No, why should there be?'

'You aren't usually up at a quarter to seven.'

'Is that the time? I haven't been to bed yet. I want you to do something for me. It turns out Selchester left some drawings to Charles. Pen and ink, gloomy scenes of Russian life by one of those oppressed types who managed to get away after the Bolsheviks took over. God knows why he wanted Charles to have them. They'd fetch nothing in the salerooms, so I don't mind them going. They're stashed in the attic, in the cupboard opposite the stairs. They weren't on the inventory, but I'll get Oliver to fix that. I don't want the lawyers asking questions when they go through the bequests. Find them, would you, darling? And then get hold of Charles, and tell him to come and take them away. I don't have his telephone number. But listen, you'll have to bring them down from the attic. I don't want Charles in there.'

'Why not? He's almost family.'

'I wouldn't trust Charles further than I could see him. Never trust a man who has blood on his hands.'

Sonia must be drunk.

'Blood? What blood? What are you talking about?'

'Didn't Tom tell you? When he escaped from Colditz, two others were with him. He made it back; they didn't.'

'I should think one in three was above the average.'

'Tom heard rumours, that's all.'

Sonia's words were casual, but Freya could hear the tension in her voice. She said, 'Besides, what would that have to do with drawings in the attic?'

'Just do as I say. I never liked Charles, and that urbane FO façade doesn't fool me. He takes care of number one.'

'So do you, Sonia.'

'So do we all, but some of us are less vicious about it than others. Must go, I'm longing for my bed. Don't forget, will you? Bye, darling.'

# Scene 2

Vivian knew that Stanley Dillon usually got to work early. She telephoned his private office number at a quarter to eight, and he answered it himself.

'Stanley?'

There was a pause, and then Stanley said, 'Who's speaking?'

'Vivian.'

'Good heavens, I didn't recognise your voice. You sound strained; is something the matter?'

'Not exactly. I'm calling you to let you know that I'm going to tell the truth.'

A much longer pause. 'The truth in what sense?'

'I'm going to come clean about Selchester's death.'

'You're going to the police? You're going to confess? Vivian, you can't. We agreed; we all agreed. It would have been bad enough then, but now . . . they'd throw the book at you. You'll be tried for manslaughter at least, maybe murder. Not to mention perjury and a few other things. And as for the rest of us—'

'I know. Don't think I don't know. And I'm not going to the police. At least, not at first.'

'Then who are you going to tell?'

'Freya and Hugo Hawksworth.'

'Freya Wryton and Mr Hawksworth?' His incredulity rang down the line. 'Why in God's name would you do that?'

'Because Freya is the one who's suffered in all this. Not just losing her uncle, but being suspected by the police, along with Lord Arlingham. He's been cleared now. There's some new evidence—'

'In which case, she's in the clear as well, and you don't need to have that on your conscience.'

'And Hugo Hawksworth because he's been investigating the murder. No, he's not police, but he works at the Hall. You know perfectly well that place is nothing to do with statistics, it's all hush-hush stuff. And Lord Selchester was involved with what they do there, during and after the war. Don't ask me how I know all this. I had my suspicions, and I've been talking to some people in London who are part of that world.'

'Vivian, the best thing you can do is keep quiet, as you've done for nearly seven years. What's changed?'

She couldn't keep back her tears. She heard Alistair's voice, warm and affectionate and so very Scottish: '*Tell the truth and shame the devil.*' This was the least she could do for him. 'My mind is made up. I'm going up to the Castle this morning. I want to catch Hugo before he goes off to work.'

'He'll go to the police.'

'I expect he will. But I can tell him and Freya exactly what happened and why. The police—oh, the police have their own view of things. To be honest, I'm not sure they'll believe me. Now Lord Arlingham's in the clear, they're planning to pin the crime on someone else.'

'Vivian, how do you know all this?'

'I told you, I have friends who are in the know. The powers that be don't want a trial. They want the whole thing just to blow over and be forgotten.'

'Why would they want that?'

'How do I know?'

'Have you spoken to the others?'

'I can't get hold of Charles. His phone is out of order. And Lionel—'

'Best not to say anything to Lionel for the moment. He'll panic. Listen, if you're really going to do this, I'll come with you. Stay there. I'll come and pick you up. Be with you in ten minutes.'

Click, and the line went dead.

# Scene 3

Mrs Partridge was chasing an errant cockerel across the front lawn when she heard a car coming up the drive. She didn't recognise it;

then she saw Mr Dillon at the wheel, with Vivian Witt beside him. What a time to come calling, with Mr Hugo about to set off for the Hall and Miss Freya already up in the Tower, clacking away on that typewriter of hers.

Mr Dillon called out to her, 'Anyone at home?'

Mrs Partridge made a grab for the cockerel and tucked the squawking bird under one arm. 'Any more trouble from you, my fine fellow, and it's into the pot you go. Miss Freya's up in her room, not to be disturbed, and Mr Hawksworth will be going to work any minute.'

That wasn't strictly true, since he didn't usually start work until about ten o'clock.

'Can you tell him we'd like a word?'

Freya had witnessed the hen drama and the unexpected arrival of Vivian and Dillon. Why were they here? Something to do with the play? Surely not, at this hour. Besides, they'd have telephoned first. She'd go down and find out what they wanted.

'I've put them in the library,' Mrs Partridge told her. 'Now I'm going up to tell Mr Hugo they're here. It seems they want to talk to the pair of you.'

'I'll get him,' Freya said.

Hugo was coming back from the bathroom, clad in an elegant brocade dressing gown. He looked sleek and, yes, dangerous. Exactly as though he had a dagger tucked up his sleeve.

'Hello,' he said. 'Looking for me?'

'Vivian Witt and Stanley Dillon are here, and they want to talk to us.'

'You don't know why?'

'No, how could I? But I don't think they want to talk about lighting for the play in the Cathedral.'

'Where are they?'

253

'In the library.'

'You go on down. I'll be with you as soon as I'm dressed.'

He vanished into his room, and Freya, wondering if she could think of a reason to include Leo in their conversation, went downstairs again.

She needn't have troubled. Leo was already in the library. He'd been sitting in an alcove, reading, when Mrs Partridge had propelled the two visitors through the door.

'Hugo's on his way,' Freya said.

Leo smiled at her and was about to leave, but she said, 'Please stay.'

Vivian and Dillon looked at one another. Vivian shrugged, and said in a tired voice, 'Why not?'

Dillon frowned. 'It's a private matter.'

'Not for much longer,' Vivian said. 'And since it's my conscience that's brought me here, why not let him hear what I have to say?' She gave Leo an appraising look. 'I suppose you're an expert on matters of conscience, given you're a priest.'

'Really, Vivian—' Dillon began.

Freya cut him off. 'If it's anything to do with Lord Selchester's death, Father Hawksworth knows as much about it as Hugo and I do.'

Hugo came in, wearing his work clothes of flannel trousers and a jacket. 'You'd better stay, Leo. We may need your keen mind on this.' He turned to Vivian. 'This is about Lord Selchester, isn't it?'

She nodded.

'Then before you say anything, I'd better tell you that I spoke to Hattie Miller yesterday—Hattie Moore, as was. I don't suppose you know the name. She was a maid here at the Castle in January 1947. On the night Lord Selchester died, she was in the passageway that overlooks Grace Hall. She saw your encounter with Lord Selchester,

Miss Witt, and only fled when your three fellow guests arrived on the scene.'

Vivian let out a long sigh. Tension drained from her face. 'Oh, what a relief.'

'Relief?' Dillon said. 'When whatever you came to say here would be deniable, and now it turns out that there's a witness?' He turned furiously on Hugo. 'Why didn't this woman speak out before now?'

'She has her reasons.'

'Has she gone to the police?'

'No. And I doubt if she will.'

'She'd be in a lot of trouble if she did,' Dillon said.

'Shut up, Stanley,' Vivian said. 'I came here to tell Freya and Hugo about what I did that night. It turns out they already know, that's all.'

'It's not all. I told you this was not a good idea, Vivian. Every word you say makes matters worse.'

'They can't be worse,' she said.

'They can, as you'll discover when you're locked in a police cell before nightfall.'

'I told you, the police don't want to hear what I came to say. Do they?' she said, speaking directly to Hugo.

He paused before he said, 'No, they don't.'

'Brushed under the carpet is what they want. A famous actress on trial, with three other distinguished and respected men charged with being accessories after the fact, or aiding and abetting, is exactly what they don't want.'

Freya was standing apart from the three of them, watching. On the other side of the room, Leo was also watching, and he now came forward. 'Shall we all sit down? And then it would be useful to hear what happened next. After Hattie fled.'

They sat down and then, as though it were a normal morning visit, Mrs Partridge came in with a tray. 'I thought you'd be needing coffee,' she said. She cast a disapproving look at the visitors. 'Even though it isn't what you'd call elevenses time, I dare say you can all do with having your wits woken up good and proper. I'll leave you to pour, Miss Freya. Hot milk in the silver jug and the other's cream.'

'Good,' said Leo. 'You have a knack of knowing just what's needed, Mrs Partridge. Thank you.' Mrs Partridge closed the door behind her with a firm click.

Leo went on, 'So, Lord Selchester has been knifed and, in falling, hit his head. Miss Witt has dropped the knife and is in a state of shock. Let's take it from there.'

Hugo said, 'Dillon, why did you and the others go to Grace Hall? You were in the library, and it's too far for you to hear any kind of fracas in that part of the Castle.'

'We were playing bridge and had finished a long rubber. Vivian went out. She said she'd left her cigarettes by the phone in Grace Hall.'

'Had you?' Hugo asked Vivian.

'No. I wanted to talk to Selchester.'

'He wasn't a stranger, was he?' Freya said. 'He told Plinth to serve a special liqueur for you. Strega. So he knew it was your favourite.'

'He could have read that in an interview in the papers,' Dillon said.

Vivian made a weary gesture. 'He didn't. He knew because we'd dined together in London. Yes, I knew him. Yes, I hated him enough to want him dead. But I didn't intend to kill him, I didn't lash out at him in anger. It was an accident. I was trying to protect myself. I snatched at the knife and caught him off balance, and he fell on it.'

'But because you knew him and had reasons to want him dead—that's a strong reaction, Miss Witt, if I may say so—you were afraid that your account wouldn't be believed. You didn't know Hattie was upstairs and saw it all and says it happened just as you describe.' Leo's voice was gentle.

'At the time, I didn't think any of that. I was horrified. I couldn't believe I'd killed him. I had his blood on my hands.'

'Let's get back to the others,' Hugo said.

'We wanted to start another rubber,' Dillon said. 'Charles said he'd go and find her. He burst back into the room just a few minutes later, saying, "You'd better come, there's been an accident."'

'Do you remember Charles coming in?' Freya asked Vivian.

'It was a little while before he came. I didn't hear him coming in. He was suddenly there. I said, "He's dead," or something like that. Charles was kneeling down beside him, I think he was feeling for the wound. He had blood on his hands. Then he lifted Selchester's head and held it for a moment. When he let it drop, it just flopped. After that he ran out, saying he was going to get the others.'

Leo looked at Vivian's ashen face and went over to the tray of drinks. He poured brandy into a glass and carried it over to Vivian. 'Drink this.'

'Not at this time of the morning.'

'Drink it.'

'Over to you, Dillon,' Hugo said. 'What happened next?'

'Tallis fainted. He always does at the sight of blood, apparently. So I pushed him out of the way. Charles had his arm round Vivian, who was shrieking, "We must call the police. It will all have to come out." Dillon cleared his throat. 'I asked her if Selchester had been threatening her. Not just physically, but in some other way. Did he have some hold over her?'

'Why did you ask that?' Hugo said.

257

'Because he had been threatening me. I won't go into the details; it was a personal matter. He was planning to ruin me, and he had discovered a means to do it. I gather he'd put private detectives to ferret out some details of my wartime activities that would be considered questionable. If he could do that me, I guessed he might be doing something of the same kind to Vivian.'

'Was he?' Hugo asked Vivian.

Her nerve returning under the influence of the brandy, she spoke more calmly. 'Yes. Oh, it was such a horrible mess. He knew I was having an affair with a married man. He wanted a hold on that man. He also—' She hesitated and looked at Leo.

'Don't mind me. There's nothing you can say that I haven't heard before. You're going to tell us that he wanted a sexual relationship with you?'

Freya winced at the words; they sounded so clinical.

'Thank you for not saying "an affair" or even "a fling".'

'Did you agree?' Hugo asked.

Freya winced. These Hawksworths were so cold. Couldn't they see what Vivian was going through? She wanted to jump up and tell them to stop. Hugo, as if sensing her agitation, put out a hand and held hers. It wasn't a gesture of affection. His grip was like iron; he was stopping her moving. Then he let her go, smiled swiftly at her, and waited for Vivian's answer.

'Yes. In the end. It seemed a small price to pay for his silence.'

'Was it a small price?' Leo asked.

'No. He was—let's just say he wasn't a considerate lover. He liked violence. I'm not going to say any more about it. I could even have put up with that, but I realised he wasn't going to keep his word. I can't imagine why I ever thought he would. When he held me and ran the tip of that knife on my breast, that was it. I never wanted him to touch me again.' She drew in a long breath. Her hands were twisting together in her lap. 'Which he never did because he was dead. I'd killed him.'

'Mr Dillon can tell us what happened after that,' Leo said. 'From the body on the floor in Grace Hall to the body buried under the flagstones. It must have been a busy few hours.'

'It was,' Dillon said. 'Vivian was in shock, and we had to haul Tallis into the passage, since every time he came round and saw Selchester's body, he swooned again. So it was really up to Charles and me. Of course, we should have called the police, and Charles went to the telephone to do so. He picked up the receiver but said he couldn't get through. The lines must have already gone down. And then Tallis finally came to his senses and told us that Selchester had been blackmailing him as well. There were some photographs of what he called an unfortunate kind. Tallis liked to take those kind of photos, and Selchester found out about it. He made Tallis hand over some that were particularly incriminating for the men in them.'

'And threatened to hand Tallis over to the authorities if he didn't play ball,' Hugo said.

'Exactly. So that was the three of us likely to face some fairly unpleasant consequences from what would come out in the course of a police investigation. An investigation that would be carried out in a blaze of publicity. Earl killed by actress? What a field day for the gutter press.'

'So, by now you were beginning to understand why you were invited to the Castle,' Leo said.

'Yes. Selchester wanted to watch our discomfort and turn the screws a little more. It seemed to suit his warped personality to have a clutch of victims there at his mercy and make them squirm.'

'Guthrie wasn't a victim?' Leo asked.

'No, he was there as a normal guest. Like Tom Arlingham and Miss Wryton.' Mr Dillon nodded at Freya.

Although Charles hadn't been entirely at his ease that evening. Nor had Tom. The atmosphere had been tense and awkward for all of them.

Except for her uncle. There'd been that outburst of fury at Tom, but otherwise he had been the perfect host. Charming, amiable, attentive to his guests. While all the time . . . Freya couldn't bear to think of what wickedness lurked beneath that impeccable exterior.

Dillon went on, 'It was actually Charles who said that perhaps there was a way out of an impossible situation. What if the Earl simply vanished? I thought that ridiculous and said so, but Charles had already thought it out. There was a blizzard blowing up. If we could bury the body and make it seem as though Selchester had, for some unknown reason, gone out, or had gone out earlier and been caught in the snow, and if we all vouched for each other, then who would ever know what had happened?'

'Altruistic of him,' Leo said.

'Who suggested the Chapel as a place to put the body?' Hugo said.

Dillon took out a handkerchief and wiped his forehead. 'Charles again. I said it would be out of the question to bury the body with the ground frozen and a snowstorm raging. Charles said we could put him in the Old Chapel. The flagstones looked as though they'd been there for centuries, but Selchester had told him that some of them had been taken up during the war when they took pipes through there. The flagstones were laid on bare earth. So we could dig down and make a grave and then put the flagstones back.'

'Didn't he think the police would search the Castle, looking for Lord Selchester?' Hugo frowned. 'It was a fantastical scheme.'

'And a risky one,' Leo added.

Freya couldn't imagine it. While she'd been nursing Magnus the kitten back to life with warm milk and strokes, this Gothic horror story had been acted out at the Castle.

'Why did Charles want to do this?' she asked. 'He had nothing to lose, and he didn't owe anything to the rest of you; you were strangers.'

'He wanted to protect Lord Selchester's reputation. He said it would be terrible for the family if even half the truth came out. He felt loyalty to his godfather, who'd always been good to him, and to Arlingham and Lady Priscilla and the rest of them. Selchester was dead, and nothing would bring him back, but this way there would be no scandal.'

'And he was right,' Freya said. 'It's inconceivable that it worked, but it did.'

'Until the body turned up,' Dillon said grimly. 'Even then, we would have got away with it if Vivian hadn't suddenly had this fit of conscience.'

'Don't you be so sure,' Vivian said. 'I don't think this is over yet. What I never told you or the others is that Selchester kept a notebook with details of what he had on us. He showed me the entry he'd written on me. No, I didn't see any of the other names. It was all neatly arranged, a page each. He flipped through a few pages; we weren't the only ones by any means. He said it was his insurance, in case anything untoward happened to him.'

'That's the little black book Sonia was looking for,' Freya said. 'I wonder how—' She fell silent. 'It's missing. No one has found it.'

'There you are,' Vivian said. 'Now you know.' She looked at Leo and then at Hugo. 'Are you going to call the police?'

'Will you tell them what you've told us? Knowing that it's almost certainly the end of your career, and probably your freedom?'

'Yes. Only will they believe me or take any notice of what I say? Aren't they used to confessions from hysterical females? If Stanley doesn't back me up, I am sure Charles and Lionel won't.'

'I don't share your scruples,' Dillon said. 'You could report all that's been said this morning to the Superintendent, Mr Hawksworth, but it's merely hearsay, especially if Hattie isn't prepared to tell the truth.'

'The police don't want the truth,' Vivian said. 'They want to close the case and be done with it. No fuss, no scandal, no revelations.'

# Chapter Twenty-Five

## Scene 1

After Dillon and Vivian had left, Freya, Hugo and Leo stood in the hall, looking at one another. Then Hugo glanced at his watch. 'I'd clean forgotten, I've a meeting with Bernard this morning. I'm going to be late.'

'You offered to let me have the car today,' Leo said. 'To visit a friend in St Enwys. I'll telephone and change the day.'

'No. If you're ready to leave now, you can drop me off. I'll catch the bus back.'

As they jolted down the drive, they saw the postman toiling up the hill on his bicycle, rather red in the face.

They stopped, and Hugo wound down the window. 'Hot work, Mr Bunbury.'

The postman balanced his bicycle against his leg and opened his bag. He extracted a letter. 'Bit of luck meeting you, Mr Hawksworth. There's just the one letter for the Castle this morning, and it's addressed to you.' He gave it to Hugo, waited for the car to go past and then manoeuvred his bicycle round to set off on the easier journey downhill, back towards the town.

Hugo went straight into the meeting at the Hall. It was as tedious as all meetings were. Sir Bernard liked to keep a finger on the pulse, as he put it, which meant reports from all departments. Hugo's mind was miles away when his turn came. He looked at the notes Mrs Clutton had thoughtfully provided for him, made a commendable effort to sound sensible and then, thank God, the meeting came to an end. As he was about to leave, Sir Bernard called him back. 'A word with you. Close the door. Sit down.'

Hugo sat. What now?

'I spoke to MacLeod yesterday. He tells me Arlingham's in the clear. I'm glad of it. It would have been tidy, but that kind of thing can bring the government into disrepute. After all, Selchester was a figure in politics, and family rows don't inspire confidence in our rulers among the general public.'

Row? Since when was patricide a row? He'd certainly changed his tune.

'Good work on your part, finding out what Arlingham was up to.'

'Miss Wryton was responsible for that.'

'Freya's doing, was it? Got a head on her shoulders, that young lady. So all's well that ends well.'

'I'm glad they've accepted the evidence of his innocence. I was afraid they might fudge some reason to doubt it.'

'Fudge?'

'The police were remarkably keen to pin the murder on Lord Arlingham.'

So had Sir Bernard been, but it was better not to mention that.

'There was some pressure from London to wrap the case up. However, they have the perpetrator now.'

Hugo stared at him. Had Vivian gone to the police after all, and confessed?

'That man who shot himself, Jason Filbert.'

Oh, he should have seen that coming. Tom Arlingham had, as it were, slipped through their fingers, and so they'd found another culprit who was dead and conveniently unable to stand trial.

'A thoroughly nasty piece of work, from what I hear, with a track record of violence. So that finishes the inquiry, and I'm glad of it. I'd like to thank you for your help. You've a knack of getting on with the locals, I hear, which I thoroughly approve of. And keep up the good work here. Nothing has shown up in the files yet, from what you said at the meeting, but if there's anything to find, I'm sure you'll find it. Slow and steady does it—nothing like a careful and methodical approach. Rather different from field work, but I can see you're settling down to your new life.'

Did he have any idea how pompous he sounded? Hugo had a frown on his face as he went back to his office, turning over in his mind what Sir Bernard had said about pinning the murder on Filbert. Who had indeed been a nasty piece of work, from what he'd heard, but even so . . .

He had forgotten all about the letter that Mr Bunbury had handed him. He hadn't even glanced at it to see who it was from. But after eating his lunch in the canteen, he remembered it and fished it out of his pocket.

It was from Henry, and what he had to say quite banished the sense of tedium that hung over him.

Dear Hugo

I was intrigued by your queries re our friend Guthrie and so did a bit of investigating on my own account. Outside strictly orthodox channels, so keep what I have to say under your hat. As a side note, when I took another look at his file and did some cross-referencing, I came to the conclusion that there are items missing. Whether they were never there or have been intentionally removed, I can't say. Anyhow, my investigation threw up a couple of interesting things that are possibly within your remit. Did you know Guthrie was married before the war to one Mitzi Rubinstein, in Vienna? This was in 1937. She was active in Communist circles, and had Guthrie not married her, given her the security of a British passport and got her out of the country, she would undoubtedly have been arrested and would probably have disappeared without a trace.

There's no record of this marriage in his file. The only marriage on his record is to Eleanor Dawkins in 1942. She divorced him, as you know, in 1949. Uncontested, on the grounds of his adultery. I haven't found any trace of what happened to Mitzi after she came to England. Maybe she went back to Austria—unwise, given the situation, or perhaps neither of them considered it anything more than a marriage of convenience, and they simply went their separate ways and she took a new name. Who knows? Although given her background, someone should have kept an eye on her.

Anyhow, Mitzi wasn't the only ardent Communist. Guthrie was a member of the same cell and was apparently a committed Communist with strong links to the Party.

It's a mystery to me how this never came up when he was vetted and subsequently joined the Foreign Office.

Anyhow, hope this is of interest. Let me know when you come to the Smoke again and we'll meet for another jar.

Yours,
Henry

Hugo stared at this missive, read it again and then went to find Mrs Clutton. 'Can you check in the index and files to see if we have anything on one Mitzi Rubinstein? Pre-war Vienna, but became a British citizen.'

'Mitzi will be a nickname, I take it,' she said.

'Yes. Could be Maria or Marie. Or Miriam.'

'Is this a priority over the other files in hand?'

Priority? 'Oh, yes, this is most definitely a priority.'

Mrs Clutton got up and went over to the bank of drawers where she had her index cards. 'I'll see what I can find.'

Hugo went back to his office and sat at his desk, staring out of the window into the distance, noticing with half his mind that there was a mist gathering over the hills.

Mrs Clutton came back into the room. 'It looks as though this is the one.' She read from the card in her hand, '"Miriam Rubinstein, born Graz, 1914, to a Jewish family, father a rabbi. Attended university in Vienna, links to Socialist causes, query Communist sympathiser". Not a lot of information, but I'll keep digging.'

'Thank you,' Hugo said. It would need to be followed up, but Henry would have got his facts right. He had a meticulous mind and wouldn't have written that letter if he hadn't been sure of what he had to say.

If Guthrie was a fully paid-up Communist back in the late thirties and had never mentioned this affiliation on his application to join the Foreign Office, then what kind of a man was he? And if Lord Selchester had known about this, then Guthrie would have been a prime target for blackmail indeed. On two counts: not only being a Communist, but possibly having contracted a bigamous marriage, too. Either would mean the end of a career in the Foreign Office.

What if he had never severed his links with the Communist Party? What if instead of being a patriotic and dutiful citizen, he was another Burgess or Maclean?

Hugo blamed himself for taking Charles Guthrie at face value. Because he was Lord Selchester's godson, he had assumed that was why he had been invited to the Castle. Instead, once the revelations about the other guests came out, he should have added him to the list of those being blackmailed, unless it was proved otherwise.

He'd need to talk to Dillon again, go through what happened that evening, with the focus on Guthrie. He went over in his mind the sequence of events, and then something leapt out at him. It was what Vivian had said about blood. What was it? Blood on Charles's hands when he touched Selchester. Blood all over his hands. Which implied that when Guthrie came on the scene, Lord Selchester was still bleeding. And unless the knife had struck an artery, he wouldn't have been bleeding like that. Dead men don't bleed.

Ergo, at that point he might still have been alive. Hadn't Vivian described how Charles had lifted Selchester's head and then it had flopped? Horribly and lifelessly.

What if the wound caused by Vivian hadn't been fatal? What if prompt treatment could have brought an unconscious Lord Selchester round? In which case, why and how had he died?

To which the answer was that Charles Guthrie had killed him. Probably through pressure on the carotid artery, an old and savage way to finish a man's life.

# Scene 2

Freya's writing wasn't going well. What did the deeds and misdeeds of a seventeenth-century heroine, however exciting, matter in the face of the drama unfolding now in Selchester? The revelations of the morning had left her uncertain and unsettled, and her mind kept returning to Vivian. How could she have survived with that on her conscience for all these years?

She covered her typewriter and stood up. She'd left a note on her desk: *Ring Charles re Sonia's message.*

She'd been up to the attic and had brought the pictures down and stowed them in the Muniments Room. A dismal set of drawings, in her opinion, although presumably some people liked that kind of thing. Undoubtedly drawn by an expert hand, and she wondered for a moment what had happened to the artist in that nightmare world of Stalin's Russia.

In Grace Hall, she picked up the telephone and dialled Charles's number. No familiar brr brr at the other end. She frowned, and rang the exchange. 'Mabel? Can you put me through to 736, please.'

'Mr Guthrie?'

'Yes. I tried to dial the number but there seems to be a problem with the line.'

'Just a moment.'

Some clicks at the exchange end, and then Mabel was back. 'There's a fault on his line. I'll report it.'

Freya put the receiver down and headed for the kitchen. Mrs Partridge was making pastry. 'Leave that alone, Miss Freya. You know you shouldn't eat raw pastry; it'll do your insides no good.' She dusted flour off her hands and went over to the oven. 'If you're done with your writing, you'd best take that horse of yours out sooner rather than later. The weather's changing.'

Freya looked out of the window. A pale cloud of mist was drifting over the hills.

'It's rising up around the river, too,' Mrs Partridge said.

Which meant that by the time darkness fell, the town and Castle would be swathed in mist. She'd just have time to take Last Hurrah out across the water meadows to Charles's house and deliver Sonia's message in person.

She ran upstairs to change into breeches, then came downstairs again to pause and pull on her boots before going out to the stables.

Ben came out to greet her, a girth in his hands. 'If you're planning to take Last Hurrah out, Miss Freya, you won't be able to. I was cleaning his tack, and look at this girth. It's frayed, and I don't have a spare except for that old one which irritates him and means he gives you even more trouble than usual.'

Freya inspected the girth. It might hold for her ride; it might not. How annoying. She stroked Last Hurrah's nose. 'No outing for you today.' She said to Ben, 'I have to call on Charles Guthrie, so I'll walk down to town and call in at the saddler's on the way.'

Freya loved Forsyth's the saddler's. She loved the smell of leather that hit you as you opened the shop door and the familiar sight of saddles perched on their racks, and halters and bridles hanging from hooks. Old Mr Forsyth was working in the back, but he came into the front of the shop to greet her, still in his long leather apron. She showed him the girth, and he pursed his lips.

'Nothing we can do for you with that. It'll have to be a new one. And not just any one, not for Last Hurrah. He's a horse won't stand for having his belly tickled, that's for sure.'

Mr Forsyth wouldn't be hurried. At last he—rather than Freya—decided on the best girth. 'Will you take it with you, or shall I send the lad with it?'

'Yes, deliver it to the Castle.' Freya paid and left the shop. She set off towards the bridge from where she would take the shortcut along the river meadows to Long Combe, where Charles Guthrie lived. It was hardly more than a hamlet, with a few houses, a farm and the church where Charles's father had been vicar. She hadn't got far along the path when she saw Charles coming towards her. 'Hullo, Charles. I was coming to see you.'

Charles kissed her cheek. 'Always good to see you. Any particular reason for the visit, or just the pleasure of my company?'

'I have a message from Sonia for you. I tried to ring you, but there's a fault on the line, and your phone isn't working.'

'So I discovered when I tried to make a call. I'm on my way to the Post Office. I have something urgent to post, and I've run out of stamps.'

Freya looked at the card in his hand. 'I think I've got some ha'penny stamps in my bag. Yes, I have, so I can spare you the walk.'

Charles handed over a ha'penny coin, took the stamp and stuck it on the card. 'Why don't you walk back with me and have a cup of tea? Or something stronger?'

'I'd better not. The mist is getting thicker. I'll come with you to the footbridge and then go back to the Castle that way.'

Charles said easily, 'It'll be clear for a while yet. What's the message from Sonia?'

'I nearly forgot, I was distracted by the mist and stamps. It's about some drawings at the Castle. Sonia says Selchester left them to you, and she wants you to collect them as soon as possible. They're in the Muniments Room. Did you know about them? That he was going to leave them to you?'

'I had no idea. Drawings of what?'

'Russia. I must say, they're fairly dreary. Are you interested in Russia?'

Charles said, 'I've never been there. I'm not sure why Selchester wanted me to have those pictures, although I do dimly remember him showing them to me. Perhaps I made the mistake of admiring them. From politeness, you understand.'

'Possibly a mistake. Still, you can always send them to the salerooms. Someone might like them.'

They had reached the footbridge. Freya was about to say goodbye to Charles, but he said, 'I'll come with you until you get to higher ground. The mist is worse here, and you might stray off the path and land up in a bog. I can take you by a shortcut. No, it's no trouble at all. I know the land around here like the back of my hand. You'll be perfectly safe with me.'

Freya protested, saying it wasn't necessary, but in truth she was getting alarmed by the fact that this mist was growing thicker by the minute.

They walked along, side by side, shadowy figures in the mist, footsteps and voices muffled. Freya hesitated, and then said, 'There's something else I wanted to tell you.' The grey web enveloping them made it all seem unreal; both their presence here by the river they could hear but not see, and the revelations of the morning. 'Vivian Witt and Stanley Dillon came to the Castle this morning.'

She sensed rather than saw Charles stiffen. 'Something to do with the play, one supposes. Odd time to make a call.'

'Nothing to do with the play. Everything to do with Selchester's death. Vivian came because she wanted to tell us the truth about the night my uncle died. She told us that she killed Lord Selchester. It was an accident, and the four of you decided—oh, for all kinds of reasons—to hide his body and say you were innocent bystanders, unaware and uninvolved in what had happened to him.'

Charles swore, the savage words jarring on Freya's ears, and then said, 'I didn't think the woman could be such a fool.'

There was a coldness to his voice that Freya had never heard before. She shivered slightly, and it wasn't the chill of the mist that made her do so. She went on, 'It's been hard on Vivian, keeping it to herself over the years. It's lain on her conscience, and she was dreadfully distressed when she described what happened. She said there was so much blood.'

'Rubbish, there wasn't much blood. Good God, it was barely enough to make Lionel pass out. For Christ's sake, why after all this time should Vivian suddenly feel she had to rake the whole business up? If we all kept our mouths shut and said nothing, we were safe. Just who did Vivian make this unnecessary confession to?'

His voice was hard. Freya said, 'I was there, and Hugo Hawksworth. And his uncle, Father Leo Hawksworth.'

'The priest? That's all it needed. I suppose even now Vivian is at the police station spilling the beans to the worthy Superintendent.'

'Actually, no,' Freya said.

'Just like a woman, fretting about blood. What does she think she's doing, playing Lady Macbeth?'

'Don't you understand at all why she had to tell someone? Don't you understand what guilt can do to a person?'

'Guilt? Guilt is nothing but a moral tale to confuse people who are too stupid to see the consequences of their actions.'

Quite suddenly, as though a ghost were breathing into her ear, Sonia's words came back to Freya: "Charles has blood on his hands."

Freya had taken that as mere malicious gossip on Sonia's part, but what if it was true? What if Charles Guthrie was ruthless enough to eliminate anyone who stood in his way?

Blood. Not much blood. *Think.* There was something she was missing. She stopped and shut her eyes, willing herself to remember Vivian's exact words. Blood on Charles's hands. But a dead man wouldn't have bled.

She couldn't see Charles, but put out a hand and found him, held his arm and blurted out, 'Vivian didn't kill Selchester, did she? You did. Why, Charles? Why did you do that?'

He wrenched his arm away, and she was alone again. For a moment, Freya thought Charles had walked away, but then she sensed he'd moved behind her. Before she could whirl round, he had pinned her arms to her side, then dragged her wrists back. She cried out, 'Charles, you're hurting me.'

Charles said, in that same cold voice, 'Sorry about this, Freya, but I have no choice. You do see that. Yes, I killed Lord Selchester. Quickly and mercifully, which is more than he deserved. I assure you, he didn't suffer. Why did I kill him? Because he was blackmailing me just as he was blackmailing those other three. You have no idea what a dangerous thing that was for him to do. Or how dangerous and unwise it was for you to go nosing about in things that are really no business of yours.'

'Why was he blackmailing you?'

Keep him talking and then maybe a miracle might happen. Someone would appear out of the mist: a woman walking her dog, a fisherman coming home . . .

'The pictures from Russia are a clue, Freya, my love. Selchester threatened my career and indeed my freedom, and that didn't make my masters happy. So he had to die.'

'Masters? Your superiors at the Foreign Office? But why—'

'Not the Foreign Office. Moscow.'

Freya twisted free, lost her balance and reached out to grab hold of Charles.

He stepped to one side, seized her by the shoulders and swung her round.

For a long moment neither of them moved; muscle pitted against muscle.

He was too strong for her, and with a sudden violent movement, he pushed her off the path.

Freya slithered into the bog, fighting to get a foothold. Breathe. Keep calm. 'Mustn't panic,' she said out loud, even as Charles loomed out of the mist.

His booted foot came down on her, forcing her deep into the evil-smelling, sucking slime.

# Scene 3

Hugo plucked his hat and mac from the hat stand in his office and went next door to Mrs Clutton's room. 'I'm leaving early,' he said, and before she could reply, he was gone. There was a bus at ten past, and with luck he might just catch it.

It was pulling away as he reached the Hall gates, but the driver saw him wave, and obligingly stopped and waited while he limped towards the bus and climbed aboard. Impatient to get back to the Castle and share what he'd heard from Henry with Freya and Leo, he regretted not having the car. It was still a slow walk from the bus stop at the other end.

His luck was in. As he got off the bus and thanked the driver, a horn hooted. 'There's Mr Graham in his van. I dare say he'll give you a lift up to the Castle,' the bus driver said.

Mr Graham got out of the van. 'I'll run you up, Mr Hawksworth, since I've got a delivery for Mrs Partridge. I'll just move that bag of carrots off the seat, and then you can hop in.'

Mrs Partridge was alone in the kitchen. She took the box of vegetables that he'd brought in and made disapproving noises. 'Just because your leg's not hurting so much, it doesn't mean you should behave as though you didn't need that stick.'

'Is my uncle back?'

'No, he isn't.'

'Is Freya upstairs in the Tower?'

'Last thing I saw of her was a while ago. She was putting on her boots to take that horse out for a ride.'

Damn it. Who knew when either of them would be back. He wanted to talk the whole matter through. He had a sense of unease, but why? He was making too much of it. Charles didn't know what he'd found out—probably didn't even know that Vivian had confessed. She was no danger to anyone, but what about Charles? He didn't like what Henry had had to say about the rumours regarding that escape from Colditz. Was Charles Guthrie a far more ruthless customer than he had any idea of?

He'd go out to the stables and see if Ben knew which direction Freya had ridden. At the door he stopped. 'Freya can't have gone for a ride. I saw Last Hurrah in his box just now.'

'Well, if she's back, I didn't see her come in. Best ask Ben.'

Hugo went out to the stables and found Ben hooking up a hay bag for Last Hurrah. 'Do you know where Miss Freya is? Mrs Partridge said she'd taken Last Hurrah out, but since he's here, she must be back. Do you know where she is now?'

Ben said, 'She was going to go for a ride, but Last Hurrah needs a new girth to his saddle. She decided she'd walk down to the saddler's to buy one.'

'How long ago was that?'

'Maybe an hour ago.'

'So she should be back soon?'

'I doubt it. She said as how she was going to call on Mr Charles. She had a message to give him and said his phone wasn't working, so she'd deliver it herself.'

Hugo said, sudden urgency in his voice, 'Where does Mr Guthrie live?'

Ben looked at him as though he were witless. 'Down at Long Combe. It's a little hamlet outside Selchester, along past the river.'

Hugo thought for a moment. 'Out to the east? How would she go there from the saddler's? Is that the one in Goose Lane?'

'It is. And from there she'd most likely head for the bridge and take the river path. And then a shortcut through to his house. It's that much quicker than going round by the road. Then she'll come back over the footbridge and up the hill.'

Hugo stared at Ben, flummoxed. There was no obvious reason to think that Freya would be in any danger from Charles. Freya was no threat to him. His reason told him to stay put and wait for Freya to return and then to tell her. But the instinct he'd long ago learned to trust told him that Charles was dangerous. All it would take would be a chance remark from Freya. She wouldn't know about his Communist past, but she was as capable of putting two and two together as he was about the blood. It might suddenly occur to her that Vivian probably hadn't killed Selchester. And if she inadvertently said anything to Charles . . . No, he wouldn't harm her; it was too risky.

Ben said, 'The mist will be rising off the river. Miss Freya will have to mind her step, but she knows the danger well enough.'

'Danger? What danger?' Hugo said, his mind still fixed on Charles.

Ben looked at him pityingly. 'All those boggy patches. It's peat around there, with a heap of streams draining into the river. The ground's soft if you leave the tracks, and some of those bog holes are big enough for farmers to lose animals in. But Miss Freya has the sense not to go falling into any of those boggy pits.'

Hugo was now seriously alarmed. If only that girth hadn't broken; Freya would have been much safer on horseback. He looked at Last Hurrah, who rolled a knowing eye at him.

'How long would it take to walk down to this footbridge?'

Ben shook his head. 'You don't want to be doing that, not with your leg and the stick.'

'How long?'

'The speed you'd be able to go, and it's not an easy path, mind, maybe half an hour, maybe more.'

'If I took Last Hurrah?'

'He'd have you off as soon as you got on his back. Besides, I can't put a saddle on him until I've got the new girth.'

Hugo made up his mind. 'Put on his bridle. I'm going to ride him.'

'I don't think you can do that, Mr Hawksworth. It wouldn't be wise. Not with your leg and on that horse, even if you can ride.'

Hugo said, 'Of course I can ride. Otherwise, I wouldn't suggest it. I'll be better off bareback than with a saddle, with my leg. Quick, man.'

There was something about his voice that silenced the objections Ben was about to make. So, clicking his tongue in disapproval, he took the bridle from its hook and went into the loose box. Two minutes later, he led the horse out.

Last Hurrah looked at Hugo, and Hugo looked at Last Hurrah. Hugo said, 'I know you don't want me to ride you, but you're doing this for your mistress, not for me, okay? So behave.'

Last Hurrah swished his tail, and if he hadn't been so concerned, Hugo would have laughed at this response. Ben silently led Last Hurrah to the old mounting block, and Hugo, regretting the days when he would have leapt easily into a saddle, dropped his stick and climbed on to the block. He manoeuvred himself on to the horse's back and took the reins from Ben. Last Hurrah snorted, tossed his head and lunged sideways. Hugo squeezed hard with his knees, to hold on.

Ben gave the horse a buffet. 'Give over with that.' He picked up Hugo's stick and handed it to him. 'You'll need this if you come off.' Then he gave Hugo directions. 'Go out of that gate and get on to the grassy path. About a hundred yards on, if you haven't been thrown off, you'll come to a ruined shepherd's hut. He'll shy there, always does, so be ready for him. There's a track that cuts across the path. Follow it downhill and that'll lead you to the footbridge. Don't stray off the path—not that Last Hurrah will let you. He's a knowing one, and as long as you stay on his back, you won't end up in the bog.'

He gave Last Hurrah a slap on his polished rump, and the lame man, his stick and the horse set off together. Hugo was using muscles he hadn't used for a long time, and he thought what a sorry and pale imitation of a knight errant he was. Galloping forth to rescue a damsel in peril? Hardly. Ben was right; he'd be lucky to make it to the footbridge.

Last Hurrah's ears twitched backwards and forwards, but the horse was giving him an uncommonly smooth ride down the hill. It was almost as though he knew what he was about. And there, ahead of him, was the misty outline of the footbridge; he could hear the gurgle of water flowing over stones.

The river.

He'd made it, and he gave Last Hurrah a kick to urge him on. But before he reached the footbridge, Last Hurrah stopped abruptly and let out a whinny. His ears were pricked forward, his head up.

The sudden halt nearly had Hugo off, but he managed to cling on, cursing Last Hurrah. Then he heard what the horse's keener ears had heard: a voice coming out of the mist. Someone crying for help.

Freya.

The voice was half swallowed by the mist, but he knew it was her.

He was about to slide off the horse's back, but Last Hurrah was on the move again, picking his way with odd zigzags, the ground making squelching sounds under his hooves.

Hugo found himself praying that the horse did indeed know what he was about. Last Hurrah was treading with infinite care but steady purpose.

Freya's voice was nearer now, and Hugo shouted to her to hold on, he was coming.

He peered through the mist and saw her, lying on her back, half-submerged in a black pool of water.

He slid down from Last Hurrah's back and sank in the boggy ground up to his knees. He pulled out one leg and then the other, hanging on to the horse.

Last Hurrah appeared to be standing on firmer ground, so Hugo edged closer to him and then dropped on to his hands and knees. He carefully inched towards Freya, stretching out with his stick. 'Hook your arm over it. Now the other one. That's it.'

He pulled a sodden and furious Freya out of the water and dragged her under the horse's belly. Last Hurrah stood rock solid on his four hooves but turned his head round to blow at her.

Freya was breathless, but managed to say, furious, 'That bloody Charles. He pushed me in. Hugo, he did it—he killed Selchester.'

Hugo said, 'I know. Where is he?'

Freya was trying to wipe mud and green matter off her face and hands. 'He left me to drown, although I was damned if I was going to.' She sniffed. 'Have you got a hankie?'

Hugo felt in his pocket and produced one. 'You did the right thing, to lie on your back. How long were you in there?'

'Not long. I'd have been all right for an hour or so, but in this mist and with night coming, no one would have heard me yelling if you hadn't arrived. You didn't see Charles, or hear him? I expect he's gone back to his house to wait for news that I was missing, so he could appear surprised and distressed. What a beast he is.' Her teeth were chattering, but her anger was keeping her spirits up. 'Let's get out of here. Hang on to Last Hurrah, he'll make sure we don't go in.'

They made their careful way back to the track, but as soon as they were on firm ground, Last Hurrah tossed his head and trotted off into the mist.

'Quick,' Freya cried. 'Catch hold of the reins. What does he think he's doing?'

'Oh, damn that horse,' Hugo said. 'Heavens, I hope we don't have to haul him out of the bog.'

Out of the gathering gloom came a man's voice, shouting, 'Get away from me.'

'That's Charles,' Freya said. 'He must have stayed to make sure I didn't escape from the bog.'

A loud whinny sounded, and then a louder cry of panic rent the air.

'Over there, by the river,' Freya said, running blindly towards the footbridge.

Hugo followed as best he could. Before they reached it, the mist suddenly cleared, wispy clouds billowing across the water, and there was Last Hurrah, looming over Charles, who lashed out with his boot, landing a blow on the horse's leg.

Last Hurrah reared up, striking at Charles with his hooves. Charles put his arms up to protect himself. Last Hurrah dropped his legs, whirled round and with a hefty kick sent Charles flying into the water.

The mist descended, thicker than ever.

Hugo was tearing off his jacket, lurching towards where he thought the bank was, but he hit the fence beside the footbridge with a thud that took the breath out of him. 'Must go in, save him,' he panted.

Freya had hold of him. 'No. The river's running fast, and the currents here are lethal. We need to get help. If he can keep his head above water, they might be able to rescue him further downstream.'

Last Hurrah came walking out of the mist. Freya put her arm round his neck for a moment and then twitched the trailing reins over his head. Looping them over her arm, she cupped her hand. 'Get on,' she said to Hugo. 'Don't argue.' She gave him a leg up and then, with a jump, was herself up on Last Hurrah's back, perched in front of Hugo.

Last Hurrah seemed pleased to have Freya back in command as she gathered up the reins and told Hugo to hang on. Then they were over the footbridge and cantering along the river path. 'There's a place we can cut through to get on to the road,' Freya said. 'As long as I can spot it in this mist. Yes, here it is. Duck, because there are overhanging branches.'

She guided Last Hurrah on to the road. 'We'll come to some houses a little way along, where we can telephone for help. Or a car might come along and we could try to stop it.'

'If it doesn't run into us,' Hugo said.

As he spoke, the beams from a pair of powerful headlamps cut through the swirling mist. Hugo knew those headlamps. The Talbot Lago rolled to a stop. Leo was at the wheel, with Ben sitting beside him.

'Oh, thank goodness,' said Freya. 'Got to get a message to the police. Charles is in the river,' she shouted as Leo got out of the car.

Ben was at Last Hurrah's head. 'Down you come, Miss Freya, and you, too, Mr Hawksworth. I'll take care of the horse; you get into the car.'

Freya's knees buckled beneath her as her feet touched the ground, but Hugo was there, holding her up. He half-carried her to the car. 'In you get.'

'I smell terrible,' she managed to say as Leo tucked a rug round her.

'There is a certain aroma,' Leo said. He handed her a flask. 'Brandy. Drink it. Which way to the police station, Hugo?'

# Chapter Twenty-Six

## Scene 1

Freya lay in the bath. She'd sluiced the green slime off herself and then slipped down into the sarcophagus-sized bath with its huge lion feet and immense brass taps. Magnus sat primly beside the bath, on the cork top of the bathroom seat. He liked bath-time and would sometimes set out on a precarious journey around the wide rim of the bathtub. Today he just sat, the end of his tail twitching slightly. Freya lay back in the bath, her mind dissolving in the hot water, oblivious to the world of hurt and betrayal that lay beyond the bathroom door.

She heard hooves and sat up. Ben must be back with Last Hurrah. She listened intently to the steady clip-clop; he didn't seem to be lame, thank goodness.

Reluctantly, she heaved herself out of the water and reached out for the large towel draped over the radiator. Back to reality. She had a phone call to make; she wanted to tell Vivian about Charles before anyone else did.

She was going to stay in her dressing gown, but after a moment she hung it back on the door and put on some clothes. The police would come to the Castle, wanting statements from her and Hugo.

It was a pity they couldn't take a statement from Last Hurrah. He knew more than any of them about what had happened down there by the river.

Down in Grace Hall, she found Hugo on the telephone. He finished his call and replaced the receiver. Even in that shadowy light, she could see how worried he looked. But his face lightened into a smile as he saw her.

'Feeling better?'

'Yes. I want to phone Vivian.'

'Better not right now. I'm afraid we're about to be invaded.'

'By?'

'The police. You must have expected that.'

She nodded.

'And people from London.'

'People?'

'Special Branch. Officials from the Foreign Office and the Intelligence Services.' He paused. 'And Sir Bernard. That's who I was speaking to on the phone just now.'

'Do we need the services of a statistician?'

He looked puzzled for a moment and then smiled. 'Ah, yes.'

'Don't worry. I never for a moment thought you spent your time at the Hall juggling figures.'

'No? Well, I don't think you spend your time in the New Tower writing a family history.'

# Scene 2

Freya didn't want the visitors in the library, which she regarded as a kind of sanctuary. The South Drawing Room was better. Georgia, eyes bright with the excitement of it all, volunteered to help remove the covers, and the two of them once more hauled the dust sheets into another room. Mrs Partridge followed to light a fire, not best pleased at the prospect of an invasion.

'I don't see there's any call for them to come at such an ungodly hour. If Mr Charles is drowned, then there's nothing anyone can do about it. If he didn't drown, then we'll hear about it soon enough. And they needn't think they'll find his body. More than half of those that have been lost in that stretch of river are never seen again. Washed out to sea and eaten by crabs is what happens to them, poor souls. Nothing ever found to give a Christian burial.'

At this moment, Freya felt crabs were a suitable fate for Charles, and then she was ashamed of herself. As she told Father Leo, but he took a brisk attitude to it. 'In your shoes, given that the man tried to kill you in what would have been a horrible and lingering way, I probably shouldn't feel much charity towards him.'

'But you'll be praying for him, just the same.'

'I will.'

'Judging by what Charles has been up to, I don't think your prayers will save him from the other place,' Hugo said grimly. He looked around the drawing room and raised an eyebrow. 'Receiving in state, are we? It's a beautiful room and quite different without the shrouded furniture and with the lights on.'

Sir Bernard was the first to arrive, with the Superintendent hard on his heels. Leo took Georgia off to the library for a game of chess, and Hugo poured out a brandy for his Chief and a soft drink for the teetotal policeman.

Sir Bernard sat back and fixed his eyes on Freya. 'None the worse for what sounds like a nasty experience? You should be in bed, resting, my dear; I'm sorry that you've got to be here to answer questions. Inevitable, I'm afraid.'

'I'm not in the least tired,' Freya said coldly.

The Superintendent shifted in his brocaded chair and produced a notebook. 'It might be as well to get the facts of the incident down before the others arrive, Miss Wryton. Perhaps you'd like to give us your account of what happened in your own words. Take your time. Then I'll have a statement from you, Mr Hawksworth, since you were there when Mr Guthrie went into the river.'

'No sign of him?' Hugo said.

MacLeod shook his head. 'No, and I wouldn't put his chances at one in a hundred. Not with the river running the way it is. And I gather he sustained an injury before he fell in. From your horse, Miss Wryton. Well, we'll get to that.'

He extracted the facts of the matter from her in an orderly manner that aroused Hugo's reluctant admiration.

'It's a bad business,' Sir Bernard said when Hugo had in turn answered MacLeod's questions. 'Guthrie turning out to be working for the Soviets. And a murderer, too. It's all a bit of a mess. We'll have to tread carefully on this one. Very carefully.'

# Scene 3

In the library, Georgia was putting away the chess pieces, arranging them in neat ranks in the box. 'You always win, Uncle Leo.'

'I'm a more experienced player than you. But each time we have a game, you play better and learn something new.'

'Still, I like to win. Daisy's father lets her win.'

'And?'

'She'd rather play with her brother because he hates losing, and when she beats him, she knows it's because she played better. Who are all those men with Hugo and Freya?' she added, ultra casual.

'The police and officials from London. Charles Guthrie was an important man in the Foreign Office.'

'Was he a spy?'

Leo was taken aback at the direct question. 'Possibly, yes.'

'Spying for us?'

'Unfortunately, it doesn't seem so.'

'Are they going to take Hugo away? He's a spy, isn't he?'

Leo heard the fear in her voice. 'There's no question of them arresting Hugo. He's on the right side, you see.'

'Not a traitor?'

'Most certainly not.'

Georgia sighed. 'Sometimes you wonder about all this right and wrong stuff. Did Charles kill Lord Selchester? Straight answer, please, Uncle Leo.'

'He probably did.'

Georgia wandered along the shelves. 'That's going to cause a bit of a stink, isn't it? Or will they hush it all up because it's top secret? I don't think murder should be hushed up, do you?'

'No.'

Georgia had taken a book down from the shelves and was inspecting it. 'I thought this was a Bible, but it isn't. It's some kind of fat prayer book. Leather with gold on the edges, very posh. It's got initials on the front: "RLHStJF".'

Leo took it from her. 'It's a missal. A Catholic prayer book. I think it must have belonged to Lord Selchester.' He opened it, and a piece of paper fluttered to the floor.

Georgia picked it up. 'It's a letter, in funny old handwriting. It's in French. Our French teacher writes like that. She says they're all taught that kind of handwriting at school.'

Leo was reading the letter when the door opened, and Freya and Hugo came in. Freya was pale and distressed; Hugo, blindingly angry.

'Have they gone?' Leo said.

'Yes, thank God,' Hugo replied. He went over to the drinks tray and poured a stiff whisky. He noticed his sister. 'Georgia, shouldn't you be in bed?'

Mrs Partridge had followed Freya and Hugo into the library. 'Yes, you should, Georgia. I've run your bath, so off you go.'

Loud protests from Georgia. 'I want to hear what those men said about Mr Guthrie. I want to know what's going on.'

Hugo and Leo exchanged glances over her head.

'I can see you making those knowing faces at one another. I'm not blind, you know. I don't want to go to bed.'

Freya sank down into a chair, her head in her hands.

'That's enough, Georgia,' Leo said. 'Go upstairs. Hugo will tell you more in the morning.'

'I bet he doesn't. With all I've done to help, you'd think—'

'Upstairs.'

Georgia yielded to the authority in her uncle's voice, and, with a withering look at Hugo, stalked out of the room.

Freya sat up, running her fingers through her hair. 'What a terrible evening. Nothing like a sense of trust, is there, Hugo? I have to say, I don't care for the people you work for. Waving the Official Secrets Act at us.'

'They made you sign it?' Leo asked.

'No, just reminded me that I signed it at Bl—during the war, and I'm bound by it more or less for ever.' She yawned. 'It's irrelevant. You know as much as they do, and you'll find out soon enough what they're up to.'

'I don't work for them,' Hugo said, his voice weary now. 'Only for Sir Bernard.'

'He's bad enough, all that not wanting to rock the boat.'

'Ah, a cover-up? I expected it,' Leo said.

'Did you?' Freya said. 'How cynical of you.'

'They can't afford to have another diplomat exposed as a spy, not after Burgess and Maclean. Where was his last posting, Hugo?'

'Washington, I'm afraid to say. Which makes matters even worse as far as they're concerned. So it's brush everything under the carpet. A tragic accident.'

'And Vivian, and the others?'

'I think that rather stuck in MacLeod's gullet, but he has his orders. I had to tell them what happened the night Lord Selchester died, that it was Charles who killed him.'

'You might have kept Vivian's name out of it. I can't believe the Superintendent won't want to have a go at her,' Freya said.

'He'll take a statement from her. A truthful one this time. And from Dillon and Tallis,' Hugo said. 'But that will be the end of it. The story will be that the police are satisfied Filbert was responsible for Selchester's death, and the case will be closed.'

'Serve them all right if Charles didn't drown and he turns up in Moscow grinning away at a press conference to announce his defection,' Freya said. 'Anyhow, it's all over now. Finished.'

Hugo drained his whisky.

It wasn't finished for him. Tomorrow, he was supposed to start the careful tracing of Charles's activities and contacts from before the war, while his opposite number in London would be examining every facet of the man's life after he joined the Foreign Office. He got to his feet. 'I'll just go up and say goodnight to Georgia.'

# Scene 4

He went slowly upstairs and paused on the landing, sitting down on a bench seat covered with a faded velvet cushion.

Finished? He longed to be finished with all this, for good. He felt a fierce stab of regret for his past life. For the days when he didn't limp, when mental and physical agility took him in and out of danger.

There was no point in being sentimental about it. He lit a cigarette and watched the smoke rise gently into the air. The times of action and adventure were interspersed with longer times of tedium, and he had even then been under the command of the men at desks. Now he was a man at a desk.

Damn them all. He'd leave the Service. He understood why they'd taken this line, but he couldn't in conscience feel it was right.

He'd said as much to Sir Bernard when he saw him to his car. Sir Bernard was having none of it. 'It's for the good of the Service, and that means it's for the good of the country. That's why we do what we do, Hugo. Guthrie was a traitor. Because of him, people—good people—lost their lives. As you'll doubtless find out as you unpick the tangle of his treachery.'

He wanted nothing to do with treachery, on either side. He stubbed out his cigarette on the stone floor. He'd do what Valerie wanted. Go back to London, get a job. There were plenty of good schools in London for Georgia.

His sister was coming out of the bathroom, pink and cross. 'Huh,' she said as her brother draped an affectionate arm around her. 'I shan't forgive you for this. Secrets!'

'I'm sorry,' Hugo said. He waited while she climbed into bed, and then he sat on the end of it while she sat up against the pillows. 'There are some things I simply can't talk about.'

'I know. It's hard, that's all.' She changed the subject. 'I checked Uncle Leo at chess this evening. I like playing with him better than the chess club at school. Miss Hartley takes it, and she talks at you all the time, telling you what you've done wrong and what you should have done and what you should do next, until you can't think straight.'

'Are you happy at school? Getting on okay?'

She eyed him suspiciously. 'Are schools about happiness?'

'They can be. You weren't happy at the last one.'

'It's much better here. And I've got a friend. I like Daisy.' She grudgingly added, 'And I suppose the lessons and things aren't too bad. Can I learn the trumpet?'

'The trumpet? Why?'

'No one else plays it, and the headmistress says it isn't a suitable instrument for a girl. But the music teacher says I can. She thinks girls ought to be brass players. Or the French horn, maybe.'

'So you like it in Selchester? Taking one thing with another.'

'Yes.' Her voice was vehement. 'It's the best place I've ever lived. I like it much more than London. And I like being here at the Castle with Freya and Mrs Partridge. And Magnus,' she said, as the brindled cat appeared and leapt on the bed. 'He sleeps here sometimes.' Magnus curled up in a cloud of gentle purrs. 'I feel safe here.'

Safe. That shook Hugo.

'Didn't you feel safe in London?'

'How could anyone feel safe in London?'

Leo had told him how Georgia had been found after the bomb hit. Trapped under a beam for hours. 'A miracle she survived.' That was a memory that wouldn't ever fade.

'We can't stay on at the Castle.'

'I know. But Daisy says Nightingale Cottage will be free soon. We can go there. And Freya's staying in Selchester when the Castle's sold. You do like Freya, don't you?'

'Yes, I do. Very much.'

Her mouth was stubborn, but he read the anxiety in her eyes. 'You aren't going back to London, are you? Because if you do, I'm not coming with you.'

It was the defiance of a child, but there was steel in her words. Heaven knew what she might take it into her head to do if he took her away.

'I shan't go back to live in London.'

'Promise? Promise we'll stay in Selchester?'

'Promise.'

'Oh good.' She slid down between the sheets, curving round Magnus. 'That's all right then. Don't turn out the light. I'm going to read.'

# Scene 5

'Is Georgia speaking to you?' Leo asked, a twinkle in his eye. 'My word, she's a strong character. Takes after your mother.'

'I think she's forgiven me. More or less.'

Freya handed him another whisky. 'You look shattered. Is that Charles's death, the men from the Ministry or Georgia's bracing ways?'

'All three. Thank you.'

'And your leg's hurting you. I don't suppose the ride did it much good. I'm grateful for it, though. I have to thank you for saving my life.'

He smiled at her. 'I think you'd have hung on until help came.' Freya was, like his sister, full of character and courage. A survivor.

He gingerly stretched his leg. It was hurting like the devil. It would be a long time before he got on another horse. He winced and then said, 'Thank God, it's all over and we know the truth about Lord Selchester and how and why he was killed. We shan't ever have to think about him again.'

'I wouldn't be too sure about that,' Leo said. 'Georgia might have been right when she said he was haunting us.'

Hugo looked at his uncle in astonishment. 'Come on, Leo, you're not saying his ghost walks? You, of all people?'

Freya handed Hugo the letter Georgia had found in the missal. 'Read this.'

'It's addressed to Lambert Halfern. Who's he?'

'They're two of my uncle's Christian names. He was Radulf Lambert Halfern St John Fitzwarin.'

Hugo read the letter, blinked, read it again and then, translating as he went, said aloud:

Oxford, May 1902

My dearest husband, for that is what you will always be to me. You have betrayed me. I leave in shame. I shall never see you again, but my heart is yours for ever. May God bless you and forgive you.

Mary Louise

'I don't believe,' Leo said, 'that we're anywhere near finished with the deeds and misdeeds of the late Lord Selchester.'

# Acknowledgements

I want to thank:
My brilliant editor, Anselm Audley.
Eloise Aston for being such a whiz beta reader.
Andrew Wilkinson and Mohsin Khan for their forensic
knowledge and assistance.
Elizabeth Jennings for being such a supportive writing buddy.
Jean Buchanan for her expertise and encouragement.
Maggie Fox for her pithy and excellent advice.

# About the Author

Elizabeth Edmondson was born in Chile, brought up in Calcutta and educated at Oxford. She is the author of eight novels, including *The Villa in Italy*, *The Villa on the Riviera*, *Voyage of Innocence* and *The Frozen Lake*, which have been translated into several languages. She has a particular fascination for the Cold War era and the mysteries it suggests to her as a novelist; above all she has a desire to enchant and entertain. Elizabeth lives in Oxford, where she writes, rings church bells and enjoys vigorous walks in the University Parks, avoiding lacrosse balls and Quidditch players on their broomsticks.